Tattoo

(A Beautiful Sin)

By Kenny Sills

For the <u>FULL</u> Tattoo experience and to hear the
Classical pieces being played, scan below
or go to www.tattooauthor.wix.com/tattoo

Contact Kenny - tattooauthor@gmail.com

Facebook - Tattoo: A Beautiful Sin

Please leave a review at - http://goo.gl/YEoXTD

Published by Dark Moon Press

P.O. Box 11496, Fort Wayne, IN 45858-1496

www.darkmoonpress.com

Edited by Karen Hawk and Sharon Lustick

Cover illustration by Mike Borromeo

To Anthony and Ozzy... you were so inspirational and I miss you both.

To my parents, for a lifetime of encouragement.

And to Syndi for believing in me... always.

A special thanks to the villagers of Walkerville, MI and to their president, Jerry Frick.

Prologue

It still comes rushing back to me, all of it. Walking down the aisle in a grocery store or just sitting on my couch watching TV and *bam*, I see one of them laying there mangled on the floor, savagely ripped apart with their dry, opaque eyes half open and staring at me, staring right *through* me.

One by one they invite themselves back into my mind, day after day after day, and make me relive it all. I remember ... I remember *everything*. When I fall asleep, I can still make out all of the tiniest nuances in my dreams and when I wake up, although it's been several years, it still feels like it all just happened yesterday.

It was the most monstrous and the most macabre murder case – murder *cases* – ever in those parts and comparable maybe only to the Ed Gein case from the '50s or the Billy Damballa case from back in the late 80's. It was truly horrific and ghastly. There's just no other way to describe everything that happened in that innocent little community and everything that these eyes have seen. Just thinking about the things I've witnessed ... I've seen things that could make a man question the very existence of God.

Until then, being a cop was simple in that quiet little Michigan town, but it was the details, the gruesome, bloody details that somehow dripped through the cracks, as they do, and into the good peoples' ears that began to transform that sleepy little speck on the map called Walkerville, into a place that no one would ever be able to look at again and call quaint.

Things were so different back then. It was a just a simple little logging community a couple hours north of Grand Rapids and just east of Lake Michigan. With only about 250 residents, it was a sweet little town. In fact , as

2

of 1908, it was officially a sweet little *village*, the kind that rolled up its sidewalks at dusk but only after they've had a good sweeping, of course.

All that changed though, once the chaos started. Everyone got scared, real scared, and then the accusations started; that's when all Hell broke loose. It wasn't just the murders – it was also the *uncertainty* that got into the heads of those folks and changed Walkerville forever. For the first time in their lives, everyone really started to step back and take a good hard look at one another. Folks formulated scenarios in their minds and started imagining that what was happening was by the hands of someone they'd known all of their lives. Could it be one of their neighbors, an old lover or even a close friend? It was a goddamned modern-day Salem witch trial right there in Walkerville and no one was immune.

You would think that in this day and age there would be more civility in a time of crisis, but they sure proved the idea of mob mentality.

Yeah, being a cop before all that was easy. Hell, back then the most action the officers in the village ever saw was some domestic disturbances or the occasional scuffle down at Seth's Place. In fact, it was at Seth's Place that all this started. I remember … it was an unusually cold mid-October night…

Chapter 1

At the bottom of the hill, surrounded by the thick, dark Manistee National Forest, sits a little country bar dwarfed by its enormous, mostly empty, gravel parking lot. The surrounding trees in the distance are barely visible, faintly lit only by the bluish moonlight and the occasional sweep of headlights as vehicles drive in or out of the parking lot. There's a warm glow that surrounds the building from the blue and red neon Bud and Bud Lite signs in the windows of Seth's.

Mostly locals hung out there; bikers and loggers. Your occasional out-of-towner, just in for a long weekend of camping, would happen by from time-to-time but, seeing the clientele, they would rarely stick around for long. Sometimes they were even invited to leave if they were dressed a little too fancy or looked at someone with even a hint of attitude. The local boys, always trying to look the toughest, liked to show off for strangers and for one another, but Seth, when he was there, kept it a mostly peaceful place and from a distance that's just how it looked.

Walking toward the entrance of the bar, the soft sounds and smells of the breezy nearby forest gave way to that of glasses clanking, pool balls smashing and patrons yelling, so as to be heard over the George Thorogood or Lynyrd Skynyrd song that was usually playing on the jukebox. All this before walking into a warm cloud of cigarette smoke that engulfs you like the summer heat embraces your body when you take that first step outside of a dark, air-conditioned movie theatre on a sweltering August afternoon.

Inside Seth's, Lathe Walthes was hitting on Syndi Bastion who was, in everyone's opinion, the best looking waitress and in most men's opinions, the most beautiful girl in Walkerville. Seth encouraged his waitresses to dress "appealing" to help bring in more customers and to boost sales. "Appealing" was left up to the waitresses and evolved over the years from mini-skirts and half-buttoned shirts, tied up at the bottom revealing their belly buttons to Daisy Dukes and short leather shorts, the kind strippers wear, and bikini tops barely covering the store-bought D cups that a few waitresses sported.

The men, and even some of the women in the village, thought it was truly an oasis in an otherwise boring town. Even in the winter, the girls tried to wear as little clothing as possible. It was no secret that drunk barflies were all too happy to throw their hard-earned cash at a fantasy, at something they knew they could never have and would never even be allowed to touch – most of them came back night after night, just in case though.

Lathe, a towering six feet five inches and 325 pounds, on a good day, was one of the biggest boys in town. He walked with a slight limp on his right side and was a giant mixture of muscle, beer and fast food. Although it was scarred, he still had a baby face under his thick, dark brown beard and mustache that he'd been growing for as long as anyone could remember, since he was a teenager at least. He was wearing his trademark blue plaid flannel shirt, both sleeves buttoned at the wrists, and a pair of washed-out blue jeans, a circle worn in the back left pocket where he kept his can of chewing tobacco.

Jobin and Travis were at the pool table in the corner arguing about the last shot – if it was, in fact, called before the eight ball dropped into the left corner pocket off of three banks. Loraine, the other waitress working, was giving hell to all eight of her customers.

The décor was plain: no sexy beer-girl posters, no street signs and no old baseball bats or mitts hanging on the walls. Seth's wasn't that kind of place: a bar; a pool table; an old forty-five record jukebox; eight tables; two dusty, old, mounted wild turkeys, one with part of an old cigarette stuck in its open beak;

and a few dark brown walls. That's it. You went there, you got drunk and you went home – or at least went away.

As midnight rolled around, Loraine yelled out "Last call, y'all!" which, as usual, was followed by a simultaneous "Aww!"

Lathe actually thought he might be getting somewhere with Syndi but she abruptly ended their conversation by telling him that her shift was over and that she couldn't wait to get home. She grabbed her purse and coat from behind the bar and headed toward the door.

"Thanks for closing for me tonight, Loraine!" she yelled as she headed for the front door, buttoning up her coat.

Not ready to give up, Lathe followed and offered to walk Syndi to her truck in the giant parking lot as he gave some onlookers a sly wink.

Syndi liked to park toward the far end of the lot. She parked away from the building simply because she liked to walk, to which she partly attributed her nice figure. Tonight it was also because she had borrowed her friend's new pickup truck while her truck was in the shop having a new transmission put in. The last thing she wanted was to get any scratches on her friend's truck.

Syndi was always careful when walking around town. She had moved back to Walkerville from New York three years ago and still had the New York mentality to always be aware of her surroundings in order to avoid becoming a statistic.

Because it was such a long walk to the back of the parking lot, Syndi answered Lathe in the fake, flattered tone that most beautiful waitresses use on their customers to ensure a generous tip, "Sure, hon, I really appreciate that. You're so sweet!" After all, Lathe was huge but harmless.

As they walked toward the back of the lot, they passed two motorcycles, three trucks and an SUV. The testament to the few completely committed patrons who were typically still there at closing time. The sounds and the light from inside the bar faded until only the gravel crunching beneath their feet could be heard. Their path was dimly lit by the waxing crescent moon peeking out from behind some slowly drifting clouds.

Although they thought they were alone, there was someone else in that parking lot. Someone hiding and watching from a distance. A man was crouched down between two trucks and was watching Lathe and Syndi as they walked together. In his hands he clinched a tire thumper, a two-foot wooden club with a three-inch lead tip. The kind truckers use to beat the mud, dirt and rocks from the tread of their tires. As Syndi and Lathe neared, the man silently rolled under one of the trucks and lay in its shadow, watching the two of them continue on to Syndi's truck.

Life in Walkerville was simple, what one would probably expect from a small town located dead in the center of a huge forest. It was basically just a bunch of rednecks and good ol' boys. All in all, good folks. It was the kind of town where you didn't have to lock up your house when you left, where you could leave your car running when you ran into the market, where parents didn't have to worry about their kids playing outside and being abducted, and where everyone literally knew everyone else.

As far as education went, most families didn't have much use for it. Many of the parents pulled their kids out of school as soon as they were old enough to drive. Sometimes sooner. Most Walkerville kids were seen as extra help for their families. There was a time when kids were used as unpaid farm hands, but that was before all the farms dried up during the droughts in the '80s. After that, most farmers joined the logging business and most men brought their boys with them to work and taught them to be loggers, too. Because of this, most boys in Walkerville were pretty rugged, burley and tough. The whole county was basically just one big pissing contest – everybody always trying to look tougher than the next guy but usually not doing a damn thing about it since they were all pretty good friends.

"Pretty cold tonight, huh?" Lathe asked as he looked down at all five feet and four inches of Syndi.

"Yeah," she responded as she watched her feet crunching the gravely ground as they walked, folding her arms to keep warm. "It already feels like winter!"

"Yeah, no doubt!" Lathe replied, slightly limping along as he tried to think of something clever to say as they walked on in silence.

"Hey!" Lathe began in a loud tone, startling Syndi. "Have you been to that new coffee shop yet? They just opened it last month!"

"Oh yeah, I went there a couple times already with one of my girlfriends. It's pretty nice!" she said as she looked up at Lathe with her deep green eyes.

"Well," Lathe continued, "they're open until one on Fridays, can you believe that?"

"Yeah, really!" she laughed. "Everything else around here usually closes around eight except for the bars!"

"You want to go get a cup?" Lathe nervously asked.

"Aww, well, I can't. I'm borrowing my friend's truck and I have to get it back to her. I told her I'd bring it back right after my shift. Thanks anyway, though!"

"Oh … that's okay. Maybe some other time . . ." Lathe said, his words diminishing as he spoke.

"Yeah, maybe," Syndi said as she smiled uncomfortably.

As they walked on toward the back of the parking lot, the man who had been hiding in the darkness beneath one of the trucks, quietly crawled out from underneath and moved stealthily between the other vehicles in the parking lot, back toward the bar. He watched Lathe and Syndi as he crept so he could duck out of sight should one of them turn around unexpectedly.

"Well, this is me," Syndi said, pulling her keys out of her purse as they neared the farthest spot in the parking lot. "Thank you so much for walking with me, Lathe. You're such a nice guy!"

"Aw," he stammered, "that's ok. I just wanted you to be safe." Smiling, he said "Well, have a good night."

"You, too, hon." She climbed up into the truck and shut the door before revving up the cold engine. Syndi rolled down her window and said, "Hey, do you want a ride back up to the bar?"

"Oh no, I'll walk, thanks anyway," Lathe said. "I need the exercise!" They both laughed and Lathe waved to her as she pulled away and out onto the main road.

He turned back toward the bar and began walking through the parking lot. On his face he felt the cold autumn breeze that worked its way through his hair and beard as the trees in the distance swayed collectively back and forth.

Lathe was halfway through the parking lot and thirty yards away from an SUV that was parked facing him between two trucks. On the far side of the SUV, a man crouched in its dark shadow. He was squeezing his tire thumper tightly with both hands as Lathe walked toward him. The man in the shadows snuck around to the back of the SUV, feeling that this would be a better position for what he had planned in his mind. However, the night was so quiet that he was unable to make his way to the back of the SUV in complete silence. Lathe stopped when he heard the sound of scuffling on gravel and looked around toward the noise. He took a few steps, passing by the hood of the SUV, and stopped at the side mirror to look around from a different vantage point. He listened intently but heard only the distant sound of the music in the bar and the wind blowing through the trees. Lathe walked cautiously toward the back of the SUV and listened for the sound that he had heard only a few seconds ago.

"What the hell was that?" he thought to himself as he reached the back of the SUV and slowly poked his head around. In the darkness, he saw nothing.

Curious, he squatted down behind the SUV and slowly and very cautiously peeked his head under to take a look, expecting to see a raccoon or opossum. However, he saw nothing but the bottom of the SUV and its tires.

"Hmm?" Lathe said as he stood back up and brushed the gravel dust off of his blue jeans, imagining that whatever kind of animal it was had now run off.

Lathe turned around and took a deep breath before heading back toward the bar. The man in the shadows had a plan for Lathe that relied heavily on the element of surprise. Knowing that he had been heard, the man had crawled back to his original spot beside the giant tire of the SUV before Lathe ever looked underneath.

Lathe tried not to be noticed as he walked back into the bar alone.

"Crash and burn, man!" bellowed a voice from behind the pool table as everyone in the bar snickered. Lathe saw Jobin looking up at his hand that was falling slowly toward the pool table accompanied by a declining whistle that ended with a loud explosion when it finally hit.

"Piss off, Jobin! And I wasn't even trying for her, so shut the hell up!" yelled Lathe who was now obviously embarrassed and bitter.

Everyone in the bar exploded in roars of laughter. Jobin and Travis leaned against the pool table, laughing so hard that their faces turned red and tears welled up in their eyes and ran down their cheeks.

With all of his girth, Lathe could have overpowered Jobin and Travis together, but everyone knew that he was what some call a gentle giant, while others just called him a big pussy. Since childhood, he had been pushed around, called names and heard the hurtful chant: "Lathe don't bathe!" In either case, he was an easy target and usually the butt of everyone's jokes.

Lathe had a buried secret though, one buried so deep that he had never told a single soul: for years he was beaten by his father during his childhood. Not the spanking or belt-whipping kind of beating that the rest of the kids in

10

Walkerville had received, but the kind of beating that would have ended him up in the hospital, several times, had his father, Bill, ever taken him there when he was through with him. Bill was mean. He was mean when he was sober, but when he got to drinking, he'd been known to be downright monstrous.

After Lathe's mother died, Bill learned to take out all of his anger, frustrations, and aggressions on Lathe, and Lathe missed a lot of school while recovering from the beatings. He missed so much school in the eighth grade that he was eventually expelled. Lathe didn't dare tell anyone the real reason he had missed school for weeks at a time; he just let them believe he was helping out on the farm or playing hooky. He knew in his heart that if he ever told anyone the truth and got his father in trouble, he was as good as dead, and, to that day, he never had. No one knew. Some suspected and figured that's where he'd gotten his limp, but no one actually knew.

The beatings that he'd received throughout the years that scarred his body also left deep mental and emotional scars and left him completely terrified of *any* kind of violence. Lathe would feel queasy and dizzy whenever anyone tried to start a fight with him; he actually threw up a couple of times right in front of a group of boys that were picking on him.

The laughter at Lathe's expense began to raise his temper and he quickly walked to the men's room and slammed his palms on the door, only to find it occupied and locked from the inside. This was just too much and everyone in the bar howled with laughter, completely drowning out the music from the jukebox. Infuriated, Lathe stormed out of Seth's through the heavy back door, pushing the outside screen door so hard that it slammed against the outside brick wall and resounded with a loud bang that echoed throughout the nearby trees before it bounced back and shut behind him.

"Stupid assholes!" he grumbled as he spat a stream of brown tobacco on the ground, unzipped his jeans, and began peeing on the wall.

11

About twenty yards behind him was the first line of trees in the surrounding forest and a few feet to his left was a large green dumpster that was pushed up against the wall. On the far side of the dumpster, peering around the edge, was the man who had been hiding in the parking lot, moving between the shadows, watching Lathe walk Syndi to her truck.

Lathe stood grumbling aloud while peeing on the wall and was unaware that a very large man, dressed from head to toe as a surgeon, complete with blue scrubs, a white surgical mask and cap, blue rubber gloves, and a white apron had stepped around the dumpster and was now quietly creeping up behind him. The surgeon's footsteps were drowned out by the blaring sounds of "Bad to the Bone" and the hurtful laughter coming from inside through the still-open heavy back door.

"Screw them guys! They think they're so smart, got no women anywhere and giving me shit for just talki--" All he felt was a brief, heavy strike to the back of his head. As his forehead bounced off of the wall in front of him, Lathe was out. He fell limply to the ground with a splash. The blood from his forehead ran down his face and dripped from the tip of his nose into the puddle of his own steaming urine in which his head now lay.

Without hesitation, the surgeon grabbed Lathe by his wrists and hurriedly dragged him, face down, across the gravel in the cold back lot of Seth's Place and into the shadowy forest. Lathe's body scraped the ground, his penis still partially hung out of the unzipped fly of his jeans. As the sounds of the bar faded, he was dragged through the woods to an old rusty Blazer parked on an overgrown logging trail that had not been used for years. No more Thorogood, no more yelling, no more smoke and noise, no more laughter. Only the silence of the forest mixed with the peaceful sounds of crickets and frogs creating the tranquil music of the night.

Lathe was propped up against the Blazer and the large brown leaves that had so recently fallen, crackled along with the dry sticks that crunched

12

beneath the weight of his body. His plaid shirt was torn open, revealing a tattoo on the right side of his chest of a smiling skull wearing a top hat and bow tie. As Lathe lay unconscious, his feet were bound together and his arms tied behind him with a thin nylon rope. His eyes and mouth were covered by pieces of duct tape. A shallow, bubbly breath could be heard coming from his nose as his body was, through great exertion, hoisted up and into the back of the Blazer and pushed inside on top of a clear plastic tarp that covered a large brown blanket.

The tailgate door shut and the surgeon got into the front of the Blazer. He turned around and smashed Lathe on the temple with the tire thumper for being so fat and making it so hard to move him. Blood ran out of Lathe's forehead, down his neck, and began pooling on the tarp. The surgeon wrapped the sides of the tarp and blanket up and over Lathe's body, covering him completely.

The trail ahead was dimly lit by the soft moonlight shining through the leafless trees mixed with the orange glow of the Blazer's fog lights. The surgeon drove cautiously until they were out of sight and away from Seth's.

A short time later, the Blazer rounded the corner into a newly developing subdivision on the other side of town, pulled in front of a beautiful two-story home, and backed up the driveway as the churning motor of the garage door opener broke the silence.

On the front of the house, giant white columns rose from both sides of the porch to the second-story roof. A large, beautiful chandelier hung between them, illuminating the elegant, heavy, mahogany front door and the fountain in the front yard.

Many of the homes on the block were still under construction, nothing more than holes and concrete slabs, while a few others had the basic framework completed and the skeletons of walls beginning to creep up. Like all development sites, the smell of lumber carried through the crisp, cool air of the entire subdivision. Once the Blazer was inside, the garage door motor churned again as it closed until the night finally fell silent once more.

The surgeon stepped out of the old Blazer that was still sputtering as it died down, and he walked around to open the tailgate door. He pulled out the large brown blanket and tarp that cocooned Lathe. Lathe's body hit the concrete floor of the garage with a muffled thud. He was dragged through a doorway that led into the lower level of the house, across a narrow hallway, and down a single cement step into a darkened room. The blanket bounced as it fell off of the step and onto the bare floor.

*****

In what could have been hours or days later, Lathe began to wake up. He felt nauseated and like all of his energy had been completely drained from his body.

"How much did I *drink*?" he thought to himself, not yet realizing where he was. He could only think about how much his head was throbbing, how much pain he was in, and that he was freezing. Shivering, he opened his eyes slowly, very slowly, to complete darkness. He reached for his covers and discovered that his hands were tied down by his sides.

Confused and still not quite awake, Lathe slowly began to realize that he was naked and was not in his bed at all but was rather laying on something hard, solid, and cold. As he tried to move around, he found that he was bound to this something – his wrists, ankles and a thick strap holding his waist down. Deprived of all light and sound, panic began setting in as he started struggling to free himself. Fear began setting in as he tried yelling for help but was only able to muster up enough energy to barely mumble the word, not even sure where he was, what had happened, or who would hear him ... if anyone. But it didn't matter. Nothing mattered. His mind raced and his fear grew more and more intense as random thoughts emerged, telling him that this was some sort of practical joke or this might be some kind of alcohol-induced nightmare. Then the pain in his head made it all too real. *This* was real and he *knew* he was in trouble. There was no longer any doubt in his mind.

His calls for help grew louder and his struggling turned into squirming as adrenaline coursed through his body. Lathe began to shiver from the cold, from the fear of the unknown, from the pain in his head and now in his wrists and ankles that began to bleed from his squirming against the thin nylon ropes. They were wrapped several times around, rubbing into his skin, holding him in place on what was now his prison.

Suddenly, Lathe heard a door open just past the foot of the platform where he lay. He looked down to see not a person, but a blurry shadow of a tall, stocky man standing behind a white sheet that covered the doorway. The light from the hallway shown over the man's head and illuminated a slit in the sheet that ran down the center of the doorway all the way to the floor. The man in the hallway pushed the sheet apart as he stepped down into the room. The hallway light illuminated Lathe's naked and badly scraped body that was lying upon a stainless steel autopsy table. Scars covered his arms and chest from the childhood beatings and on his chest, just above his right nipple, was the tattoo of a smiling skull wearing a top hat and bow tie.

Lathe was now completely filled with fear and, with all of the energy he could muster, yelled, "Who are you? What the hell's goin' on here?"

Seeming not to have even heard Lathe, the man in the doorway, now silhouetted in the light from the hallway behind, tilted his head slightly and gazed at Lathe as if he were looking at a beautiful Picasso, admiring it as an exquisite piece of artwork and for its aesthetic beauty. Lathe watched as the man reached up behind the sheet on the wall and flipped a switch that lit up the room like the flash of a thousand suns all beaming at once. The sudden, burning brightness too much to bear, Lathe squeezed his eyes shut; the light immediately made his head pound even more furiously than before.

For a moment, all he could do was listen helplessly as he heard the man shut the door, walk into the room and head toward Lathe, stopping just next to his head. Lathe began to shiver more violently, but this time it was from fear as the reality of the situation started to truly sink in. As he lay there, he could feel his heart beating faster and faster in his chest and he started breathing hard, as if he had just run a mile.

Lathe struggled to open his eyes as he heard his captor fidgeting around briefly followed by a deafening silence. Seconds passed that seemed like hours in Lathe's now exceedingly paranoid mind. He lay helpless, listening to the stranger's deep nasally breathing, until, without warning, the melodious sounds of a classical music piece began to play loudly. Lathe had heard the violin music somewhere before, perhaps as a child in a cartoon, but he didn't know it to be the sound of Mozart's "Eine Kleine Nachtmusik." The very first note instantly swallowed up the silence of the room and made the horror of the situation suddenly far more horrifying.

The music played on as he lay captive on the table, still struggling to free himself. Lathe heard a high-pitched whistling that he instantly recognized as water running through pipes. Although he could tell the sound was coming from just a few feet away, he couldn't hear any water splashing into a sink. Curiously, he didn't hear the splash of water at all – only the whistling of the water through the pipes.

Beginning to cry softly, Lathe forced his eyes open, slowly and quite painfully, his head throbbing all the while with every beat of his heart. Through his blurred vision he could see that just above him was a very bright round surgical light inside of a shiny metal reflective dome, the kind surgeons use above their tables when operating; it was blinding when he looked at it directly. As his eyes slowly started to adjust, he looked down and saw the stainless steel table on which he was bound.

There was an inch-deep trench running completely around the table, just inside the outer edge and, although Lathe couldn't see it, just above his head was a quarter-sized hole in the table. Beneath the table, a nine-foot piece of rubber hose connected to the bottom of the hole and ran down deep into a sewer-pipe in the cement directly under the table. Beside him, Lathe saw various metal oval rings running the length of the table. They were welded solidly, two inches inside of the trenched edge of the table.

Lathe then turned his attention to his own body and saw blood covering his chest and arms in large, somewhat dried, reddish-brown patches.

There were no windows in this room and, oddly, the ceiling was covered with a thick dark brown shag carpet. All four walls were hidden by clean white sheets hung by clear plastic shower curtain rings attached to a wire that ran around the tops of all four walls.

Just to Lathe's left were two silver meat hooks hanging on chains that were bolted into the ceiling. They were six feet off the ground and two feet apart and to his disgust, he could make out what appeared to be small bits of meat embedded in dried blood on both hooks. To his right, he could see a small stand with a blue towel draped over the top. By the contours of the towel, he could tell that there were several different items hidden beneath and he tried, albeit in vain, not to imagine what they could be. Against the far wall to the right was a freestanding two-door orange metal cabinet and to the left of it, an old green, five-wheeled swivel chair.

"Please let me go!" he mumbled in an almost inaudible voice as he sobbed while the sounds of playful violins continued. He looked around and found a very large, very strange man who was dressed as a surgeon in light blue medical scrubs, a clean white apron tied around him, blue rubber gloves on his hands, and a white surgical cap that covered his entire scalp tied snugly around his head. The surgeon had just finished tying a white surgical mask on his face so all Lathe could see were the man's eyes peering down – his evil, vacant, sunk-in eyes – before he turned to the small stand next to the autopsy table and picked up the blue towel, revealing several pristine surgical instruments that gleamed as they were uncovered. Lathe gasped at the sight of them.

As the music played on, the surgeon crisply folded the blue towel four times into a small square, laid it on the lower shelf of the stand, and began separating the instruments, one by one, and making sure they were all a thumb's width apart and in order from shortest to longest with the bottoms all neatly lined up.

He began with a set of forceps, then aligned three scalpels, two pairs of long, skinny scissors, a pair of double hinged pliers, a set of long tweezers, a small rotary saw, and, at the very end, oddly, lay a dull and rusty old pocket knife.

Next to the tools sat a rectangular stainless steel dish that contained a clear, pungent liquid that smelled of chlorine. It was a sanitizer for surgical instruments and the strong odor made Lathe feel even more nauseated, causing him to gag. As he did so, the surgeon looked at Lathe almost quizzically before turning and walking toward the orange cabinet. As he walked away, Lathe noticed that the surgeon wore black rubber boots that were wet from the ankles down. He couldn't see it, but the faucet that he had heard being turned on had a seven-foot piece of garden hose attached that ran over the two-tub sink and onto the floor. The water rushing out of the hose created a shallow puddle that spread out six feet around the table and flowed inward toward the open drain in the floor, which was partially blocked by the rubber hose that ran down into it from the bottom of the table.

The deep, soft sounds of cello's playing Beethoven's "Ode to Joy" began playing as the surgeon returned with an unopened bar of soap that he sat on the counter of the sink before adjusting the water flow and returning to the tray of instruments.

Lathe's eyes widened as the surgeon picked up a scalpel with his right hand while running a finger of his left hand around the two-inch high tattoo of the smiling skull wearing a top hat and bow tie. Lathe could see the surgeon's eyes wrinkle and squint as he began to smile with the first touch of his latex covered fingertip to Lathe's skin.

"No, man," whispered Lathe from the back of his throat as he tried desperately to hold back his tears. "Please don't hurt me. Don't do it. Please don't do it! I never hurt nobody!" His voice began to rise and quiver. "PLEASE! I'll do whatever you want!"

The surgeon slowly brought the scalpel to rest on Lathe's chest, an inch above the skull's top hat where he waited, silently tormenting Lathe. Seeming to not hear Lathe's pleas, the surgeon's eyes closed and he began to lightly sway to the music.

As the music drew toward a crescendo, Lathe's eyes widened and his cries instantly turned to guttural screams as the first cut sliced deeply into his skin. The surgeon pulled the scalpel backwards over the tattoo and Lathe's blood rushed to the surface and spilled out of the newly sliced skin as his horrified screams continued.

The surgeon slowly raised his free hand, palm to the ceiling, in attempts to direct Lathe to scream louder, like a conductor directing his orchestra. The surgeon stopped cutting only halfway across the top of the tattoo when Lathe's screams became uncontrollable and the overwhelming pain caused his body to convulse. His back arched and slammed down over and over onto the autopsy table followed by his head rising and crashing down again and again and again, almost rhythmically with the music. The thin ropes around his wrists and ankles cut more and more deeply into his skin with every move. His screams persisted, seemingly louder during the brief decrescendo; the thick dark blood flowed freely down both sides of his chest and onto the table.

With each convulsion, blood splashed onto the surgeon's clean white apron and mask and onto the floor and disappeared into the steadily flowing puddle of water. The sight of this made the surgeon's smiling eyes gleam with excitement as the music played on. He turned the stereo up to match the volume of Lathe's screams of pain, then lifted his scalpel in the air and began to use it as a conductor's baton. Blood flicked from the end as he directed his invisible symphony. The surgeon pointed his scalpel towards Lathe and, with the other hand, placed a bloody finger to his facemask and hushed Lathe to no avail, directing him to make his screams softer as the music had now drawn toward another decrescendo.

With clenched fists, Lathe continued to convulse and writhe in pain, his body still slamming up and down on the table as he screamed. The pain, the terror, the odor of the sanitizer – it was all too much for Lathe to bear and he vomited violently onto his face, shoulders and chest, which added texture to the already gruesome canvas as it mixed with the dried and fresh blood. The incision above his tattoo stung as the acid from his vomit entered the wound.

The surgeon dropped his scalpel into the sanitizer, danced across the room and sung in Italian to the music and to Lathe's screams until he reached the tall orange cabinet where he pulled out a three-inch thick leather strap resembling a weight lifter's belt.

Playfully, the surgeon danced his way back to the autopsy table and stood above Lathe's head, looking down at him with those evil black eyes and grinning beneath his mask at Lathe who was spitting out vomit between his screaming and crying. As tears ran down Lathe's pale face, the surgeon slipped the leather strap through one of the oval rings bolted on the table to the right of Lathe's neck, laid the strap across his throat and threaded it through a metal ring that was bolted on the left side, then pulled the strap back tight, and buckled it securely.

Instantly, Lathe's screams were silenced and his thrashing stopped immediately. His face quickly turned from pale to red as the blood and oxygen were trapped inside of his head. His eyes, filled with tears, were fighting once again to stay open.

With his blood-soaked hand, the surgeon rubbed the hair on top of Lathe's head, as if to somehow comfort him as one would comfort a child who had just fallen off of his bicycle.

The choir was now singing joyfully, their ode, in unison with the symphony.

Fighting desperately to get a breath past the neck restraint, Lathe started drooling and frothing at the mouth as low growling and choking sounds barely escaped his constrained throat. The surgeon picked up a pair of forceps from the instrument stand and used them to pick up a two-inch gauze square, which he dipped into the dish of sanitizer. Once the gauze was drenched in the liquid, the surgeon rubbed Lathe's tattoo with it, removing the blood and vomit and making it easier to see before the fresh blood again rose up from the incision above the skull tattoo. Lathe's eyes squeezed shut and his teeth clenched tightly as the sanitizing liquid entered his wound and burned him from within. The incredible pain caused Lathe's body to shake uncontrollably.

Once the tattoo was cleansed, Lathe opened his eyes and frantically followed the surgeon as he picked up a clean scalpel from the instrument stand, inserted it into the gash created by the first scalpel, and resumed cutting just as the choir began singing the masterful main phrase of "Ode to Joy."

Lathe's body shook as the surgeon finished the line above the skull's top hat. He continued drawing the scalpel slowly, meticulously, cutting down the left side of the tattoo. He continued across the bottom of the tattoo and back up the far side to meet at the point from which he had started, creating a perfect square a half-inch outside of the entire tattoo.

The massive amount of blood that was now spilling out of Lathe's chest and onto the autopsy table ran down both sides of his body and collected in the trench that ran around the table. The blood flowed toward the hole just above Lathe's head, down the hose beneath, and deep into the sewer pipe in the floor.

As the beautiful choir persisted, Lathe's bloodshot eyes looked far, far away and his body began to relax. His shaking subsided as his pain, his terror, and his grasp on reality began to slowly fade away.

The surgeon laid the bloody scalpel in the sanitizer, turning the liquid a deeper shade of red and picked up the double-hinged pliers in his left hand and a small razor blade in his right. He pinched the top right corner of the freshly cut skin with the pliers, pulled it back slightly, and began separating the flesh and muscle from the ribs beneath with the razor, using small, slow, scraping motions.

Once he had the top right corner cut away, he dropped the razor blade into the sanitizer and picked up the rotary saw. The blade on the saw was about the diameter of a quarter and sounded like a dentist's drill as it revved up to full speed. The surgeon pulled the skin back with the pliers and, using the saw blade, began to cut away the rest of the skin from the ribs until he could pull the entire square of skin completely out of Lathe's chest.

"A perfect cut!" The surgeon thought to himself as he turned the saw off and ejected the blade into the sanitizer. He returned the saw to the instrument table and dropped the pliers into the sanitizer. He held his new prize, the bloody, tattooed slab of skin, with both hands and examined it closely under the bright, round surgical light. The angelic choir sang as the blood dripped out of the skin and onto Lathe's stomach.

"Perfect!" the surgeon whispered as he began smiling and chuckling to himself. With the music rising and seeming to encourage his endeavor, the surgeon began swaying back and forth. He picked up the hose from the floor, rinsed the skin and his gloved hands of blood and dropped the half-inch thick tattooed slab of skin into the right sink tub that was filled with soapy water. The surgeon watched in amazement as the skin drifted toward the bottom of the sink tub while small bubbles escaped from within.

When the skin had fallen deep beneath the murky, soapy water and out of sight, the surgeon returned to the autopsy table. There on the instrument stand sat the unused rusty pocket knife which he quickly picked up, inspected carefully from end to end, and then wiped down using the blue towel that had previously covered the surgical instruments. He looked closely, making sure that there were no fibers or pieces of debris on the handle or the blade. When he was through, he laid the towel back on the instrument stand and leaned over Lathe, pocket knife in hand, examining the fresh wound a bit closer.

The surgeon thought to himself how precise the incisions looked, how perfect the extraction of the skin, and how pitiful that he would now have to ruin his own beautiful work. With that thought, he began scraping at the inner wall of skin with the pocket knife, tearing at the perfectly cut walls, sawing at the skin, the ribs below, and the connective tissue in between. The surgeon hacked furiously at the wound as the choir and the symphony raged on.

When he was finished, the wound looked as if the skin had simply been ripped right out of Lathe's chest – like an animal had chewed on and made a meal of the flesh. The surgeon looked at the hole in Lathe's chest and shook his head in disgust before reaching down and cutting the ropes off of Lathe's lifeless body with the rusty and now very bloody pocket knife.

Lathe's bloodshot eyes peered into the distance, still half-open with the faint, yet unmistakable, look of terror still in them. As he unbuckled the leather strap that had stopped the flow of air in and out of Lathe's body, the surgeon could hear the wheeze of Lathe's lungs letting out their last, trapped breath. He rinsed the strap with the hose and set it on the sink counter before returning to the orange cabinet where he retrieved a bottle of bleach.

"No DNA," he whispered to himself. "No evidence."

He opened the bottle and laid the cap on the sink counter and proceeded to pour the bleach all over the leather strap before turning to the table and dousing Lathe's body. He started with the right foot and poured the bleach up his leg, onto his arm and chest, into the wound on his chest, and down his left side, not missing an inch of skin in the process. The bleach mixed with the blood and vomit, and ran off the body, onto the autopsy table, and into the trench around the table. The disgusting concoction of fluids followed the course that flowed down into the hole just above Lathe's head.

When the surgeon had saturated the entire body, he asked Lathe, "Care for a drink?" before pouring some bleach inside of Lathe's mouth. It filled up quickly and overflowed, drenching his beard that instantly began turning from dark brown to beige.

"Almost clean," the surgeon said as he poured the bleach all over Lathe's hair and finally, tipping it over completely, poured the remainder of the bottle onto Lathe's face, being sure to get some inside of his nose and ears.

When he was through, the surgeon threw the bottle away in a nearby trash bin, placed his hands on the sink and closed his eyes as he listened, quite intently, to the beautiful music in the room, humming along and swaying.

When the piece ended, the surgeon picked the hose up and began spraying the autopsy table, rinsing it completely of every drop of blood and diluting the strong fumes of bleach. When it all had been rinsed away, the surgeon dropped the hose and turned the faucet and the stereo off.

In the silence, he sat down on his green swivel chair, taking a few deep breaths as he folded his hands in his lap and leaned back, looking at the brown-carpeted ceiling, finally relaxing, although briefly, for the first time that night. As he sat, the last of the water on the floor rolled down into the drain beneath the table. A moment later, however, realizing that there was still work to be done, he slapped his lap, stood up and stretched. He left the room, went across the hall and into the garage where he grabbed a clean, clear tarp and a fresh brown blanket from a stack on a nearby shelf. The surgeon returned to the basement, laid the blanket on the cold, damp floor next to the autopsy table and laid the plastic tarp on top, spreading both of them out fully.

He walked around the table, careful to not get snagged on the hooks that hung from the ceiling. With one hand on Lathe's shoulder and one on his hip, the surgeon rolled Lathe's body off of the table. Lathe landed solidly, face down on the tarp. After straightening Lathe's body and arranging his arms to his sides, the surgeon wrapped the damp blanket and tarp around Lathe, grasped the blanket at Lathe's ankles, and with a few grunts, dragged the body up the steps, across the hall and back into the garage where the Blazer sat silently, its tailgate still open.

The surgeon set the rolled blanket up against the back tire of the Blazer and, using his last ounce of strength, grabbed around the blanket and hoisted Lathe's body up and into the back. Once inside, the surgeon shimmied Lathe's body until the bottom of the blanket was up and past the tailgate. Satisfied, the surgeon returned to his skinning room and began removing his apron, scrubs, gloves, cap, mask and the ropes he used to tie Lathe down. He tossed them all into the large silver trash bin before pulling out the plastic trash bag, tying it up tightly, and taking it into the garage where he threw it in the back of the Blazer on top of Lathe's body. After the surgeon slammed the tailgate shut, he climbed into the drivers' seat. As he started up the engine, the garage door lifted and the Blazer drove back out into the night.

Chapter 2

As morning broke, the village stood in shock as all four of Walkerville's squad cars, sirens blaring and lights flashing, sped toward the growing crowd that circled the pale, naked, mutilated body of Lathe Walthes. He was covered in old scars, fresh scratches, and a new gaping wound from which small trails of blood ran down his chest, almost as if it were crying.

It was 7:00 a.m. on Saturday and, as usual, news had gotten around town pretty quickly. Lathe's naked body was sitting up against the tire of a logging truck in the Ace Logging and Lumber Company's parking lot. His eyes and mouth were still half open as his head drooped downward. Whispers could be heard about the wound on his chest as well as all of the scars on his body.

As the first car pulled up, the Walkerville sheriff quickly got out and ran over to examine the body. The sheriff was shorter than most men in town and a bit on the heavy side. His thinning, light brown hair fluttered in the breeze when he removed his hat as he ran. Three more squad cars sped into the area and three deputies; Julian, Tim, and Charlie, exited the cars and immediately began moving the crowd back and putting up 'Police Line–Do Not Cross' tape around the crime scene. The deputies were all tall and slender and were wearing their tan uniforms, caps and jackets, each with a shiny silver star pinned above their hearts.

"Aw, Lathe, what have they done to you, boy?" the sheriff said breathlessly as he squatted down next to Lathe, careful not to touch him. "*I want everybody's names and I want everyone out of the area!*" he yelled, eyes still fixed on Lathe.

The sheriff noticed the beige color of Lathe's hair and beard. As the wind kicked up, he caught the odor of bleach, which made the situation even more confusing.

"Why did he bleach his hair?" the sheriff asked himself. The deputies began taking names and phone numbers, first from the people trying to inconspicuously walk away and then moving on to the rest as they herded the entire crowd into the lumber warehouse, out of sight of the body.

The sheriff called to one of his deputies, "Julian! Get the Grand Rapids Homicide Department on the phone for me." The sheriff stayed with Lathe to prevent anyone from touching him and to shoo away any curious varmints that might come up for a quick snack. Fortunately, it was too cold to have to worry about ants and flies or rapid decomposition of the body, for that matter.

When Deputy Julian returned with the phone, the sheriff began to explain the situation. "Yes, sir," he began, "this is Sheriff Anthony Kerry of the Walkerville Sheriff's Department. We've got a dead body here. There's a naked young man here with a hunk of his chest ripped out."

"Yes, sir – naked! I can't imagine why he would be out here naked, though!"

"Just above his right nipple."

"Yes, sir, Captain Parker, I do. His name was Lathe Walthes, he was thirty years old, single white male, about six foot three, and about 350 pounds. Brown hair and brown eyes and a brown beard and mustache but it looks like he bleached his hair and beard recently. In fact, I can still smell the bleach a little bit."

"Yes, sir, scars all over his body, too many to count. They're all over his arms, legs and chest. Fresh scrapes on his stomach, too," Sheriff Kerry commented, noting the scrapes that Lathe received on his stomach as he was dragged across the gravel behind Seth's Place.

"I don't know. Could be from a small animal scratching at him maybe."

"Well, sir, he's pretty torn up, looks like it was ripped or chewed out. He's sitting up against a tire in a logging yard but the strange thing is, there's no trail of blood leading up to him on the gravel. I'd think that if he was attacked by a wild animal, he would have left a trail."

"Well, could have been a bear or a coyote maybe, but there's no bite marks or claw marks on him, just the one wound and the little scratches."

"I don't know. He could have been murdered!" Sheriff Kerry said, sounding almost as if he couldn't believe what he was saying.

"Yes, sir, about two hours then. We'll be waiting for you. I'll put my deputy on the phone to give you directions. We'll see you soon then."

"Yes, sir, goodbye."

As the sheriff handed the phone back to Julian, he told the deputy to bring him Lathe's father's address. Julian walked back to his car, giving the captain directions from Grand Rapids to the Ace Logging and Lumber Company. Sheriff Kerry stood looking into the nearby forest and wondering if whatever or whoever did this was out there, watching.

"Was it a wolf, a coyote, a drifter? Could it be someone in the lumber warehouse being questioned? Who could have done this to Lathe and why?" he asked himself.

"I've got Lathe's father's address, sir, do you want me to drive up there?" Julian asked nervously.

"No, I'll do it myself," Sheriff Kerry replied. "Tell you the truth, I'm surprised he hasn't already heard."

"Yeah," Julian replied solemnly. "Doesn't take long for news to travel around here. Goes even quicker when it's *bad* news."

Sheriff Kerry looked down at Lathe. "I'm gonna wait until after forensics gets here and does their thing and takes him away first. Lathe's father is too old to see his boy in this condition. It's gonna be hard enough just trying to explain it to him."

"Yeah, I'd hate to be in *your* shoes, Sheriff." Julian said as he turned and walked back toward the annoyed crowd in the lumber warehouse.

Two hours later, sirens were heard throughout the village as a dark blue squad car with the words 'Grand Rapids P.D.' led two plain, unmarked brown Ford Crown Victorias into the Ace Logging and Lumber parking lot. Sheriff Kerry walked toward the cars as two men stepped out of one of the Crown Vics, three out of the other and one out of the blue squad car. All six men were white. Four of them were of average height and weight, carried a briefcase and wore the standard mirrored sunglasses and gray suits under beige overcoats.

One man, who was a little overweight, was wearing black shiny pants and a thick jacket that was zipped all the way up with 'Crime Lab' printed on the back. His thick black mustache resembled his thick black belt that held his gun, flashlight and a pair of handcuffs. He carried a large case in one hand that bore the same words that were printed on the back of his jacket.

Finally, from the blue squad car stood a tall man wearing a blue police uniform and sharp-brimmed hat, the kind that state troopers wear. He was well built and under his hat he had a full head of thick brown hair that he combed straight back. He carried himself with a noble demeanor and had an unmistakable, no-nonsense presence about him. He removed his dark sunglasses and walked toward the sheriff, never taking his eyes away from him as the other men spread out behind and looked around as they surveyed their surroundings.

"Sheriff, I'm Captain Lucas Parker," he said as he flipped his worn wallet open, revealing his shield and ID badge.

"Pleased to meet you, sir," Sheriff Kerry said as he shook the captain's hand. "If you men will follow me, Lathe is right over here."

Sheriff Kerry led the way as all six men followed him through the rows of logging trucks to the body. When they were close enough to see Lathe, Captain Parker stopped, as did everyone else, including Sheriff Kerry.

"Let's not go any further," Captain Parker said to the sheriff. "We don't want to take the chance of contaminating the scene."

It was at that point that the crime scene squad started their investigation. For the next hour, they moved in a circle, starting about twenty yards from Lathe, and slowly working their way inward. One of the men began taking photographs of the body and the surrounding areas from every angle imaginable. Two of the others donned black rubber gloves and began looking carefully for any traces of evidence, getting on their hands and knees and using tweezers to pick up random slivers of metal and other foreign objects and placing them into plastic resealable evidence baggies. They placed small numbered flags next to each item and photographed them in their natural state before placing each item in their own resealable baggie.

When they had finally reached Lathe's body, the crime lab detective approached and opened his briefcase revealing rows of empty test tubes and occupied tubes containing fingerprinting dust that were among various swabs, plastic bags and rolls of clear tape. He walked carefully toward the body, took swabs from his briefcase and began collecting samples from inside the chest wound, the mouth and nose, the anus, penis and from many of the scrapes on the chest. He stored each swab in its own test tube and wrote from which part of the body each sample was taken on the labels.

Meanwhile, Captain Parker was trying to get a better picture of the situation. "Was there anyone around the body this morning, Sheriff?"

"Yes, sir. Unfortunately when I arrived there was a crowd of folks around. They're back in the lumber warehouse now being questioned by my deputies."

Captain Parker turned to two detectives standing nearby, both without any expression on their faces. Without speaking a word, the captain motioned for them to go into the lumber warehouse. They both nodded before turning and heading toward the visibly irritated crowd that had unwillingly been sequestered therein.

Once inside, one of the detectives called the deputies to the side while the other detective, smiling warmly, climbed atop a three-foot stack of wooden pallets and spoke out, "Can I have your attention, please? Folks, please, listen up!"

As the confusion of the crowd began to settle down he continued, speaking loudly so as to be heard clearly by everyone in the warehouse. "Good morning, ladies and gentlemen. My name is Detective Carter. This is Detective Williams." He said as he motioned toward the other detective. We will be taking you aside, one by one, just to ask a few questions. Please be patient and with your cooperation, this will all be over very shortly!"

The crowd, very unhappy with the news that they had just been given, began responding with their disappointment.

"We didn't do anything wrong, we were just lookin'!" one man yelled over the growing murmurs of the crowd.

"Yeah!" another man roared. "We don't have all day to stand around here answerin' your questions! We've been here for over two hours already!"

A man was heard from the back of the crowd yelling, "I can't stay, I've got to get to work!"

Detective Carter stood unfazed, removed his sunglasses, and looked at the crowd. He tilted his head slightly downward, his smile fading and his expression becoming cold and adamant. His face now showed the years of seeing things that most people could never even imagine and interrogating the worst lowlife, insane criminals that the world had to offer.

31

Seeing this, the mumbling of the crowd subsided and everyone in the warehouse began to quiet down as Detective Carter plainly said in a gruff, matter-of-fact tone, "I'm sorry, but I simply must insist."

As the intent in his chilling voice was absolutely understood and felt by every man, woman and child in this small-town crowd, silence filled the warehouse as they were all temporarily stunned by the seriousness in the detective's voice and the uncompromising expression on his face. There was no question that he was now in charge.

The silence finally broke as Detective Carter smiled and said pleasantly, "Now, let's begin." He pointed to a man in front of the crowd and called him over to begin questioning. The man quickly complied. Detective Williams dismissed the sheriff's deputies and picked a young woman, two small boys in tow, out of the crowd and began to question her.

The deputies, a bit confused and not quite knowing what to do next, returned to the parking lot, where Sheriff Kerry and Captain Parker were examining the body.

"Sheriff," the Captain asked, "did this man have any enemies?"

"Naw, everybody liked Lathe. He was a big ol' teddy bear. He never caused any trouble or messed with anybody. He got picked on a bit, but nobody ever really wanted to hurt him."

"Did he have a wife, girlfriend – or *both*?"

"No, he was single his whole life. Had a couple girlfriends that I can remember, one of em' he was pretty serious with, but it didn't work out. That was about five, six years ago now," Sheriff Kerry said, thinking back.

"Hmm, what about family?" Captain Parker asked.

"Well, all he had was his father. They didn't really get along though. Rumor was his daddy used to beat him good, and by the looks of all the scars on his body, it seems like the rumors were all true! Since Lathe grew up and moved out though, he didn't go to see his daddy all too often from what I've heard. I think I heard someone say that Lathe went up there a couple months ago to help him move an old broken-down tractor. His momma died quite a while back, when he was just a little boy, and he didn't have any brothers or sisters so, basically, it was just him and his daddy."

The captain, looking very disappointed at Sheriff Kerry, said, "I see. Well, that doesn't really give us much to go on now does it?"

"'Fraid not, sir," Sheriff Kerry said solemnly. "I wish I knew more."

"Well, maybe his father might have some information we can use. Have you gone to see him yet?"

"No," said the sheriff. "I was gonna' wait 'till Lathe's body was removed so he wouldn't come down here and risk messin' up the crime scene."

"Good thinking, sheriff. How far does the father live from here?"

"Oh, only about fifteen minutes away."

"Great. My men should be done marking the ground and taking pictures in about an hour or so. Would you mind driving me over to his father's house?"

"Um, sure," Sheriff Kerry said, a bit surprised. "I gotta' warn ya' though, he's a nasty ol' son-of-a-bitch, and I don't know how he's gonna take this!"

The captain nodded, and then turned to one of his detectives. "I'm going to see the father. I want you to get the body out of here ASAP."

"Yes, sir," came the response from one of the detectives who had been looking at the wound on the body through a magnifying glass, searching for hairs or any other tiny fibers that might be stuck in the blood before they transported the body to the morgue.

Sheriff Kerry and Captain Parker walked to the sheriff's car and got in. Sheriff Kerry started up his car and turned off the stereo, which had been playing quiet piano music, before pulling out of the parking lot onto B-96 and driving east toward Woodland Park.

The two men rode quietly for a couple of miles until finally, wanting to break the uncomfortable silence, Sheriff Kerry spoke up,

"So, how long you been on the force, Captain?"

"I started at a juvenile detention center back in 1979 when I was just twenty-one." he replied as he looked out his window into the endless brown and leafless wall of trees that was blurring by.

"Yeah?" said the sheriff. "I've been on for about twenty-five years now myself. If Lathe *was* murdered, this is only the second one since I've been here in Walkerville. Not a whole lot happens around here really. How many murder cases do you think you've worked on, Captain?"

"Oh, I don't know, a few hundred maybe," he said in a monotone voice, keeping his eyes fixed on the trees lining the road. Sheriff Kerry's mouth dropped open with astonishment but noticing the captain's indifference to the conversation, Sheriff Kerry decided to change it.

"You grow up in Grand Rapids?" he asked.

"No, I moved there about ten, twelve years ago from St. Louis. I was transferred to Grand Rapids after finishing a case in a little town called Cape Girardeau. It's a couple hours south-east of St. Louis, just a little college town. Nothing really there to speak of." He said, suddenly realizing that the sheriff was trying to make conversation. Not wanting to be rude, he turned his focus to the sheriff.

"What about you? Have you been the sheriff of Walkerville all twenty-five years?"

"Oh, hell no. I've been here for seventeen years now. I actually moved here for this job. I was up north on Mackinac Island before that. I served up there first."

"See much action?"

"No, not really," the sheriff continued. "It's mostly just a summer resort island. The big old hotel up there is the major attraction. It draws a lot of folks from all over the country. They all just came to relax and ride the horse and buggies and such. Just upper-class white folks wanting to enjoy the atmosphere, so not too many problems at all, really."

"So no murder cases up there then, huh?" The captain asked as he let out a slight chuckle.

"Actually, there was one! Took people by surprise so much that someone actually went and wrote a book about it. That was before my time though." The sheriff said, feeling pretty proud of himself for enlightening the captain.

"Is that right?" The captain asked, coolly.

"Yep, good ol' Mackinac Island. Guess I'm just a small town kind of guy."

"Yeah, I hear ya," replied the captain, again looking out of his window.

They drove on until they came upon a dirt road. A rotten wooden post leaned slightly to the right with an old mailbox barely hanging onto the top. Sheriff Kerry turned left onto the road and a cloud of dust followed them as they drove toward a run-down trailer home at the end. Forty acres of dirt and a few trees surrounded the home – no grass, no shrubs, just dirt. In the driveway was Mr. Walthes's gray '79 Ford pickup truck and on the side of the house was the old rusted shell of a '58 truck, same make and model. Off to the right was a large barn, which looked as if it should have been condemned twenty years ago. Its doors hung open on rusty hinges and exposed the eerie darkness within. Mr. Walthes kept nothing in the barn but some old farming tools that were scattered about and the broken-down tractor that Lathe had helped him push inside a few months earlier.

The sheriff and the captain exited the sheriff's car and walked up three rotting wooden steps to the front door of the house. Sheriff Kerry, looking quite anxious, knocked loudly on the torn screen door but with no results.

"I know he's here, his truck's here," said the sheriff, now banging on the door. "Bill, open up, it's Sheriff Kerry!"

They heard some mumbling coming from inside the house, growing louder as Bill arrived at the door. Pulling the curtain to the side and standing behind the dirty glass panel in the wooden door, a lit cigarette hung loosely from the corner of Bill's tightened lips and bounced in rhythm as he yelled out, "What the hell you doin' out this way? Wadda ya want?"

His face was weathered and scruffy and his greasy gray hair clumped together and stuck up in spots as if he had been sleeping.

Sheriff Kerry replied, "Bill, this here's Captain Parker from down in Grand Rapids. You mind if we come in for a minute?"

Bill pulled the curtain open a little more to see the captain standing next to Sheriff Kerry, who gave a polite smile and nod. Knowing he didn't really have a choice, Bill mumbled in annoyance and opened the door. As he did, the blaring sounds of 'The Price is Right' escaped from the living room in the back of the house.

It was easy to see where Lathe got his height, as his father was six feet, one inch and had actually shrunk a couple of inches in the past few years. He was sixty-two and looked quite frail, although working the farm for so many years made him as strong as an ox to this day. There was a time when Bill was quite muscular; he had been a farmer his whole life. But ever since his crops dried up in the drought of '81, he'd done nothing but drink a little heavier, smoke his Pall Malls, and sit around watching the six channels of television he received on his blurry TV set. The only time Bill left the house was to drive into town, cash his check from the government, and stock up on groceries and supplies.

"What's this all about?" he said, as he took his cigarette out of his mouth.

"You mind if we come in for a minute, Bill?" Sheriff Kerry asked.

36

Bill's eyes were darting from the sheriff to the captain, and back. In a rather uninviting tone Bill said, "Yeah, come on in." and he turned toward the back room. The two officers removed their hats and sunglasses and entered the home.

Bill's house was disgusting. Upon entering, Sheriff Kerry was immediately overcome by the overwhelming stench of cigarette smoke, rotting food and what smelled like a dead animal. He covered his nose and mouth as discreetly as possible. As the three men walked through the house and into the living room, they saw stacks of soiled dishes in the sink, next to the sink, on the kitchen table and on the floor. Not surprisingly, most of the dishes had mold growing on them and some still had old, rotten food left on them. Between the dishes, Captain Parker saw some large cockroaches scurrying for cover as they felt the vibrations of the men's footsteps. A few of the unluckier ones had been crushed and smeared on the floor.

As they entered the smoke-filled living room, the earsplitting sounds of a chewing gum commercial were interrupted as Bill turned the volume down and sat down in his old, tattered recliner.

"Go ahead, sit down!" Bill said as he motioned for the men to sit on the couch. Sheriff Kerry turned and sat down only to bounce straight back up when he saw Captain Parker still standing.

Unfazed by the captain and the sheriff still standing, Bill took a long drag from his cigarette and, with smoke exiting his mouth on every word, spoke in an obviously annoyed tone. "Well, we're all here now, what the hell is goin' on?"

Captain Parker gave a nod to the sheriff, and then took a step back. Sheriff Kerry took a step forward and began, "Bill, I'm afraid I have some bad news."

"What? What the hell did I do? I didn't do nuttin'!" Bill said in a loud crotchety voice, now visibly becoming more and more agitated.

"Bill," Sheriff Kerry continued with a shaky voice as he fidgeted with is hat, "last night there was … an accident."

Bill sat up and looked at the sheriff straight in the eyes and said in a very slow and deliberate tone, "Well, what the hell does that got to do with me? I was here all night!"

"Well," Sheriff Kerry continued, as he lowered his head and looked at his shoes, "it's about Lathe, he was hurt real bad."

"Goddam it, get to the point!" Bill roared.

"Sir," Captain Parker interrupted with words that cut the tension like a knife, "your son, Lathe, was killed last night. I'm very sorry."

Sheriff Kerry looked up at Bill's expressionless face. Bill sat motionless and silent for a moment, knowing that what he was just told was the God's honest truth. He stared off into the distance as his memory faded to a time when things were better for him and better for his family.

Bill looked toward the kitchen; the dirty dishes seemed to vanish as he was drawn back somewhere in time. Lathe was only eight and his mother, Sonja, was still alive. Bill could see his son's beaming face. Lathe would run around the farm as a boy, chasing the chickens, having conversations with the cows, and running for hours on end through the cornfields behind the house, his arms outstretched and slapping the corn stalks as he ran past them and his dog, Zena, always following just behind, barking all the while. Bill's memory drifted as he saw Lathe lying in bed, wearing his Spider-Man pajamas, hair still damp from his evening bath, sleeping peacefully with his *Rupert the Rhinoceros* book lying on the bed at his side. Bill found it hard to not kiss his boy on the forehead just before he backed out of the room, turning off the light and silently shutting the door.

Just then, Bill's thoughts took a violent turn as they went from his angelic son to his lazy bitch of a wife. Bill jerked at the flashes of his iron fist landing on her cheek, throwing her backwards over the kitchen table. Bill's eyes began to turn red and tearful as he dropped his cigarette into the ashtray on the floor, folded his hands together and pushed them against his quivering lips. He stood from his recliner and wandered out of the room in silence toward the kitchen. Captain Parker and Sheriff Kerry watched Bill as he touched the kitchen table. His mind flashed again and he saw himself throwing it out of his way, the empty beer bottles on top flying through the air and crashing to the floor. He could see himself climbing on top of Sonja who had crawled underneath the table in terror. He began smacking and backhanding her in the face, all the while screaming at her for burning his dinner.

"You stupid, lazy bitch, what are you trying to do, make me sick? Is that what you want?" Sonja's pleas for Bill to stop were drowned out by her sobs and his demonic screams. Now enraged, Bill began throwing punches at her face between his sentences, just to emphasize his point.

*"You just love pissin' me off, don't you, woman? **DON'T YOU?** You good-for-nothing bitch, I work all god damn day out in them fields while you sit here on your ass and you can't even cook me a decent meal? Why the hell can't you do anything right?"* In the midst of all of the punches, Sonja tried feverishly to explain that she was taking care of Lathe, cleaning the house, and running errands, which only further enraged Bill.

"I didn't ask for your whole life story goddam it!! Excuses, that's all them is!" Bill ended each sentence with another blow to his wife's bloody face.

"Excuses are like assholes, everybody's got one! What the hell was I thinking when I married you? I could have married a good woman, what the hell was I thinking?"

Just then, Bill's mind took him to one of the most disturbing images he had ever seen. One that he had kept buried in his mind for years. He saw himself stand up, looking down at his wife, blood covering his still-clenched fist. He had beaten her so badly that she now struggled just to lift her head from the black-and-white checkered floor. Bill tried fighting the memory that came rushing back, but to no avail. He remembered turning around to see his handsome young son, his pride and joy, whose wide, tearful eyes were filled with horror. Too scared to cry, Lathe stood at his opened bedroom door, just off of the kitchen, frozen in place except for the slight uncontrollable shaking caused by seeing, for the first time, his father brutally beating his mother. Lathe had lately heard their arguments getting louder, punctuated with more curse words, but never anything like this! Too scared to move, a steady stream of urine began to run down Lathe's leg and onto the black-and-white tiled floor as he looked into the evil, red eyes of his father.

The sheriff and the captain watched in silence as Bill yelled "Oh, no! Oh, *God*, no!" as he slammed both hands down on the kitchen table. Thunder crashed in his mind, thrusting him back to Sonja's funeral. Father Goshi, dressed in black robes, stood next to Sonja's casket and recited from his Bible while a young man next to him held a black umbrella over the priest's head. As Bill stood in the rain and held his little boy's hand, he fought back the tears and looked down to see Lathe crying uncontrollably, his chest shaking from the sobs.

Bill bent down and whispered into Lathe's ear, "Don't cry, Lathe, be a big boy. Everybody's lookin' at us!"

Confused, Lathe continued crying and started calling to his mother, hoping and praying that she would hear him from inside of her coffin and come out to hug him again.

"Mommy, don't leave me, *please* don't leave me!"

"Goddamn it, boy!" Bill whispered as he began squeezing Lathe's hand harder and harder. "Stop that cryin'! That's not gonna bring your momma back! She got the cancer. She's dead Lathe, and she ain't *comin'* back!"

With that, Bill loosened his grip and Lathe pulled his hand out of his father's and ran to the side of his mother's slowly descending casket. Lathe fell to his knees beside the hole, dropped his head into his hands and continued sobbing and yelling, "Mommy, I love you, don't leave me! Mommy, please come back … please take me with you! I'll go with you!"

Bill snatched Lathe up by his collar and lifted him completely off of the ground as everyone watched in disbelief. "Look what you've done to your new suit! You got it all muddy!" he yelled in his crying child's swollen face. "Go wait in the truck!"

Bill put Lathe down as Sonja's sister, Teresa, ran over to Lathe, picked him up, and held him tightly.

"What the Hell's the matter with you, Bill?" she asked as she carried Lathe over to her warm, dry car. Once inside, she continued holding and rocking Lathe as he cried and screamed for his mother. Soon they were both crying together, holding each other as tight as they could. Feeling a little part of Sonja in each other that they never wanted to let go.

"Are you OK, Bill?" Sheriff Kerry asked quietly as he patted Bill sympathetically on the back. Since Sonja died, Bill had learned to direct all of his anger onto Lathe and Bill cried out as he remembered seeing Lathe, about twelve years old, covering his face while Bill whipped him with an old, frayed extension cord.

"God dammit, boy, I told you to clean them tools! We're gonna' go broke if this drought keeps up. I can't afford to go buyin' new tools!"

"But, Daddy, I – " Lathe screamed out.

"Don't you 'but Daddy' me, you little bastard!"

Lathe's face and arms were cut and bleeding as he cried out, trying feverishly to explain to his father that he went out to the barn and found that they were out of oil so he couldn't clean the tools. Bill wouldn't hear a word of what Lathe had to say. Instead, he continued whipping his son in the arms, chest and face, leaving welts and open cuts with every strike. This memory was too much for Bill to handle and he lost control of his mind and his emotions as he threw the table over. The stacks of dirty dishes flew everywhere and smashed upon the floor. Bill turned around and threw a wild punch that landed squarely on Sheriff Kerry's left cheek, knocking him back and into the stove, sending a stack of soiled dishes crashing to the floor beside him as rotten and moldy food splashed onto his face and uniform.

"*AAAH! FIGHT BACK GODDAMN IT! YOU NEVER FIGHT BACK, BOY*!" Bill screamed, blind with rage, as he continued throwing punches in the air imagining it was Lathe that he was attacking.

Without hesitation, Captain Parker jumped in, deflected one of Bills punches, entered in to get a hold on him, and quickly took Bills legs out from underneath him, throwing him solidly to the putrid floor and momentarily taking his breath away. Bill fought to stand back up but lost the battle as Captain Parker restrained him, simultaneously wrenching one arm behind his back and choking his throat. Bill fought for a few more seconds until he began losing consciousness. Captain Parker released the pressure from Bill's neck and stood back up. Bill lay on the floor amongst the broken dishes and filth and began to cry.

"That boy never did fight back," Bill said in a quiet voice, shaking his head and crying. "He never did fight back."

Captain Parker turned to Sheriff Kerry, making sure he was all right. Bill just lay on the floor curled up, covering his face with his hands while he sobbed. No matter how bad their relationship had become, the reality came crashing down on Bill that he had just lost his only child.

Chapter 3

Back in Walkerville, the village was at a standstill. Everyone had but one thing on their minds – the fate of Lathe Walthes. The questions on everyone's lips were "How could this happen?" and "Who would do such a thing?". Emotions were running high, ranging from disbelief, to horror, to anger and revenge. Fingers began to point and threats were being made, even though no one had the slightest idea yet of what had really happened to Lathe or even if it was the result of man or beast. The human response is to expect the worst and that was the fire that began burning in the minds of everyone in Walkerville.

As they spoke, ideas were imagined and everyone began creating their own story of how it probably happened. From there, ideas grew into rumors until everyone was sure that Lathe had been murdered. It just didn't make any sense. Lathe had always been one of the gentlest, most easy-going people in town. He never got too upset and was never violent. He was just a calm, quiet, local boy. So why would anyone want to kill him? Why Lathe? After all, there were so many other people in the village that no one would have really minded if they were found murdered. Just like in any other town, there were a few bad seeds, but no one could ever say that about Lathe. The ideas continued: maybe it was someone just visiting, someone just passing through town that didn't even know Lathe!

As Sheriff Kerry and Captain Parker returned to the sheriff's department, a reporter from the *Walkerville Ledger* was waiting restlessly on the outside steps, tape recorder in hand. His name was Jim Richardson and he was a young man of thirty-two with short dark hair that was parted neatly on the right side and wearing a sharp gray suit. He was small in stature but big in ambition. Some people in Walkerville called him "a small-town reporter with delusions of grandeur." In his mind though, he knew that some day he would be writing for the *New York Times*. It was just going to take a big story to get their attention and he knew this story was the break he'd been waiting on for eight years! He could already see the headline: "Mutilated Man found in Manistee National Forrest" by Jim Richardson.

"Sheriff, Sheriff, can I have a few moments of your time?" he asked anxiously.

"Not now, Jimmy," Sheriff Kerry responded dismissively as he and Captain Parker walked by and headed through the glass door into the office, seemingly not even noticing Jim's presence.

Jim followed them inside, his voice slightly rising, but not so much so as to upset the sheriff and blow his chance at the biggest story of his career. "Sheriff, this is the worst thing to happen in Walkerville for as long as anyone can remember! Everyone knows that Lathe was killed and they're all confused and upset and everyone's going to be reading the paper tomorrow morning to find out exactly what happened!"

"Jim," Sheriff Kerry said in a matter-of-fact tone, "Captain Parker and I just got back from Bill Walthes's house where we had to tell the man that his son was killed last night."

"But, Sheriff," Jim said cutting him off, "the people *need* to know what happened! How did someone get a hold of Lathe? Why was there a hunk of skin ripped out of his chest? Was it done by an animal or a person? Do you have any leads yet? Were there any fingerprints? The more people know, the less they're gonna make up their own versions of the truth and start blaming the wrong people. Things *could* get out of hand, Sheriff!"

Sheriff Kerry looked at Captain Parker and back at Jim. "Jimmy, we honestly don't have any details for you right now. We got a call this morning from Frank, the owner of the logging company who found Lathe early this

45

morning as he was opening for the day. We don't know yet why he was naked, why there was a chunk taken out of his chest, if a person or an animal did it, when exactly, or why. These things take time. Time I should be using to figure this out instead of talking to you! Now go write your story and let me do my job!"

Jim stood in silence as Sheriff Kerry and Captain Parker turned and walked to the back office with its heavy wooden door shutting solidly behind them.

In the sheriff's office, Grand Rapids Detectives Alan Carter and George Williams were waiting to debrief the sheriff and the captain.

"What do you have, boys?" asked Captain Parker as he and Sheriff Kerry took off their hats and sat down with well-deserved sighs.

"Well, sir," started Detective Williams as he looked down at his notes, "we know that the victim was at a bar called Seth's Place last night. Some patrons remember seeing him there until just before closing time, which was around midnight. He was said to have walked one of the waitresses: a – " he paused as he looked down at his notes, "Syndi Bastion, to her vehicle around that time, returned inside the bar about ten minutes later and left through the back door shortly thereafter. His truck was still in the bar's parking lot when we got there. We did find fresh urine on a section of the back wall and a trail of blood and drag marks starting from the same spot and leading into the woods. We're assuming he was peeing on the wall when he was attacked if the blood samples do prove to be that of the victim. We're pretty sure they're going to be a match."

Detective Williams continued, "We did a search of his residence but we didn't find anything out of the ordinary; no forced entry, no signs of a struggle, and the only prints we found were that of the victim."

Captain Parker nodded his head and asked, "Do we have any fingerprints, hairs, fibers on the body or in the wound?

responded Detective Alan Carter spoke up. "No, sir, nothing, it's all clean. Whoever did this took their time to do it right. There was severe trauma to the back and front of the skull and neck as well as stress marks and wounds on the wrists and ankles that suggest he was tied down for a brief period. Also, there were slight traces of a sticky substance running horizontally over the eyes and mouth."

"Duct tape," said Captain Parker knowingly.

"Yes, sir, I'm sure that was it, but we're running some tests to give it a positive ID. His eyes and mouth must have been taped shut during the ordeal."

"Well, that doesn't explain how he died," said the captain, unconvinced. "He didn't sustain a mortal wound. Although the skin on the chest was missing, no major arteries were cut so he couldn't have bled out."

Detective Carter responded quickly, "No, sir, but there were exploded blood vessels in the eyes, so we assume the victim was choked to death. There were no fingerprints on his neck and his windpipe wasn't crushed so we don't think it was from someone's hands or a rope; we did find some minor rub marks going across his throat and chest, so we think there may have been some sort of thick material wrapped around his throat. Something was probably made into a tourniquet which obstructed the flow of air and blood."

"Sounds like we've got a real sicko running around, Captain," said Sheriff Kerry a bit nervously. "Poor boy," he looked towards the ground and slowly shook his head in disbelief.

Detective Carter continued, "Sheriff, do you know how long the victim had worn facial hair?"

Sheriff Kerry raised his head and responded sadly, "His name was Lathe." He didn't want to see Lathe referred to as just a statistic, as just another dead body.

Detective Carter nodded apologetically accompanied by a quiet, "Sorry." He looked from the sheriff to the captain who nodded in agreement.

"It's ok." Sheriff Kerry responded. "Lathe has had a beard ever since I met him about twelve years ago. Not sure how long he had it before then, why?"

"Well, during our investigation of the body," he caught himself, "of *Lathe's* body, we found that not only his chest, arms, and back were riddled with scars, but his face was, too. Most of them had been there for a long time. Any idea who did that to him, Sheriff?"

"You know," stated Sheriff Kerry, "I didn't even know he had scars on his body until this morning, let alone on his face! His father is a pretty mean old bastard; I would bet that he gave Lathe those marks," he said as he rubbed his sore jaw.

Captain Parker, thinking back on that afternoon and their meeting with Bill Walthes, agreed, "Yeah, that wouldn't surprise me a bit."

"We have a list of people who were in the bar last night at closing time," Detective Williams said.

"OK, let me have that. Looks like I'm going to meet some more locals today," Captain Parker said with a slight hint of sarcasm in his voice before going through the details of his unusual encounter with Lathe's father. When he had finished, he asked Sheriff Kerry to give him directions to everyone's house on the list.

"Well, don't you want me going along?" Sheriff Kerry asked, confused by the very idea of not going.

"No, I'd rather do this myself. Everyone knows you so they might be more inclined to hold something back." The Sheriff thought though that Captain Parker just didn't want him to get in the way. He figured the Captain just saw him as a small town man with small town ways of dealing with people and it just wouldn't work in a murder case. Either that or he might interfere with Captain Parker's methods of getting the information he needed.

Seeing the Sheriff's disappointment, and not wanting to create any friction, Captain Parker added, "Sheriff, I'm just afraid that since everyone around here seems to like you, they just might feel too comfortable with you there. That's *not* what we need right now. I hope you understand."

"Well, yeah," said Sheriff Kerry half-heartedly, "I guess I can see your point."

"Ok, then," Captain Parker said as he handed Sheriff Kerry the list of the patrons that were at Seth's Place the previous night. "Do me a favor then and give me directions to these people's homes and to Seth's Place and I'll get started."

"Oh, no need for that!" Sheriff Kerry replied. "You'll be able to find all these folks down at Seth's tonight. They're there *every* night and since all this happened, I'm sure they wouldn't be anywhere else tonight!" Sheriff Kerry proceeded to draw a map to Seth's Place for the captain.

"Very good," said Captain Parker turning to his detectives. "You boys go on back down to Grand Rapids and get to work on this. Oh, and be sure to positively identify the substance on Lathe's face. I'll stay in the All Seasons Motel that we passed on the way in here and meet up with you in a few days back in Grand Rapids.

Late that evening, having paid for his room, Captain Parker cleaned up a bit inside before heading down to Seth's Place. The mood at Seth's was strange and somber that night. There was no music on the jukebox, no one playing pool and, eerily, there was no yelling – quite uncommon for the usual crowd. Everyone had been drinking and talking for hours and the conversations were flowing in a natural progression from "Poor Lathe!" to "Why did this happen?" to "Who would have wanted to kill him?" to "He really was a good guy" and finally back to "Poor Lathe!"

They had been reminiscing and taking turns telling their personal anecdotes about Lathe. They all knew him and some of them were actually pretty close friends growing up and were unable to hide their tears.

Earlier in the night, Jobin told everyone about the night that he and Lathe and a couple of other boys went out driving in the back roads.

"We must have been seventeen, eighteen maybe. We were out looking for road signs to decorate my bedroom walls. We got down to 'The Bottoms,' you know, the back roads near the lake? Well, we were in my mom's Malibu and came up on this big orange 'Road Closed' sign in the middle of the road. It was just propped up against a traffic horse, the kind with the yellow blinking light on top. You know the kind."

"Yeah." Came the response from a few patrons sitting nearby.

"Anyway, me and Lathe jumped out of the car and grabbed the sign. Turns out, with the huge adrenaline rush we had, we didn't realize that the sign was too big to fit in the car. So we're standing there, freaking out, thinking that the sheriff is going to be coming down the road at any minute and we're all going to go to jail. So we finally realize that if we slide the sign in at an angle, then held it horizontally over everyone's head, it would fit. So that's what we did. Me and Lathe slid the sign in and jumped back in the car. So now all four guys in the car are holding this sign up against the ceiling and yelling and screaming 'cause we just got away with this huge sign! So I hit the gas, still thinking that there's gonna be a cop around so I wanted to get the hell out of there and get back home to unload this sign."

Everyone in the bar was quietly fixated on Jobin's story.

"So we're driving for about fifteen seconds when all of a sudden *spoosh*! This *nasty*, green water comes splashing in the open windows; we're stuck in the middle of a flooded-out piece of the road. The water, mind you, is washed over from the sewage lagoon down there after a really heavy rain, and it's just about up to the windows. We were all completely silent for a second, no one knowing what to say about this predicament we've now found ourselves in. Just then I looked up at the sign we were all holding and after about two seconds of thought, said 'Road Closed!'"

The somber mood of the bar broke instantly and everyone roared with laughter. Jobin started pounding his fist on the table as he laughed and said, "It was like the light went on in everyone's head at the same time and everybody in the car yelled 'Road Closed!'"

One other man in the bar said, "Yeah, holy crap, I *remember* that! I was one of the guys in the back seat!"

This just put everyone in the bar over the top. They were all belly laughing and wiping the tears from their eyes. They were tears of laughter but also tears of sorrow as they remembered and missed their friend.

There was a unique mixture of emotions in the bar that night. Everyone in the room was feeling sorry for Lathe and, although no one had brought it up, most of them felt ashamed for letting their friendship with him slip away and always making him out to be the fool.

Captain Parker pulled into Seth's parking lot and parked his car. As he walked toward the bar, he felt a strange static in the air. He could hear everyone in Seth's talking and laughing and he knew what the topic of conversation was before he even got to the building. Like a predictable old movie, the talking and laughing stopped immediately when he walked through the front door. The bar was instantly silent and everyone's smiles fell slowly into solemn blank faces. Virtually all movement came to a standstill as the tension in the room solidified. Everyone stared nervously at the captain as he stopped and looked around, unfazed and expressionless. From his experiences through the years, he could tell by their reaction that they would not give him much trouble when he started asking questions. He surveyed the room while he walked up to the bar.

Syndi looked around nervously and asked him quickly, "What can I get you, sir?"

"Top shelf bourbon," he coolly replied.

Syndi was aware of everyone staring at her and the captain as she turned to get his drink. When she returned and handed him his bourbon, the noise slowly started up again. He thanked her for the drink and turned back to look around the bar. Although it was almost 11:00 p.m., there were still twelve people there including the two bartenders, Syndi and Loraine. All of the patrons were congregated on the left side of the bar so they could share their stories about Lathe.

Captain Parker walked over to the crowd and asked them who was there last night at closing time. Of the fifteen patrons, six men and two women raised their hands. They knew better than to lie because if they were caught later, it would make them look suspicious.

"Well folks, if you don't mind, I'm going to need a few minutes of your time," Captain Parker said in a friendly voice. The groans and distressed looks on their faces told the captain that they were none too happy about being questioned, some of them for a second or third time that day.

"Oh, I forgot to mention, next round is on me!" he said with a giant smile. The tension broke immediately as everyone looked at each other and began smiling and laughing again.

"I guess he's not so bad," he heard one man say.

Captain Parker took each person, one by one, to the farthest table at the other side of the bar and ran through a standard battery of questions. Everyone cooperated and told all that they knew or could remember, depending on their state of mind currently or the night prior. Because they'd been drinking all night, most of them gave the captain all the information he wanted and in some cases, much more, but he knew that was to be expected when conversing with a drunk.

When he was through, he questioned the bartender, Loraine. She wasn't much help. No one really was, though, because no one saw anything after Lathe left out the back door. Finally, he called Syndi Bastion over to the table. She was dressed in a tight black mini-skirt, a black bikini top and black high heels.

"Would you mind sitting with me for a few minutes so I can ask you some questions?"

"Um, sure," Syndi responded.

"Last Call folks!" Loraine yelled over the crowd.

"Aww," followed the familiar reply.

Syndi and Captain Parker sat down in the empty corner of the bar.

"Hi, I'm Captain Parker," he said as he offered her his hand. "And you're Syndi Bastion, right?"

"Yeah, how did you know that?" She said nervously as she shook his hand.

"I knew it the minute I walked through the door. You fit the description," he said jokingly. "I've read a lot of testimony today and your name came up quite a few times. You're described as five foot four, Caucasian, athletic build, blondish brown hair to the middle of the back, green eyes, and some of the guys interviewed went on to talk about how beautiful you are and then into measurements, but we don't need to get into all of that," he said with a slight grin. Seeing that Syndi was a little uncomfortable and embarrassed, he digressed.

"Well, why was *my* name brought up so many times?" she asked pointedly.

The sheriff cleared his throat before responding in a more professional tone, "Seems Lathe walked you to your truck last night around closing time."

"Yeah, he did." Syndi said.

"Well," Captain Parker continued as he looked through some of his papers, "according to the testimonies, about ten minutes later he came back in the bar through the front door and almost immediately exited through the back door. That was the last anyone had seen of him. So I'm wondering," he said looking up from his papers and smiling politely, "what happened in those ten minutes while you two were outside?"

Surprised at what she thought he was implying, Syndi quickly responded, "Nothing! I park all the way in the back of the lot just so I can get in a little exercise. I park at the back of the lot usually wherever I go – the store, church, the movie theatre, wherever really. So it took about three or four minutes to get to where I was parked."

"So did Lathe try anything while you two were alone? Did he get physical in any way?"

"Oh, God, no!" Syndi responded. "He would never do anything like that, he's too … he *was* too shy for that. I knew he liked me, he always found reasons to come up and talk to me and I'd always catch him sneaking a peek at me when he thought I wasn't looking, but he never did anything about it. He never even asked me out. He was just too shy." She sighed and looked down at the table, noticeably saddened by the thought that Lathe would never again sit in her bar, talk to her, or offer to walk her to her truck.

"Did you see anybody else in the parking lot when he walked you out?"

"No, it was just me and him. Nobody came or left while we were out there."

The captain continued, not trying to hide his inquisitive tone, "So after you got in your truck, he made the walk back to the bar alone?"

"Yeah, I offered him a ride back up to the front, but he said he'd just walk. To be honest, I was kind of relieved. I thought it might get uncomfortable and thought he might strike up a conversation and I didn't really have time to talk so I told him that I was late for dropping off my girlfriend's truck. I'm borrowing it until mine gets fixed; it's in the shop right now getting a new transmission put in."

"Oh, I see," responded the captain.

Syndi went on, "Yeah, my friend is waiting up for me now so I can drop off her truck and she can drive me home. I actually get *my* truck back tomorrow! Are we about done here? I really don't want to piss her off."

"Well, I do have some more questions I need to ask you, but I'll make you a deal… I let you go now if you'll meet me tomorrow so we can finish this up."

"Deal!" Syndi said as she stood up from the table and extended her hand to shake his.

"Very good then," Captain Parker said as he stood up and shook her hand. "What time do you work tomorrow?" he asked.

"Besides getting my truck tomorrow, I don't have any plans," Syndi stated and said, "Why don't we meet at the Eat Rite Diner for lunch?"

"Sure!" Captain Parker responded, a bit surprised. "How about 1:00?"

"I'll be there!" Syndi said, smiling. "Thank you so much for understanding."

"Oh, not at all. You have a good night Ms. Bastion, and I'll see you at 1:00 tomorrow."

Syndi turned and started to leave but then spun around and said, "Would you mind walking me to out to my truck, captain? There's no way I'm walking out there alone in the dark any time soon!"

"Sure, be happy to, ma'am," he said with a smile as he reached into his wallet and laid a fifty-dollar bill on the table for the round of drinks he bought, then laid another fifty on the table in front of Syndi as a generous tip. As Syndi smiled and picked it up, all eyes were on her and the captain as they walked out the front door.

As they walked, Syndi asked, "Well, you've been asking questions all day, how's about you answer a few?"

"Sure, what would you like to know?" Captain Parker asked with a laugh.

"Where are you from?"

"Well, actually I was called up here from Grand Rapids."

"Ahh," Syndi mused, "A *city* boy, huh?"

"Yeah, I guess you could say that. Been a lot of places really, I go where the job takes me."

"Oh, I see," Syndi responded. "An all over kind of guy?"

"That about sums me up, I guess," he said with a smile. Their conversation drew on until finally they found themselves at the back of the parking lot by Syndi's truck.

Seeing flakes lightly falling from the sky and landing on the fur collar of the captain's black coat, Syndi said, "Oh, it's starting to snow! Can I give you a ride back, captain?"

"You know, I kind of like walking, too. I think I'll be all right," Captain Parker said as he smiled and bid her a good night.

As Syndi pulled out of the parking lot, Captain Parker walked back toward Seth's Place, taking almost the same path that Lathe had taken when he walked back to the bar the night before. The Captain listened carefully to the giant parking lot as he wondered if Lathe had heard anything on his long walk back.

The captain walked by the vehicles and looked between each one as he passed, which was a trait that he had acquired while being on the job. As he neared the bar, he veered off to the right side and walked around to the back where it was much darker due to the lack of windows. Feeling the cold flakes melting as they landed on his cheeks, he noticed that the air was uncommonly still and, when he looked up, he could see that the sky was thick with clouds hiding the stars and the moon. As he ducked under the yellow police tape surrounding the area behind the bar where the trail of blood was found, he walked past the green dumpster, pulled a small flash light from an inside pocket of his coat, and shined it on the screen door and the heavy black back door. The door which was the last one that anyone would see Lathe walk through. After examining the doors, Captain Parker turned to his left and shined his light on the dumpster and the lid that covered the top as he walked over to look under it, wondering if his team had possibly missed anything.

As his light shown below the dumpster, he reached his hand under, pushing further and further until his shoulder pressed up against it. As he lay on the cold, gravely ground, he felt around, trying to find anything out of the ordinary. Having found nothing, he pulled his arm out from underneath and stood back up and put his hand in his coat pocket to warm it up. The captain's light flowed from the dumpster to the gravelly ground and up onto the wall, almost to the very spot where Lathe's forehead had bounced after he had been bludgeoned on the back of his head with the lead end of a tire thumper the night before. On the ground, just four feet below the circular outline of the flashlight's beam, was some of the dried urine and blood that had spilled from Lathe's body.

Captain Parker turned back toward the heavy black back door and just as he neared it, he heard a rapidly advancing noise coming from behind him. He pulled his pistol and turned quickly to see the golden eyes of a frightened raccoon racing toward him before turning sharply toward the forest as it was startled by the captain's surprised yell.

After regaining his composure, the captain chuckled and walked back to the dumpster to have a look inside figuring that the raccoon had been scared out when he was reaching around beneath it. Using a branch from the ground to open the lid, he saw only a day's worth of trash inside. He looked toward the forest and said jokingly, "Well, I guess there goes this town's only real lead."

Chapter 4

Early the next morning, the captain met Sheriff Kerry at the sheriff's office to discuss their plans for the day. Captain Parker told the sheriff that he had a meeting at 1:00 that afternoon to question one of the townspeople. He was wearing a pair of khaki pants and a black buttoned-up shirt with the sleeves rolled up twice.

"People are less comfortable talking to me when I'm wearing my uniform. I guess I might look a little intimidating in it," he said.

"Well, sir," Sheriff Kerry responded with a laugh, "you don't really look that much less intimidating in civilian clothes!"

By the forced grin on Captain Parker' face, the sheriff knew that he shouldn't have said anything. As his face became flush, he continued, "Who are you meeting with?"

Captain Parker replied, "I forget the name, I've got it written down in my car." Without hesitation, he continued, "Sheriff, would you mind sticking around here today in case anyone calls with any leads? It's really very important because most informational call-ins occur within forty-eight hours after a murder. If a person calls with information, it's only after they've done a great deal of mental preparation to get past their fear of calling because they think that what they know may either be brushed off or make them look like a suspect. Nine times out of ten, if they don't get someone of authority the first time, they'll just hang up and will never call again."

Sheriff Kerry responded, "Well, I hadn't planned on it, but I can see your point. Sure, I'll take care of it, Captain," he said assuredly.

The two men discussed the best places for the captain to visit to get more acquainted with Walkerville and to get a better feel for their way of life in this little village in the middle of the forest. Sheriff Kerry drew up a map of some of the local establishments for the captain to check out. "Here's where the church is," Sheriff Kerry said. "Being that it's Sunday, that's a good place to start. And down the road here," he continued as he drew, "is the flea market. That place is pretty crowded on the weekends." He continued mapping out various places where he thought Captain Parker would have the best chance of finding a crowd. When he was finished drawing, the captain took the map, thanked the sheriff for his help and headed out of the building.

"Boys, I'm going to be holding down the fort today," Sheriff Kerry told his deputies.

"Julian, I want you and Tim to ride together. Charlie, I want you to just go out and make your presence known. Just talk to folks, or rather, get them talking to you. You're the one with all the charm! Just see if you can get any information about what happened to Lathe, but don't make it *look* like you're trying to get information."

"Yes, sir, I can do that," Charlie said with a grin.

"OK then, you boys get going and call me on the radio if anything comes up."

*****

At ten minutes to one, Captain Parker sat waiting for Syndi at the Eat Rite Diner. He always made it a habit to be a little early for appointments. He knew it was more professional to be early than to be late. His father used to tell him "Better late than never, but better never late!"

Moments later, Syndi walked into the diner wearing a pair of tight blue jeans and an unzipped black leather coat. Beneath her coat was a brilliantly white oxford with the top two buttons unbuttoned, exposing her cleavage and just the very top of her pink satin-laced bra. She wore very little makeup, but she was a natural beauty and didn't really need any. Her long dirty-blond hair was pulled back into a ponytail, accentuating the curves of her face.

When Sheriff Kerry saw Syndi, he stood up as she joined him at his table. He waited for her to remove her coat and sit down across from him before he started to sit back down, trying desperately not to look at her cleavage.

"Thank you for meeting me today," Captain Parker said politely.

"Well," Syndi replied, "I told you I would be here and I wouldn't want you hunting me down for not showing up!" She laughed and Captain Parker grinned. They continued their pleasantries until their waitress came and took their lunch orders.

"I do have a few more questions for you, Ms. Bastion."

"Oh please, my mother is Ms. Bastion. Call me Syndi."

"Well, thank you, Syndi." Captain Parker said, not offering the same. "I'd like to know more about your friend, Lathe," he said, trying to lead Syndi into the conversation.

"Well, honestly, we weren't that close of friends really. Not any more anyway. We went to grade school together. He was a couple of years older than me, but he was always really nice to me, even back then. After he was kicked out of school, we never really saw each other anymore."

"He was kicked out of school?" Captain Parker interrupted.

"Yeah, he used to skip school all the time. It got to where he skipped so much that they finally just told him not to come back."

"I see," Captain Parker said as he began writing in his note pad. "So then you really didn't see much of him after that?"

"Well maybe we'd pass each other in a store or restaurant every now and then, but you know how it goes," she said. "As the years went by, we'd have less and less to say to each other, then it turned into just a smile and a wave from across the room until finally we'd see each other but wouldn't even act like we did. Well, at least I'd act like I didn't see him. I knew he was looking at me, though. Why does it always have to be like that? You know what I mean?"

"Yeah, I know what you mean. I'm guilty of it myself," Captain Parker said. "So when did all that change? When did you start talking again?"

"A few years ago, Lathe moved out of his dad's house and got his own place here in town," she said. "He came in to Seth's one night and I was behind the bar. He just came right up to me and said 'Hey, remember me?' Of course I did, even though for years I acted like I didn't. We sat and talked for most of the night, just catching up from the years gone by and talking about all the people we used to go to school with, what's changed in the town and how much it's stayed the same, just stuff like that."

Captain Parker interrupted, "So, you were friends from then on?"

"No, I wouldn't really say that. We were 'friendly' toward each other, but I wouldn't say we were actually friends. I really only saw him at Seth's when I was working. We never got together or called each other on the phone or anything like that. It was more of a bar-friend kind of thing."

"But you felt comfortable having him walk you to your car at night, huh?"

"Yes, I did. Lathe was the kind of guy you just *knew* was all right. I never understood why everybody picked on him but when it got to be too much, I would usually step in and put a stop to it and I think he appreciated that. He really was a good person; I could just tell he had a good soul."

"I'm sure he appreciated it, Syndi," the captain said.

Throughout their lunch, Captain Parker asked question after question and tried to get a feel for who Lathe really was, what he was all about, and if anyone would have reason to want him dead. Talking with Syndi was insightful, but he knew that she had no idea who might have been behind the murder or anyone who would have wanted him dead.

"So," Syndi asked, "what's on your agenda now?"

"Huh?" Captain Parker responded quickly, sounding quite confused. "What do you mean?"

"Well, are you going back to Grand Rapids today?"

"Oh," he said, finally understanding. "No, I thought it would be better if I stayed in Walkerville for a few days and worked on the case here while the other guys on the team worked in the office back home. I'm going to just explore the town today, kind of get to know the place."

"Do you know where everything is?" Syndi asked.

"Well, Sheriff Kerry mapped out a few places for me," said Captain Parker, pulling the hastily drawn map out of a metal folder and handing it to Syndi. She took the paper, gave it a quick once-over, noticing the grocery store, flea market, hardware store and church that were marked on the map.

"Well, what about the new little coffee house they just built, or the ice skating rink, the movie theatre, oh, or that Chinese Restaurant that everyone goes to?"

"Um, well, I don't … really know." Captain Parker said, not knowing what answer to give and not actually knowing if the question was rhetorical.

"If you really want to experience Walkerville, and not just the places that Sheriff Kerry frequents, I could really show you around!" Syndi said.

"Well, that would be great! I'd appreciate it," said Captain Parker, not fully understanding her intent.

"Then why don't you pick me up around 7:00 and we'll hit the town. We can start at Sijo Lee's Chinese restaurant!"

"Great!" Captain Parker said, stunned at how quickly their lunch meeting had turned into plans for dinner and a night out. Syndi wrote down directions to her house on the back of the map, along with her cell phone number in case he got lost, and handed it back to Captain Parker.

"You go ahead and check out the places on the map that Sheriff Kerry made for you and tonight I'll show you the rest!" Syndi said.

"Ok, I'll see you at 7:00 then." Captain Parker said as they stood up and shook hands.

"It's a date!" she said with a smile as she slipped her coat on, turned and walked past the large front window of the diner and out the door. Captain Parker stood for a moment in disbelief as one of the most beautiful women he had ever laid eyes on climbed into her truck and drove away.

As the day went on, Captain Parker checked out the places the sheriff had noted on his map and talked to most of the workers at each spot and some of the people on the streets in between. No one came forth with any information – any *useful* information anyway, that would give any insight as to who murdered Lathe Walthes.

"But at least I've made my presence known a bit more today," the captain thought to himself. "If there was anyone in this town that didn't know I'm investigating Lathe's murder, I'll bet they'll know by the end of the night!"

Captain Parker caught up with the sheriff back at his office where they filled each other in on their day. Sheriff Kerry told the captain that no one had called with any leads. Captain Parker filled the sheriff in on his lunch meeting, his jaunt around town, and his plans for later that night.

"Where the hell do you keep that rabbit's foot?" Sheriff Kerry said as he looked playfully around the captain.

"Huh? What do you mean?" the captain replied, quite confused.

"You've got a date with Syndi Bastion? Nobody gets a date with her. She never goes out with *any* of the boys around here!"

"Well," Captain Parker said in an uncharacteristically humorous tone, "I ain't from around here!"

Sheriff Kerry stood momentarily motionless, his mouth wide open before he laughed out loud while the captain just grinned.

*****

At five minutes to seven, Captain Parker pulled into Syndi's driveway. He'd been involved in countless investigations throughout the years and had dealt with tens of thousands of people in the process – car thieves, gang

members, rapists, child molesters, the mentally insane, and even serial killers –
but for some reason he found that just walking up and knocking on Syndi's
door was terrifying. Because he had immersed himself in his work for so many
years and devoted all of his time and efforts to the job, he had not made much
time for friends or women in his life.

Syndi opened the door and greeted the captain with a warm and excited
smile. "Hi there, Captain Parker. I see you found the place all right."

"Sure did, but under the circumstances, why don't you just call me
Luke?"

"All right then, Luke," Syndi said, delighted as she attempted to hold
back a smile. "Well why don't you come on in and have a seat?" She offered
him a drink, which he graciously refused, before she said, "I'm just about ready
to go." She was *not* just about ready to go. In fact, she was still dressed in the
same outfit she had been wearing when they met for lunch earlier that
afternoon. Luke sat down and watched as Syndi walked into her bedroom.

"I'll be right out," she said, shutting the door behind her.

As he sat waiting, Luke became aware of things that most calm people
don't usually think about.

"Was it really that hot in here?" he thought to himself. "Should I have
worn something besides my black slacks and this red shirt? My palms are really
clammy. Are they always this clammy?"

Twenty minutes later, as he sat pondering his discomfort, Syndi opened
her bedroom door and came into the living room.

"OK, I'm ready to go!" Luke turned to see Syndi standing in the
doorway and his mouth inadvertently fell slightly agape. She looked perfect.
She had taken her hair out of the ponytail and let it fall, the loose curls reaching
the middle of her back. She was wearing tight black suede pants and black high
heels with a big purple cashmere sweater that accentuated her large, full breasts
and thin waist and was pulled down on the sides exposing her soft, smooth

shoulders. Luke noticed Syndi's wet red lips that she had painted and her dark green eyes that sparkled even more brilliantly than before, surely the result of the makeup that she was now wearing. He stood up and smiled, unable to actually speak for a brief moment as he caught a slight whiff of her freshly applied perfume, which actually warmed his lungs as he breathed her in.

Syndi asked, "Is everything ok?"

"Oh, yeah," Luke said, fighting the urge to tell her how beautiful she looked and sounding exactly like every other guy she'd come in contact with over the past fifteen years. "Just fine! Ready to go?" Luke walked with Syndi out of her house and down to his car.

"Sijo Lee's then?" Luke asked as he opened the passenger door on his blue squad car.

"Hey, this'll be the first time I get to ride up *front* in one of these!" Syndi said, ignoring his question.

Luke tilted his head slightly, eyebrows raised, and looked down at Syndi.

"Ha! Got ya!" she said as she began to laugh.

Luke smiled widely and shut her door once she was seated. "All that and a sense of humor too!" he thought to himself as he rounded the front of the car and got in. "So the Chinese restaurant, then?" he said and smiled.

"Absolutely! We'll need some energy for the rest of the night!" she said with a slight grin.

*****

Later that evening, as they were enjoying their desserts and each other's company, the conversation had drifted from one getting-to-know-you topic to another until they had firmly covered each other's families, friends, favorite movies, career ambitions, pets, hobbies' and home towns.

Eventually, Syndi said "So … what about Lathe?" Her eyes looked directly into Luke's and she was obviously concerned about what had happened and what would be happening next.

"I'm sorry, but I'm not really at liberty to talk about the case to anyone outside of the investigation." Luke said.

"Oh, well I can certainly understand that," she said, disappointed. "It's just so unbelievable! I guess it has me, well, it has everybody a little freaked out. The person that killed Lathe is out there somewhere but nobody knows where! That's the scary part. He could be three states away by now or he could be five feet away from us at the next table! We've always felt so secluded and safe up here, away from the insanity of the real world."

"Well I've got some of the best men in the state on the case," Luke said. "I would never tell anyone that they're a hundred percent safe, but as long as you keep your head up, stay aware of what's going on around you and you're careful, chances are a lot better that you'll stay safe."

"I feel pretty safe with you around," Syndi said with a smile as she reached across the table and briefly touched Luke's hand.

With his heartbeat suddenly increasing, Luke responded, "Well you certainly should because I'm not going to let anything happen to you while I'm around, that's for sure!"

They both smiled, Syndi feeling even safer and more at ease than before. Just then, a Chinese waiter approached their table and asked if they would like any more coffee. Luke responded negatively in the waiter's native language and asked for the check. The waiter smiled and laughed as he shook his head and turned around.

Turning back to Syndi, Luke said "So you say you lived in New York for a while, huh?"

Completely taken aback, Syndi responded, "Did you just talk to that guy in Chinese?"

"Well, actually, I spoke to him in Cantonese," he said modestly. "It's a dialect of the Chinese language. I heard him talking to one of the other waiters so I knew what language he spoke. I spent some time overseas and picked up a little bit when I was in Hong Kong."

Syndi responded, obviously impressed, "That's *amazing!*"

Luke laughed it off humbly and said, "OK, enough about me... tell me about New York!"

"Well it's not as exciting as living in Hong Kong probably," Syndi said. "I went up there for a modeling job a few years ago. It was pretty fun at first, but after a year or so of getting up at 4:00 a.m. to have my makeup and hair done and then going to different locations for the shoots, and then the parties every other night, it got pretty old and I got tired. I was only there for about a year and a half, but that's like a lifetime in New York! It can really change a person. Know what I mean?"

"Yeah," Luke said, "I know what you mean. Life's a little different in New York than it is in Walkerville!"

The waiter returned with a small tray that held the bill and two fortune cookies. As he stretched to set the tray on the table, Luke noticed a tattoo of an old Chinese man in a long white robe carrying a long black staff on the waiters' forearm. "Interesting tattoo!" Luke said in Cantonese.

"He's a Chinese symbol of good luck!" the waiter answered in his native tongue as he smiled and bowed slightly before leaving their table. Luke took the bill off of the tray before motioning for Syndi to pick up a fortune cookie.

Smiling widely at Luke's conversation with the waiter, she broke her cookie open and read aloud, "An unexpected surprise is in store for you." She thought for a moment and then giggled.

"What's so funny about that?" Luke asked with a smile.

"You have to put 'in bed' at the end of your fortune!" Syndi replied. "It always makes it funny!"

Luke thought for a second and then smiled mischievously.

"What's yours say?" Syndi asked.

Luke cracked open his cookie and read the paper inside, "Fruits of your labor will be rich and sweet indeed."

Luke and Syndi looked at each other and couldn't help but laugh. Luke leaned toward Syndi and asked in a quieter tone, "Have you noticed how many people have been watching us since we got here?"

"No, not really," Syndi said with some surprise.

"Yeah, at first I caught a few guys looking, so I figured they were just checking you out, but then I noticed some women and even some kids watching us. I could tell they were talking about us, too."

"Well this *is* a small town," Syndi said. "Not to sound vain or anything, but guys do look at me a lot wherever I go. I really don't notice it anymore, but now I'm here with *you*, the Captain of the Grand Rapids Homicide Department. You can bet that everyone here knows who you are by now, and now that they've seen us together, the tongues will be waggin' tomorrow at the water cooler, I guarantee you that!" Syndi turned sharply to catch a couple at a nearby table, staring.

"Hi there!" she said loud enough for half of the restaurant to hear her as she waved. "Enjoying your meal?"

Syndi turned back to see Luke who, for the first time, looked completely shocked. Syndi simply said, "Well!"

They both broke out in laughter, not even trying to hide it from the numerous onlookers.

"Let's get out of here," Syndi said. They both stood up and walked toward the door as Syndi held onto Luke's arm. "The night is young and we need to make the best of it. What say we go to the new coffee shop? They make the *best* iced lattés! I've got a friend that's going to be playing his guitar in there tonight, too!"

"Sounds good to me – this is your town, you're in charge tonight!" Luke said. He helped Syndi into the car and they headed toward the other side of town. They were only a half mile down the road when a red minivan passed them headed in the opposite direction. Kathy Peters, a local hairdresser was at the wheel. She was a young woman of twenty-eight, a little on the heavy side, but pretty in the face and a genuinely nice person.

She was headed for the Kwik-Mart, which is the last building on Main Street before it turns into Harrison Road and becomes nothing but fields and woods for what seems like an eternity. Kathy needed to pick up a few things and since it was past 9:00 on a Sunday, the grocery store was already closed for the night. She pulled into the Kwik-Mart parking lot, parked her car, and went inside. She was only in the store for a moment when a very large man wearing blue surgical scrubs, blue rubber gloves and a white cap and surgical mask tied tightly around his head stepped out from the shadow of a truck in the back of the parking lot. He ran to Kathy's minivan and tried opening the tail door. Finding it locked, he quickly headed to the driver's side door and found it unlocked. He climbed inside and quietly closed the door behind him. Once inside, he lumbered around the passenger bench seat and squatted down behind it in the back storage area. The surgeon peered over the bench seat and out the front windshield as he tried to control his rapid breathing and silently lay down so as to not be noticed when Kathy returned to her minivan.

In his mind, he had all of his bases covered; since her minivan was the only vehicle in the parking lot not belonging to the two employees inside, he knew that if she opened the rear door, he could attack and control her and ultimately knock her out, get her into the minivan, and drive off. It was just a waiting game at this point.

Moments passed slowly in his mind and the surgeon was getting even more anxious. His adrenaline raced. He could feel his heart pounding harder and his breathing becoming more rapid. As he was trying to calm himself down, he waited and listened. In the distance, he could hear the thump of rock music that was steadily growing louder and louder. He raised his head ever so slightly to look out of the side window where he saw a shiny black '72 Charger pulling into the parking lot.

The surgeon quickly dropped back down on the floor of the minivan as the Charger parked just to the right. A long-haired teenage boy got out of the driver's side, while his girlfriend waited in the car while he went into the Kwik-Mart to pick up some cigarettes. The Surgeon remained pressed to the floor of the minivan for a few more seconds before slowly lifting his head again to look out of the side window just in time to see Kathy walking out of the Kwik-Mart. He instantly dropped back down as she walked toward her minivan, holding a bag of groceries.

The surgeon reached into the pocket of his scrub pants and pulled from it a round, white toothbrush case. He hastily opened the case, revealing two shiny, metal scalpels inside. He pulled one out, shut the container, and shoved the case back into his pocket. He clenched his fist around the scalpel and gritted his teeth as he prepared himself physically and mentally for what he knew he must do next. His mind raced as he tried to decide if he should jump out and run away as fast as he could when Kathy opened the rear door or if he should stick to his original plan, knowing that if the girl in the Charger saw him abduct Kathy, surely he could knock Kathy out and jump into the driver's seat and get away before the girl in the Charger could run into the Kwik-Mart and call the police. And she wouldn't be able to describe the surgeon anyway since he was wearing his surgical garb.

Kathy approached the minivan and the surgeon heard her lift the door handle. No more time for thinking, now he had to act. Kathy opened the

70

driver's side door and climbed in, lying her bag of groceries on the passenger seat beside her before starting up the engine and turning around to look out of the rear window of the minivan while she backed out of her parking spot. She pulled out onto Main Street and headed for home. In the back, the surgeon carefully wiped some beads of sweat off of his forehead and rubbed his hand on his blue scrub pants, not wanting his sweat to be found in the van later.

As Kathy drove, the surgeon watched out of the back window to keep track of where they were. She had turned off of Main Street and onto a rural side road. Once they were safely away from the lights of downtown Walkerville, the surgeon saw that there were no other cars or buildings around, only open fields and trees beyond them. He lay back on the floor of the van gripping his scalpel and taking a few quick, short breaths. All at once, he threw himself over the passenger bench landing on the floor behind the driver's seat.

Kathy screamed at the top of her lungs and, with a jerk, lost control of the minivan and began swerving all over the country road. Her groceries were thrown about in all of the chaos, smashing against the passenger door, the dashboard and Kathy's body. As she fought to regain control of the vehicle while simultaneously trying to see who was behind her, the minivan spewed dirt and gravel, sliding from one side of the road to the other and narrowly avoiding a large drainage ditch.

Kathy screamed uncontrollably as she straightened out the van, slammed on the brakes, and opened the door to jump out. As she twisted to throw herself out though, she was suddenly aware that she was unable to move her head away from the headrest. The surgeon had a tight grip on her hair, which he was pulling backwards through the hole between the headrest bars. She looked in the rearview mirror to see his other hand shoot forward from the darkness, holding a scalpel which he placed on her well exposed throat.

"*Stop screaming!*" he yelled. "*If you keep screaming, I'll slice your fucking throat!*"

Kathy looked into her mirror again to see the Surgeon's wild eyes fixed on hers. She held her breath momentarily as it was all she could do to control her screams.

"Now, if you even touch my hand, I'll make you wish you hadn't," he said in a low, growling voice, rubbing the scalpel up and down her neck. "Shut your door and drive!"

"What do you want from me?" Kathy asked through her sobs.

"I want you to *drive*! Didn't I just *say* that?"

"You're going to kill me if I do."

"You don't know that! But I *will* kill you right here, *right now* if you don't!"

"OK" Kathy whispered in a shaky voice. "I'll take you wherever you want to go." Shaking uncontrollably, she closed her door and began driving again, her hair still in the surgeon's grip and his right arm around her throat, the scalpel resting heavily on her left jugular vein.

"Where are we going?" she asked.

"Just go until I tell you to turn," he said angrily. "Why don't you turn on the stereo? It'll help you relax."

With a trembling hand, Kathy switched on the stereo, which was set to a Country and Western station.

"*Turn that shit off*!" the surgeon screamed.

Startled, Kathy jumped, causing the scalpel to nick her throat. A tiny drop of blood filled the nick as the surgeon commanded, "Turn it to the classical station!"

Kathy clumsily turned the dial until they heard violins and a piano softly playing Rachmaninoff's "Rhapsody on a Theme of Paganini."

"There," he said sarcastically, "don't you feel more relaxed now?"

"Turn left at that dirt road!" he said as he pulled her hair harder against her headrest.

Kathy was trying to keep as calm as possible but was unable to stop crying. She drove down the dirt road for a few minutes until the surgeon told her to turn again into a thicker part of the forest.

"I'll do whatever you want," Kathy said quietly through her tears.

"What's that?" the surgeon asked.

"I said I'll do whatever you want. Just please don't kill me. I won't put up a fight, I promise. I don't want to die!" Kathy started crying harder as the idea of her death and her funeral overcame her thoughts and emotions.

She spoke through her tears, "You can do what you want to me and then take my minivan! I can't see your face, so I can't identify you. You can just drive away! I won't even tell anybody, I promise! I don't even have a cell phone and it would take me at least an hour to walk back to town anyway, so you've got plenty of time to get away!"

Now deep in the thick, silent forest, the surgeon pulled again on Kathy's hair and said, "I like the sound of that. Turn left here." Kathy turned onto a dirt path and drove a short distance.

"Stop the van," the Surgeon growled. Kathy stopped the van and put it into park. The surgeon released her hair, keeping the scalpel to her throat, and reached around the left side of her seat and ran his hand under Kathy's jacket and began rubbing her stomach and squeezing her breast through her shirt. Kathy whimpered as the surgeon kneaded her breast while he moaned softly behind her.

"Now open the door and get out, slowly!" the surgeon said. He reached around the headrest and gripped her hair again, keeping the scalpel to her throat as he scooted around the front of the driver's seat and out of the driver's side door behind Kathy. The only visible light was coming from the headlights of the minivan shining on the trees ahead through the freshly upturned dust that moved slowly with the gentle breeze.

The surgeon released Kathy's hair, grabbed her throat and pushed her back against the van. He brought his face an inch from hers and stared into her horrified eyes. He leaned to her side and sniffed her hair, then her neck, then her shirt, pushing his nose down into her cleavage. He began to laugh quietly. Kathy started shaking and squeezed her hands and eyes shut.

The surgeon stood between the open door and the driver's seat and guided Kathy closer to him as he sat down on the seat.

"Bend over here, bitch!" he said as he held onto her neck with one hand and kept the scalpel to the side of her throat with the other until she was bent all the way over with her hands on her knees to brace herself so she wouldn't fall forward. The surgeon pulled Kathy's head forward until he could feel her warm hurried breathing on the crotch of his blue scrub pants. He held the scalpel and her hair in his left hand, while his right hand reached under her shirt and bra and began squeezing her breast and pinching her nipple hard until she yelled out in pain.

"Ever think you could feel this alive?" the surgeon asked in a deep growl.

Frozen in fear, all Kathy could do was look up at him and cry. The surgeon brought his hand out from beneath her shirt and reached back to give Kathy a hard spank.

"Oh, I'm really going to *enjoy* this!" he said happily. He untied his scrub pants and slid his blue rubber gloved hand inside of his underwear. "Open your mouth, and close your eyes and I'll give you a *big* surprise!"

Kathy shut her eyes and slowly opened her mouth as she tried to slow her uncontrollable crying. Still holding her hair in his left hand, the surgeon quickly pulled his legs into the minivan, grabbed the door handle with his right hand, and as Kathy's eyes opened wide, he slammed the door shut on her head, pinning it just above her ears. Blood squirted out of the gashes on her temples and out of her nose at the same time. The surgeon pushed the door back open and Kathy collapsed to the ground in a heap.

The surgeon got out of the minivan and studied Kathy's still body lying on the ground for a moment before tying his pants back up. He squatted down and felt the beating pulse on her neck before standing back up. He pointed down at her and said, "Don't go anywhere," before casually walking away from her and the minivan, down the dirt path and disappearing into the darkness of the forest.

Kathy lay motionless and completely alone on the dead brown and orange leaves that blanketed the ground. The only sounds were that of her minivan's running engine and the wind gusting from time to time, blowing the dead sticks and leaves around. Neither the frosty, damp ground nor the cold blowing wind could stir Kathy from her deep unconsciousness.

Moments later, the surgeon's Blazer roared from out of the forest and stopped just beside the minivan. The surgeon stepped out of the Blazer, walked over to Kathy and straddled her before squatting down and applying an eight-inch length of duct tape securely over her mouth.

Blood covered the sides of her face from the open gashes on each side of her forehead. The surgeon pulled Kathy's shirt up and wiped her face of the fresh blood before applying another strip of duct tape over her eyes. He then leisurely rolled her over onto her stomach and proceeded to tightly tie her ankles together before tying her hands behind her back with the same type of thin nylon rope that he had used on Lathe. Once finished, the surgeon lifted Kathy from the ground and walked to the back of the Blazer where he tossed her atop a plastic tarp that covered a brown blanket.

Once satisfied that Kathy was secured, the surgeon got into her minivan and drove it back out onto the main dirt road while opening all of its windows. He drove just a short distance before turning onto a long path that was overgrown with high grass and reeds. A minute later he entered a circular clearing that was once used as a lumber storage area. A few old logs littered the ground on the far side of the clearing in a scattered pile.

The surgeon parked Kathy's minivan in the middle of the clearing and exited it, leaving the driver's side door open. He looked around at the openness and stillness of the clearing and smiled beneath his surgical mask before turning, leaving the clearing, and beginning his hike back down the overgrown path toward his waiting Blazer and toward Kathy.

He wondered if her minivan would be found right away or if it would be weeks or even months until it was found. He grinned as he imagined it taking a month or more, the day that it was finally found, and what they would all say about the addition he had planned for its roof top.

"The police would only check the ground in its vicinity for prints, blood and signs of a struggle," he thought to himself as he walked down the path in the darkness, knowing that they would never check the area, over 300 yards away, where he had actually spilled Kathy's blood.

"We didn't drive the Blazer into that area either, so there's no tire tracks from it, and because of the thick layer of dead leaves on the ground, there's no need to worry about footprints that could lead the police back to the actual scene of the crime. Even if they dusted the minivan, they wouldn't find our fingerprints because we're smart enough to wear latex gloves and the windows are all open so dust, leafs, rain, bugs and animals will all contaminate the inside of the minivan making it even harder for forensics to find anything at all when they finally do find it." Pondering this reassured the surgeon that he was far too clever to get caught and he laughed and shook his head as he returned to his Blazer.

He climbed back inside and looked behind him to make sure Kathy was still unconscious before he pulled the sides of the tarp and the blanket up over her. The surgeon drove back toward the Kwik-Mart, using the same path they had taken to get there. When he was about a half mile away, he turned off of the main road onto a long dirt road that wound back into the thick forest. He pulled the Blazer to a halt and quickly climbed out to retrieve a mountain bike that was lying just off of the side of the road in a ditch. He opened the back of the Blazer and threw the bicycle inside. He listened but didn't hear any groans when it landed on top of Kathy.

Earlier that night, he had ridden his bicycle from his Blazer that was hidden a few miles away in the forest, back towards the Kwik-Mart and stashed it in the ditch on the side of the dirt road before walking a half mile through the woods to the Kwik-Mart parking lot where he awaited his victim. He had taken no chances of being caught and had thought hard about the best way to pull off this abduction.

He needed to be at the Kwik-Mart and needed to have his Blazer far away and deep in the forest where it would not be seen accidentally. His bicycle was the natural solution for getting from the Blazer to the Kwik-Mart with the least amount of energy spent.

"Ah, the cleverness of me," he thought to himself as he climbed back into the Blazer and drove away.

*****

From some other time, it seemed, a melody played softly. Not yet completely awake, Kathy didn't realize that she was hearing Chopin's "Piano Concerto No. 2." It had begun seeping into her unconscious mind, and it was beautiful. Before all the pain and terror Kathy was about to endure, she was at peace. She was one with the wonderful piano music that had surrounded her as she, unfortunately, started to regain consciousness. Like walking towards the sun lit opening out of a long, dark tunnel, Kathy started to become more aware of the things going on around her. The music seemed to grow louder and the lights seemed to grow brighter as she became conscious of becoming conscious.

"Ahh... good morning, sleepy head!" she heard a cheery voice say from just to the right of her. Kathy snapped her head to the right but because of the trauma to her head, her right eye had shifted in its socket and she saw two blurry images of a giant surgeon standing next to her, still wearing his cap, mask and gloves but with the addition of a clean white apron.

He was straightening his surgical instruments on the cart, being as precise as possible to get them all lined up perfectly– scalpels, double-hinged pliers, razor blades, small rotary saw and the rusty old pocket knife. Each tool sparkled from the light above and each was a thumb's width apart from the next. Kathy looked down to see that besides her red panties, she was naked. Her legs and arms were tied down to the cold steel table with thin nylon rope and a leather strap held her midsection down. She wasn't quite aware enough to verbalize her thoughts and emotions, but in her mind, the flash of an idea sparked, telling her that she would probably never leave this room alive.

As she became more conscious, the sounds in the room grew louder and she became aware of a high pitched whistle and a scratching sound coming from somewhere close. She tried to see what was making the noises, but was unable to distinguish from where they were coming over Ravel's "Boléro" that was now playing loudly on the stereo. As Kathy confusedly turned her head back to see the surgeon, her mind recalled a vision of him from earlier that night. She saw the light bounce off of the scalpel in his right hand and into his dark, void eyes and remembered seeing them staring at her in her rearview mirror as he held her against the seat with a scalpel to her throat.

Now she could see the double image of his blue mask moving in and out, faster and faster as, with each breath, he grew more and more excited about the job at hand. Kathy took a deep breath and mustered up enough energy to say "Please let me live." The surgeon put the latex finger tips of his left hand to her quivering lips.

"Shh... It'll be ok," he said in his deep, gravelly voice.

He turned his head to look at her red panties and rubbed them, just in front of her right hip. He slid his scalpel under her panties and rubbed her skin beneath with the flat, cold edge of the blade.

Kathy squeezed her eyes shut, yelling over the music, "*Oh my God, oh my God, oh my God!*"

With a quick jerk, the surgeon cut the thick waistband of the panties open, revealing a small tattoo of a butterfly with pink and blue wings situated just between Kathy's hip and vagina.

"Haven't seen *that* one before!" he said with wide eyes. His voice raised in octaves, he said "Good thing I peeked earlier!" He put his fingers to his mask to cover his mouth. His shoulders rose and fell while he giggled as if he were a small child who had just successfully snuck a cookie out of the kitchen.

The scratching sound that Kathy had heard earlier, persisted. As she began to cry softly, Kathy imagined the surgeon's intentions.

"Now this is going to sting a little," he said as he brought the scalpel to rest an inch above the tattoo on her pelvis. Without hesitation, he pushed down hard and pierced into the soft skin.

Kathy's blood bubbled out as she began screaming again and again, deep within her throat as she fought against the ropes and the leather strap holding her down to the table. The surgeon continued, paying attention to both Kathy's screams, and the incision that he was creating around the pretty little butterfly tattoo, humming all the while to "Boléro." The music, the whistling, the incessant scratching noise, her horror and her pain grew more and more intense as she felt the surgeon continue to cut deep inside of her pelvis. As the scalpel drew across her flesh, blood welled up in its wake as Kathy's skin pulled apart and separated, exposing the fresh pink dermis inside.

Stretching his words out, seemingly oblivious to Kathy's screams, the surgeon said "Almost done..." as he worked the scalpel around the butterfly.

"There, that wasn't so bad, now was it?" she heard him say in a pleasant voice between her screams.

Kathy opened her eyes and looked down to see two blurry images of her butterfly tattoo covered in her own thick blood that was flowing out of the four cuts around it and pouring down both the inside and outside of her thigh and onto the table. She squeezed her eyes shut again and screamed at the top of her lungs as an even more intense wave of pain rushed through her body.

The surgeon said, "Now all we have to do is remove it and we're done!"

Kathy's eyes opened wide and her screams continued as she watched the Surgeon turn to the nearby table and pick up the double-hinged pliers and a straight razor blade. Kathy cried out, "*No, no, no, no, no!*" as she tried, frantically, and in vain, to free herself from the table. The nylon ropes binding her wrists and ankles to the metal loops on the table and the leather strap across her waist made her escape impossible.

The surgeon gripped the bottom right corner of the tattooed skin with the pliers, pulled it back slightly, inserted the razor blade and began to slice the skin off from beneath. He took his time in scraping it away from the muscle with small short strokes, carefully pulling the skin so as to be sure it didn't tear.

With the increased loss of blood, Kathy's screams began to diminish as she grew increasingly pale.

With the pliers tightly locked onto the newly cut skin, the surgeon turned to the instrument table where he dropped the bloody razor blade into the dish of sanitizer before picking up the small rotary saw, its blade no larger than a dime. He gave the power button two quick taps to be sure it was working properly, then pulled the flesh back as far as it would stretch until the fatty tissue beneath the skin was visible.

The surgeon inserted the rotary saw beneath the tissue and began severing the rest of the flesh from the muscle below. Kathy mustered up another scream as her eyes and fists squeezed shut. When he was done, the surgeon ejected the blade into the sanitizer and sat the saw back on the table. He turned to Kathy and pulled the thin piece of tattooed skin free of her pelvis. It lifted out with tiny strings of skin and muscle hanging from its sides.

"Just beautiful," he said as he held the skin in the middle with his thumb and index finger, between the wings and moved it up and down quickly to make it appear as if the butterfly tattoo was actually flying.

Blood flicked from the skin as he flapped the wings over to the sink and dropped it into the right tub that was filled with warm soapy water. Kathy's screams diminished completely as she slipped slowly into shock, her eyes stared up at the brown-carpeted ceiling as her entire body began to shake.

"Well, *that's* no fun!" the surgeon commented before cutting the ropes off of Kathy's hands and feet and removing the thick leather strap that secured her waist to the table before flipping her shaking, naked body over and onto her belly. The blood on the table splashed up over the lip, onto the puddle of water on the floor, and down into the drain below.

The surgeon walked around to the other side of the table, careful to avoid the two meat hooks hanging from the ceiling, and adjusted his overhead light to shine directly onto a black Playboy bunny tattoo on Kathy's right shoulder. Kathy's body continued to shake as the scalpel entered her shoulder and sliced an inch above the bunny's ears. As the surgeon pulled the scalpel out, the blood ran down her shoulder on the right side and down her spine on the left, pooling at her lower back and running down both sides onto the table. The scalpel dripped with blood before he pushed the point down deep into her skin to cut along the right side of the tattoo.

From her silent stillness, Kathy suddenly screamed the loudest scream the surgeon had ever heard. Her body began to flail, splashing the blood off of both sides of the table and onto the surgeon's face, eyes, his clean white apron, the white curtain that covered the wall behind him, and the floor beneath.

81

Surprised, and blinded by Kathy's blood, the surgeon took a step backward, leaving the scalpel embedded deep in Kathy's shoulder.

Stumbling backward, he fell into the sharp meat hooks that were hanging from the ceiling, one hook narrowly missing his right eye. Kathy pushed herself off of the table and away from the surgeon. Her naked body landed with a splash on her left side in the puddle of water on the floor.

Through blurred vision, she could see the legs of the autopsy table that went down into the cement, the large puddle of water in which she lay that encircled the table and spread out about seven feet, the garden hose that was connected to the bottom of the autopsy table, the drainage pipe that the hose and the puddle ran down into and the bottom of the white apron and the black rubber boots of the surgeon that were now quickly making their way around the head of the table toward her.

"No, *NO!*" Kathy screamed as she pushed herself up off of the floor and hobbled as quickly as she could toward the two blurry images of the only door in the room, which was partially hidden behind a slit in a white curtain, and toward the mysterious scratching sound that she had heard earlier.

Kathy's torn red panties hung from her left thigh as she pressed firmly on the gaping wound on her right pelvis which burned as she touched it, causing her to scream uncontrollably. Blood ran down her leg from the missing butterfly tattoo. Dried, splattered blood patches stained both sides of her head where the minivan door had slammed on it earlier that night, and fresh blood ran down her back from her shoulder, where the scalpel was bouncing as she limped quickly toward the door.

The surgeon hastily made his way around the table and he tripped as he passed the corner, sending him falling forward. He knocked over the instrument stand, sending all of the tools and sanitizing liquid flying into the air and toward the ground where they, along with the surgeon, landed solidly in the water.

Kathy was just a few steps from the door when the surgeon lifted himself up off of the floor and lumbered forward as he yelled loudly, trying to catch Kathy before she escaped the room.

Screaming hysterically with her hand outstretched, she threw the door open and heard a slight thud as it swung. Just then, she felt the weight of the surgeon as he tackled her. As she fell forward onto the floor in the hallway, her right ankle smashed into the cement step that led out of the basement. Kathy felt the scalpel in her shoulder penetrate through her body and emerge from the front as the surgeon's body fell on her. All of his weight squeezed more of her blood and all of the air out of her body. Kathy was unable to scream or even breathe.

As he lay on top of her, the surgeon growled angrily into Kathy's ear through gritted teeth, "I'm gonna' tan your hide for that."

He picked Kathy up by her hair, pulled the door handle, and slammed the door shut. Her arms hung limply and the scalpel blade protruded from the front of her shoulder. Blood ran down her bare chest and stomach as the surgeon dragged Kathy back through the water, lifted her up and carelessly dropped her face down on the metal table. As her shoulder hit the table, the scalpel seemed to sprout out of her back, exposing the blood covered handle. The surgeon tied Kathy's hands and feet down to the table, finishing with the thick leather strap holding her waist down.

Kathy could now only moan.

The scratching that she had heard earlier began again and grew more feverous until the surgeon finally yelled, *"Quit your damn scratching!"*

The scratching stopped immediately. Kathy's head was turned toward the surgeon. She could see him picking up everything off of the floor, but there was nothing she could do to stop him. She had lost too much blood and was physically exhausted to the point that she could no longer scream and could barely even move.

The surgeon opened the orange cabinet against the far side of the room and took from it a new bottle of sanitizing liquid. He poured some into the dish on the instrument stand until it was almost full. When he had finished, he put the bottle away before returning to Kathy. The surgeon grasped the bloody handle of the scalpel, pulled it from her shoulder, and dropped it into the dish of sanitizing liquid.

Kathy could do nothing but listen to Pietro Mascagni's light classical piece, "Cavalleria Rusticana" that was playing on the stereo.

The surgeon picked up a new scalpel, walked around the head of the table and touched the tip of the blade to Kathy's skin, just beside the Playboy bunny tattoo. He thrust downward until the curve of the blade was buried deep inside. A low gurgling sound escaped Kathy's throat as the surgeon continued to cut deeply and carefully into the skin around the entire tattoo. He worked more slowly than before, taking his time to ensure straight and even cuts and making sure Kathy felt the sharp pain for as long as possible.

When he was through, he dropped the scalpel into the dish of sanitizing liquid, picked up a clean razor blade and pliers, and flayed the top right corner of skin away from the body. Tears ran down Kathy's pale face as the surgeon continued his work.

"We're getting there," he said while dropping the razor blade into the sanitizing liquid. Again, he picked up the power saw, pulled the corner of skin back with the pliers and proceeded to completely remove the Playboy bunny tattoo from Kathy's shoulder. When he was done, the surgeon pulled the skin free of the body with the pliers before walking around the table and releasing it into the sink that already held Kathy's butterfly tattoo. The surgeon dropped the pliers into the blood red sanitizing liquid and then pulled his gloves off of his hands, turning them inside out in the process, and dropped them into the plastic bag in the silver trash bin. He opened the cabinet under the sink, reached all the way to the back and pulled out a box of salt and a paint can with streams of dried white paint running down its side.

He sat the can on the counter next to the sink, opened it with a screwdriver and pulled from it a chamois cloth that was rolled up and secured with a loose rubber band. The surgeon removed the rubber band and unrolled the chamois to reveal Lathe's skull tattoo which looked quite different than before. The skin was now very thin, a bit smaller, and had a light layer of salt on it. The surgeon poured more salt on the skin covering it entirely and rubbed it in with his fingertips. He poured another layer of salt on the tattoo, rolled it back up in the chamois, put it back in the paint can and returned it to the cabinet under the sink.

"I've got a little something for you," the surgeon said happily as he poured a small amount of salt out of the round box and directly into the open wound on Kathy's back. He smiled as he heard her moan in pain from the salt burning the inside of her wound.

The surgeon put on a clean pair of rubber gloves that he pulled out of a box in the cabinet and looked at the opening on Kathy's back. Partially diluted salt and fresh blood filled the cavity and ran over like an overflowing pool. Kathy watched the surgeon walk across the room to the orange cabinet and take from it a half-inch thick, two-foot long rail road spike.

The music on the stereo had changed to "Canon in D major."

"I love this piece," the surgeon said as he closed his eyes and used the spike to direct his symphony. "They played this at our wedding."

He continued directing for a moment as he walked slowly toward the autopsy table, then opened his eyes and brought the point of the spike to the opening of Kathy's left ear. Her limp body lay still, yet her eyes opened slightly and looked up at the surgeon. With a grunt, the surgeon jumped up and dropped his weight, thrusting the spike down quickly, through Kathy's head. He heard several quick crunches as it made its way through her head, out of her right ear and ended with a clang as it hit the steel table beneath. Kathy's eyes opened wide and a stream of blood ran out of her left ear, down the side of her face, across her left eyeball and down the bridge of her nose where it dripped silently onto the table. Her body convulsed and twitched for a few seconds more before becoming perfectly still.

The surgeon removed his mask and smiled as he stepped back a few feet to take in the depth of what he had just accomplished. He watched in delight as the blood ran out of Kathy's ear and down her face. The surgeon enjoyed the sight for a moment before walking back toward Kathy and bent down, staring in her eyes and smiling.

His attention next turned toward the line of warm blood streaming down her face. The surgeon's lips parted and he licked the blood off of Kathy's face from the tip of her nose up to her temple. Her blood dripped from his tongue as he brought it back into his mouth slowly, as if he were tasting a rare delicacy and wanted to savor it for as long as possible. His eyes closed again as he swallowed the warm blood and he breathed a sigh out of his nose in appreciation for what he had just received.

After indulging in his treat, the surgeon walked around to the other side of the table, grabbed the spike in one hand and lifted Kathy's head with the other before pushing the spike further through. Once there were even amounts of the spike sticking out of each ear, the surgeon grabbed the ends and lifted Kathy off of the table and hung each side of the spike on the two meat hooks that hung from the ceiling. Kathy's body hung limply from the meat hooks.

"Here, let me help you with those," the surgeon said as he removed Kathy's red panties that clung to her left thigh.

She was a ghastly sight. Her eyes were wide open, her left eye looked straight and the other looked slightly to the right. Blood oozed out of her naked body from her forehead, ears, and nose, as well as from the two open wounds where the tattoos used to be and from her shoulder which was pierced straight through with the surgeon's scalpel. Her warm blood cooled as it streamed down her body and dripped off of her toes into the puddle of water below.

She swung slightly back and forth and the surgeon said happily, "Why... I'd *love* to dance with you! Thank you so much for asking!"

He bowed bringing one hand to his chest in acceptance. With that, he took Kathy's left hand in his right, wrapped his left arm around her waist, and rested his cheek against hers as he began dancing to "Minuet in G." which was now playing softly on the stereo.

"A *wonderful* piece to dance to, wouldn't you say, my dear?"

The surgeon and Kathy swayed to the music. Holding onto her tightly, the surgeon spun around several times until the chains holding her up would spin no more. He stepped back and covered his mouth as the chains unwound and he watched Kathy gracefully spin alone in the air. Amazed at what he was seeing and hearing, the surgeon said "You're like a beautiful ballerina, my love!"

When her spinning had slowed, he again took her hand and waist and continued their dance. At the end of the song, he drew back and looked at Kathy's naked body, following the streams of blood that ran down and dripped off of her toes and into the water.

"You *are* beautiful; do you know that? We're very lucky."

He smiled and grabbed her bloody face with his gloved hands and pulled her head toward his. Their lips met and he began kissing her, thrusting his tongue into her mouth. His hands traced her face and traveled down her shoulders and down her back until he was grasping her buttocks. He continued kissing her as he pulled her closer to him, moaning slightly as her groin met his.

Chapter 5

Monday morning came and the routine of going to work and school did nothing for the uneasiness that the Walkerville locals felt. Lathe's death was all that anyone could talk about. The fact that it was Sheriff Kerry's only day off that week only made them more anxious, especially when they knew that Captain Parker was still in town. He intimidated them all, which only added to everyone's steadily increasing nervousness.

From dawn to dusk, Captain Parker and Deputy Tim drove around Walkerville. They talked to various people on the streets, asking if they had seen anyone unusual or had any information as to who killed Lathe. No one had noticed or seen anything out of the ordinary and no one really had any solid proof as to who was responsible for what had happened to Lathe, although everyone had their own ideas of who they thought was responsible and most of them were more than happy to inform Captain Parker and Deputy Tim who they thought was to blame and what should be done about it.

Around 3:00 that afternoon, Sheriff Kerry called into the station to ask if there was any news. Answering the call was Linda Franklin. She was in her mid-fifties, very petite and wore a brown officer's uniform. She was the sheriff's office secretary and dispatch agent. She was also the book keeper, office manager and organizer – the person who took care of the many important duties that kept the office running smoothly. Linda assured the sheriff that they hadn't received any new information about Lathe but then informed him that Kathy Peter's boss called from the beauty shop to report that Kathy hadn't shown up for work today.

"Really?" Sheriff Kerry replied.

"Yes sir," Linda said, sounding a bit worried, "Captain Parker and Tim drove over to her house but she wasn't home and her minivan wasn't in her driveway."

Sheriff Kerry paused before he responded. "God, I hope she's okay! Do the boys know to keep an eye out for her?"

"Yes sir," Linda said. "They all know. We've been talking about it and thought maybe she went out of town or maybe she got drunk somewhere and she's just sleeping it off." Linda sounded as if she were trying to convince herself.

"Well, let me know if you hear anything," Sheriff Kerry said half-heartedly.

"Will do, Sheriff," Linda replied.

"What do you suppose happened to Kathy?" Deputy Tim asked Captain Parker as they drove through one of the neighborhoods of Walkerville.

"Your guess is as good as mine," Captain Parker responded. "It's really too early to tell."

Tim took off his brown cap and sat it on the seat between him and the captain. His short, light brown hair was tussled. Keeping one hand on the steering wheel, Tim scratched his head and sighed. He and the captain rode along in silence for a short while longer before Tim spoke again. "I know everyone is going to think she was taken by the same guy that took Lathe. It's just human nature. I'm worried about how everyone in Walkerville is going to react if she does turn up missing."

"Well," Captain Parker replied calmly, "We'll have to cross that bridge if and when we get to it."

*****

The next day, just before sunrise, the cold, peaceful morning turned chaotic with Captain Parker's first phone call of the day.

"Captain Parker here," he said in a groggy voice as he lay in his motel bed, barely awakened by the sound of the phone ringing.

"Captain, it's Sheriff Kerry. We've got another one!" he said anxiously.

"Another *what*?"

"Another body. She's a local too! It's Kathy Peters!" Sheriff Kerry said, his voice rising. "What the hell!"

Captain Parker could hear the anxiety and confusion in the sheriff's voice.

"OK sheriff, where are you?"

"We're out in the forest. Wait till you see what that sick bastard did *this* time! How long until you can be ready?"

"Uh" Captain Parker said, still trying to wake up and fully understand the conversation, "I can be ready in fifteen minutes."

"OK, I'll send one of my boys to pick you up and bring you out here. There's no way you'd find this place on your own."

"OK, I'll see you in a little while," Captain Parker responded and hung up the phone.

Soon after, Deputy Tim met the captain at his motel and hastily drove him down a maze of paved, gravel and dirt roads until finally they came upon a narrow, overgrown path and parked at the entrance to a small clearing in the middle of the forest. It was only about twenty yards in diameter and parked right in the middle was Kathy's minivan with all of its doors and windows completely open.

Captain Parker saw the sheriff and Deputy Charlie standing at the perimeter, toward the front of the vehicle, looking up at the roof where they could see the naked body of Kathy Peters. Deputy Tim and Captain Parker got out of the squad car and walked around the perimeter to join the others. The captain watched the minivan and the body on top as he walked around the clearing, noticing the bar sticking out of Kathy's ear.

She was lying on her back, her eyes staring into the endless reaches of the sky above. Her hands rested on her vagina, her right wrist covering the lesion where the butterfly tattoo had been removed. Kathy's hair was white and her mouth hung open. Everyone could see that the skin wore loose on her body and had turned a bluish gray in the cold weather.

Sheriff Kerry and his deputies looked at Captain Parker, awaiting his response. "What in the HELL?" he said, articulating each word. "And a *bar* through her head? Sheriff, what do you have?" he asked as his breath turned to mist in the cold morning air.

"Well, a couple of deer hunters came across her a little over an hour ago. They said they ran for about a mile back to their truck to call us."

"Where are the hunters now?"

"They followed my deputy, Charlie, back to the station for questioning right after we got here and are still there," Sheriff Kerry said as he looked around the clearing. "I've got their addresses, phone numbers and all that," he said and handed the notes to the captain. "They're good guys, I've known them both for years."

"Sheriff," Captain Parker started gruffly, "those two men should have been separated the minute you got here, and they should have ridden separately back to the station so they couldn't collaborate on their story on the way there!" Without giving the sheriff a chance to reply, he continued, "Did they touch anything?"

"No," Sheriff Kerry said, sounding a bit nervous. "They said they walked up to the minivan but didn't put their hands on anything."

"Has anyone else been out here today besides those two and us?"

"No," Sheriff Kerry replied, "Not to my knowledge."

Captain Parker turned his head slowly, surveying the clearing and asked, "Can you have one of your deputies be at the station in a couple of hours? I called Grand Rapids before I left and a team is on their way now."

"Yeah, I'll call Charlie and have him wait there after he's done questioning those hunters," Captain Parker said.

"Be sure those hunters don't go anywhere, my men will question them when they get here."

Knowing he didn't have a choice, Sheriff Kerry agreed. "Hey Tim," he said, motioning for his deputy, "why don't you go on back into town and do some rounds?"

"Yes sir," Tim said with an uneasy tone in his voice. He climbed into his squad car and drove back down the overgrown pathway and out of sight, leaving Deputy Julian with the captain and the sheriff.

"So, this is the beautician that was reported missing yesterday, right?" Captain Parker asked as he pulled out a small notepad and pen from his coat pocket.

Sheriff Kerry stood with his hands in his pockets in an effort to keep them warm as he filled Captain Parker in on the details. "Yeah, that's her," he said grimly as he looked up at her body. "Kathy Peters. She was a real friendly girl, never in any trouble or anything."

"Was she married, have any kids?" Captain Parker asked.

"No, she was married a while back, but that didn't work out and luckily they didn't have any kids. I'm not sure if she had a boyfriend or not. Last I saw her, she was living with a girl named Julia. They lived on the north side of town."

"I'll need the contact information on her ex-husband," Captain Parker said, still writing in his note pad.

"Sure, I'll have it for you this afternoon," said Sheriff Kerry. Captain Parker looked up from his pad and asked blankly, "Any ideas at all who might have done this, sheriff?"

"None!" the Sheriff responded as he looked down, shaking his head.

"Well, there's nothing we can do until forensics gets here," Captain Parker said. "Let's all just sit in the cars and keep warm for now." Sheriff Kerry instructed Julian to go sit in one car while he and Captain Parker sat in the other.

"We're dealing with a real psycho here!" Sheriff Kerry said as he and Captain Parker sat down in the car and shut their doors.

"Yeah," Captain Parker agreed. "These are the kind I *love* to catch! They always think they're so god damned smart and think they'll never get caught."

Sheriff Kerry watched as the captain squeezed his fist tight as he spoke. "They almost always intentionally leave something to be found, taunting us in their own sick, disturbed way. I worked on a case years ago where the killer always left his victims eyeballs for us to find. He was a real sick kid!"

"Did you catch him?" Sheriff Kerry asked excitedly.

"Yeah, we found that guy all right… found him swinging from a rafter in his house! He hung himself because he knew we were onto him!" Captain Parker said angrily.

"Well God damn!" Sheriff Kerry said as Captain Parker sat fuming. The two men sat, mostly in silence, listening to the radio and the police scanner just to pass the time until the Grand Rapids Crime Scene unit arrived with Deputies Tim and Charlie leading the way.

Captain Parker and Sheriff Kerry stepped out of their car and met the Crime Scene unit to fill them in on what they knew so far.

"Be sure to look for tracks in the soil, too!" Captain Parker yelled out. "Whoever did this probably didn't walk all the way back to town, or wherever he is now. We're miles away from civilization."

"Yes sir!" came the reply from one of the many men who were now collecting, marking and photographing possible evidence. For over an hour they moved in a circle around the minivan, starting just outside the perimeter of the clearing and working steadily inward. When they finally reached the minivan, it was dusted thoroughly for fingerprints, both inside and out, before a ladder was set up next to the vehicle so the photographer could take pictures of the body on the roof.

The photographer yelled down to Captain Parker after reaching the top of the ladder, "Sir! Besides the bar running through her ears, it looks like the body has trauma wounds on both sides of the forehead and there's a small incision on her left shoulder. The body was drained of quite a bit of blood, and it's been drenched with bleach!"

"*Damn it!*" Captain Parker yelled back.

"I know this might be a stupid question, but why would they drench her with bleach?" Sheriff Kerry asked.

Without taking his eyes off of the photographer, Captain Parker said "It gives a false positive when we're looking for blood. Her entire body, hair to toe will look like it's covered in blood when we run our test. Bleach is also like a DNA eraser." Captain Parker looked at the sheriff and said in a foreboding tone, "This guy knows what he's doing."

Once the photographer had finished taking pictures of the body, another ladder was set up next to the minivan and two men began removing Kathy from the roof.

"Sir, you'll want to come and take a look at this!" one of them yelled down.

Captain Parker climbed one of the ladders to get a good look at Kathy's body for the first time. Her skin was shriveled up like she had been in a bath tub for too long. Captain Parker saw a jagged wound on her pelvis and the small slit from the blade of the scalpel on her left shoulder.

"And look back here," the investigator said as he rolled Kathy's body over slightly. Her entire body moved as one; the result of rigor mortis. Captain Parker looked at the gaping hole in her back shoulder where the Playboy bunny had so recently resided.

"Okay," Captain Parker responded coldly, "get pictures of the wounds on her pelvis and the front of her shoulder, then take her down and get pictures of the back of her shoulder."

"Sheriff, she has two wounds, similar to what Lathe had on his chest," said the captain. "One on her right pelvis, the other on her back left shoulder."

"You've got to be friggin' kidding me," Sheriff Kerry responded.

"I wish I was," Captain Parker quietly responded.

"So we've got a *serial* killer in Walkerville?" Sheriff Kerry asked.

"Well, officially there have to be at least three murders with the same M.O. before it can be considered a serial murder, but just between you and me, I don't think it's going to hurt anything to assume that that's what we're dealing with here," said the captain. "Let's hope we can find out who did this before there is a third!"

"Oh my God," Sheriff Kerry said slowly as he shook his head and looked down at the ground.

Because he didn't want the sheriff to think that he wasn't being involved in the cases, Captain Parker asked, "Sheriff, would you mind driving me to Kathy's apartment? I need to question her roommate Julia."

"No, not at all," Sheriff Kerry responded.

"OK, great." Captain Parker said as he turned back toward the minivan. "My men will clean up this mess."

*****

As they drove toward Kathy's apartment, Captain Parker's cell phone rang. He looked at the screen and saw it was Syndi. He calmly opened his phone and began talking. "Captain Parker here."

"Hi Luke, it's just me, Syndi. I hope I'm not bothering you!" she said timidly.

"No, not at all, what can I do for you?"

"I was just calling to see if you were going to be busy later on tonight."

Captain Parker said, "I believe my schedule is still open, why?"

"Well, there's a new Bruce Willis movie out that I want to go see and I just hate going to the movies by myself. I feel like such a loser and I was just wondering if you'd like to go along and keep me company."

"I think I can arrange that," he said. He heard Syndi let out a slight giggle.

"Something funny?" he asked as Sheriff Kerry turned to see the confused look on the captain's face.

"You're with someone on the force right now, aren't you?"

"Uh, yes ma'am, I am," Captain Parker said, solidifying her suspicion of why he was sounding so official during their phone call. "I'll call you back to confirm the time later," he continued.

"Yes sir!" Syndi said as she giggled a little louder. "Talk to you later. Bye bye."

Captain Parker put his cell phone away and sat in silence as Sheriff Kerry drove towards Kathy's apartment. Although the sheriff wondered, he didn't ask the captain whom he had just spoken with. He figured if it were relevant to the Walkerville situation, the captain would have filled him in.

As they pulled into Kathy's apartment parking lot, Captain Parker finally spoke up. "If you don't mind, sheriff, I'd like to run the questioning here. Again, I'm just concerned that she might hold something back if she's dealing with someone she's comfortable with."

"Oh sure, sure, you just do your thing," Sheriff Kerry responded as they both got out of the squad car and headed toward Kathy's apartment.

*****

Their knocks on the door were greeted by a petite, pretty young woman of about twenty-five with short, straight red hair who was wearing blue satin pajamas and was only half awake. Seeing the two officers, Julia Allen's eyes opened wide with surprise. "What's wrong sheriff?" she asked.

"This is Captain Parker from down in Grand Rapids. Can we come inside for a few minutes, Julia?" Sheriff Kerry asked.

When they were all inside, Julia shut the door as Captain Parker said, "Miss, I'm afraid I have some bad news." Fearing the worst, Julia began to shake.

"What's wrong?" she asked anxiously, thinking that something terrible had happened to someone in her family.

"Early this morning, we found the body of your roommate, Kathy Peters."

"Oh my God!" Julia said expelling all of her breath in those three short words as she leaned over and tried to control her breathing. Sheriff Kerry saw Julia start to cry and he put his hand on her back to try and comfort her.

As she stood back up, she wiped the tears from her eyes and said, "I thought something had happened to someone in my family! Oh my God, you gave me *such* a scare!" Julia let out a slight laugh. "Oh man!" she exclaimed with a smile.

"Well aren't you upset that your friend is dead?" Sheriff Kerry asked, sounding quite surprised.

"I couldn't give two damns about that bitch! I'm sorry she's dead, but I'm not gonna get all torn up over it. I kicked her out a few months ago after I found out she was sleeping with my boyfriend! I do feel sorry for her family, though. How did it happen?" She motioned for the two men to sit down on the couch as she sat across from them in a chair.

"I'm sorry," Captain Parker responded as he and Sheriff Kerry sat down, "but we can't disclose many of the details yet."

"Do you think it was the same guy that killed Lathe Walthes?" she asked, growing more concerned.

"Well, we're just not sure yet. It seems like the killer used the same method of operation, though."

"Did she have skin cut off of her body too?" Julia asked as her face distorted, making her look as though she had just tasted something awful.

"Yes, yes she did," Captain Parker said. "She had two pieces cut off, one on her rear left shoulder and one on her right pelvis. I'm only telling you that because we think it could mean something to you. Does it?"

Julia covered her mouth in disgust. "She had a tattoo of a Playboy bunny on the back of her left shoulder!" she said. Sheriff Kerry, wide-eyed, looked at the captain.

Captain Parker continued quickly, "Did she have a tattoo on her right pelvis?"

"I... I don't know, we weren't that close of friends really. She just answered an ad I had put in the *Ledger* for a roommate. She was moving here from up north – Indian River. She only lived here for about three months before I found out about her and Gary. I'm sure *he* would know if she had a tattoo there," Julia said angrily.

Sheriff Kerry and Captain Parker took down information about Julia's schedule – where she worked, what she did in her spare time and the information about her ex-boyfriend, Gary Davis.

The Captain stated, "I'm sure you were pretty upset with Kathy for sleeping with your boyfriend, huh?"

98

"Well of course I was! Anybody would be! But I know where you're going with that and I didn't kill her!"

"Some people might think you had the right to…" Captain Parker said in an attempt to lead Julia on to say more than she wanted to.

"*I didn't kill her*!" Julia responded harshly. "Believe me, I wanted too, especially when I first found out about the two of them, but I got over it. Gary and I had only been seeing each other for six months before I found out about him and Kathy. After I got over the initial shock, I just let it go."

"Okay, okay," Captain Parker said in a soothing voice. "We're not saying you killed her, and we're not saying you didn't kill her either. We're just trying to get some useful information to help us find out who *did* kill her. Until we get this all straightened out, we'll need you to stay here in Walkerville." Captain Parker stood up, followed closely by Sheriff Kerry and Julia.

"Thank you for your time Miss Allen, we'll be in touch," Captain Parker said as he shook her hand and headed out the door. Julia watched through the curtains with a slight grin on her face as the two men got back into their squad car and drove off toward Gary Davis' house.

"Think she's got anything to do with all of this?" Sheriff Kerry asked the captain. "I mean, I might be able to understand her killing the girl that stole her boyfriend, but I don't think she ever had a problem with Lathe! And there's no way she would be able to drag him around anyway, she's just a little thing!"

"Well," Captain Parker said, "this wouldn't be the first time I've caught someone that killed a few extra people to cover up killing the one person they actually wanted dead! And it's possible that Julia had an accomplice that helped her with both of the murders. There could be a ton of different scenarios connecting her to the murders but we don't really have anything to go on, so I'd like for you to put one of your guys on her for a few days."

"You mean a stakeout?"

"Yeah, your guy would need to stay out of sight but able to watch her to see where she goes and what she does. Think you could take care of that, sheriff?"

"Absolutely!" Sheriff Kerry said eagerly. "I can have my deputies do rotating shifts."

*****

Captain Parker and Sheriff Kerry arrived at Gary Davis' house only to find that his younger sister, Mary, was there house sitting for him since he'd been gone on a business trip to St. Louis for the past eight days. When given the news about Kathy Peters, Mary became upset and started to cry.

"Oh my God, she was such a nice girl! How could anybody be so cruel to someone so sweet?" she said through her tears.

Over the past four months, Mary and Kathy had become very good friends while Gary had been dating her. Mary had hoped that her brother might get serious with Kathy, but now that would never be. Mary picked up a picture of her brother and Kathy from a nearby table and tears streamed down her face.

"I *am* sorry ma'am," Captain Parker said. "We will need to get in touch with your brother. We have his cell phone number. Do you think we'll be able to reach him on that number?"

Mary set the picture back on the table and answered through her hands that were covering her sobbing face, "Yeah, he's always got that with him."

*****

Sheriff Kerry was pulling out of the driveway as Gary answered his phone.

"Hello. Gary Davis," he said in a quiet and kind voice.

"Hello sir, this is Captain Parker of the Grand Rapids Police Department. I need a minute of your time."

"Of course!" Gary responded, sounding surprised. "Give me just one minute – I'm in the middle of a meeting."

Captain Parker could hear Gary apologizing that he had to leave the meeting and step out into the hallway.

"OK, sorry about that. What's going on captain?"

"Sir, I'm sorry, but I must be the bearer of some very bad news."

"Oh my God, what's wrong?" came Gary's trembling voice.

"Sir, we found your girlfriend, Kathy Peters' body this morning out in the woods here in Walkerville. She was murdered. I'm so sorry."

The captain's words cut Gary like a knife in his chest. *"No you didn't!"* Gary roared, his kind, passive demeanor now miles away. *"Who is this? This isn't true! This isn't funny!"* screamed Gary angrily, trying to will away the cruel feeling that had now grabbed him by the heart. The door to the office where he had just been in a meeting quickly swung open as everyone rushed out into the hallway to see what was going on.

Gary was always a soft-spoken and pleasant man. He was never boisterous or aggressive. He was the kind of guy you might not even remember meeting at a party. He just tended to fade into the background wherever he was. But now tears filled Gary's wide eyes and ran down his face in the silence as everyone in the office looked on. With red, tearful eyes, Gary began to tremble as he looked into the faces of his coworkers and yelled, "Some asshole just told me that my girlfriend was murdered last night!" For some strange reason, Gary felt that by saying it out loud, it would somehow make it untrue. Captain Parker handed the phone to Sheriff Kerry, a familiar voice that Gary would trust.

"Gary? This is Sheriff Kerry. I'm afraid it's true. We found her this morning, I'm so sorry, Gary."

"How the hell can this be happening?" Gary said as his mind raced and his heart began to break. He ran his fingers through his hair and walked down a hallway, toward the exit of the building, seeming not to even notice the growing crowd of curious onlookers.

"Do you know who did it?" he said angrily as he clinched his fist so tight that it shook.

"No, we don't have any leads just yet."

"My sister called me a few days ago and told me that Lathe Walthes was killed too. It's the same guy, isn't it Sheriff?"

"We don't know yet, Gary. We've been working on it day and night, though, and we've got the Grand Rapids forensics department helping us out. We're going to find who did this. I promise!"

"I don't know what to do, Sheriff." Gary said with a trembling voice.

"Why don't you just come on home, Gary? Catch the next flight out of St. Louis and just get home. Your sister is pretty upset, too; we just left your house."

"Oh man, my sister and Kathy were getting to be really good friends, I'm sure she's a mess right now."

Gary walked through the crowd of concerned coworkers, out of the building, sat down on a near-by bench and began to sob, dropping the phone from his ear and covering his face with his other hand.

"Gary?" Sheriff Kerry waited in silence. "Gary, you OK?" he said, trying to get Gary to bring the phone back to his ear.

"No. No, I'm not OK at all."

"Gary, you just get yourself to the airport and give me a call when you get your flight information. We'll have someone pick you up when you get here."

"I've got to ask you one thing before we get off of here, Gary. I'm sorry to have to ask this, but did Kathy happen to have a tattoo on her right thigh?"

"Yes ... yes she did. It was a little butterfly."

*****

102

Later that night, Captain Parker headed towards Syndi's apartment, moving his experiences from the day to the back of his mind. Over the years, he had become a master of controlling his actions and emotions, which gave him a reputation of being cold and bitter, maybe even cynical, but to the captain, it was just his way of dealing with the madness of his work, day after day after day, without going mad himself.

When he arrived at Syndi's house for their movie date, she was standing in front of her garage, talking to her neighbor. "Oh, hi, Luke!" she said with a concerned look on her face.

"This is my friend, Lola."

"Nice to meet you, Lola," said the captain pleasantly.

"Lola just told me that they found Kathy Peters' body out in the woods this morning! What happened?" Syndi asked, sounding quite scared.

"Well, we're not really sure yet," Luke said, finding himself in an uncomfortable situation, unable to disclose any details. "We had the team come back from Grand Rapids to collect evidence and they're working on it now as we speak. We don't want to be late for that movie. Are you ready to go?"

"Oh, yeah," Syndi said, suddenly realizing that she had just put Luke in a very awkward spot. "Well, I'll talk to you later, Lola," She said as she turned toward Luke's car.

"Nice to meet you, ma'am." Luke said as he took Syndi gently by the arm and helped her in.

*****

Meanwhile, in the newly developed subdivision, the surgeon stood in front of a brightly lit, large wooden table in his basement that was just around the corner from his skinning room. The table was raw, old and pitted. A few chips of finish were the only reminders of a once beautiful mahogany dining room table. To the right of the table was a large wooden bookshelf. Each shelf was packed with various types of horns, tools, glass eyes, bottles of chemicals, and paints. On the wall to the right of the bookshelf was a tall, stainless steel door leading to a walk-in cooler.

On the top left corner of his table stood a stately raven, stuffed and perched upon a small branch of the pine tree that is so plentiful in Walkerville. On the right side of his table was a mounted fleshing machine used for separating the meat of an animal from its hide. It resembled the turntable of an old record player standing up on its side. Behind the two-foot high round guard was a blade that began to silently whir as the surgeon flipped a switch.

Lying in the very middle of his table were two moist tattoos – a small pink and blue butterfly and a black Playboy bunny, both from the body of Kathy Peters.

The surgeon picked up the Playboy bunny, which was the larger of the two tattoos, and began to rub the gelatinous tissue beneath the skin, over the fleshing machine's blade. The blade was smooth and curved outward into a sharp edge, making it easy to detach the flesh and fatty deposits below from the beautiful artwork above. He slowly grazed the skin across the blade, watching each time as a wafer-thin piece of tissue fell to the table below until he was left with a lean piece of tattooed skin that resembled a slice of raw bacon. Content with his work, he laid the skin, tattoo side down, on a chamois before picking up the butterfly tattoo and repeating the process, stripped it of its underbelly meat.

When he had finished the second tattoo, he laid it, too, upon the chamois, tattoo side down, and brought them into the skinning room where he poured salt on both of the tattoos, rubbed it into the meaty side of the skins with his rubber gloves, and then rolled the chamois up, tattoos inside, and placed it inside the now-empty paint can under the sink. "See you tomorrow, ladies," he said quietly, smiling as he shut the cabinet door, walked across the room and reached behind the slit in the curtain to flip off the light.

Chapter 6

"Good morning Captain!" Sheriff Kerry yelled as he exited his squad car after seeing Captain Parker standing at the top of the stairs outside of the front office doors.

"Morning Sheriff! So today is Lathe's funeral." Captain Parker said as Sheriff Kerry opened the door offering for the captain to go in first.

"Yeah, it's gonna be a sad day, that's for sure," Sheriff Kerry said in a quieter tone as they both entered the building.

"Morning Linda," Sheriff Kerry said, half-heartedly smiling and waving as they passed the front desk and headed his office.

"I hate to ask this of you, Sheriff," Captain Parker said as Sheriff Kerry shut the door behind them, "but I'm going to need you to go to that funeral today and talk to Bill Walthes to see if he knows anything about a tattoo on Lathe's chest. I would go myself, but I have to spend the day with forensics to go over the evidence they've collected so far on Lathe's and Kathy's cases. I need to see what they've gotten since the other day and figure out where to go from here."

"Sure Captain," Sheriff Kerry said. "I was planning on going anyway to help out with traffic and to make sure there's no problems. You know – keep away any weirdos that might show up just for the novelty and excitement of being a part of all this mess. I'll talk to Bill while I'm there and see what I can find out."

"Be sure and watch for that right cross!" Captain Parker said with a grin. Sheriff Kerry laughed nervously as he shook his head.

"So," Sheriff Kerry said with a serious look on his face, "What have the guys in Grand Rapids found out last you heard?"

"Well, it's a bit disturbing, but we know that Lathe and Kathy were both tied up by their wrists and feet, had duct tape covering their eyes and mouth, and their tattoos were cut off of them while they were still alive, that is, if it turns out Lathe *did* have a tattoo on his chest."

"Somebody cut the tattoos off of them before they were dead? You have *got* to be kidding me," Sheriff Kerry said in an obviously disturbed tone.

"No. I wish I was," Captain Parker said. "Living tissue releases histamine and some other chemicals when it's lacerated, dead tissue doesn't. And even though we couldn't see it with the naked eye, it was obvious to forensics on the cellular level that the skin cells were still active after the trauma. Chemically, the skin in the wounds of Lathe and Kathy were metabolically active after the tattoos were removed."

Sheriff Kerry covered his mouth and his eyes squeezed shut as he imagined the horror and the incredible pain that filled Lathe and Kathy's last moments.

*****

After the morning briefing with the captain, the sheriff and his three deputies headed over to St. Michael's Church and with somber faces, greeted some of the town's people who came to pay their last respects.

"Morning Sheriff!" said the familiar voice of Jim Richardson, the local reporter from the *Walkerville Ledger.*

"Jimmy," Sheriff Kerry responded, sounding a bit surprised, "What are *you* doing here?"

"I just came to say goodbye to Lathe, Sheriff."

"You better not be here interviewing any of these good people, Jimmy!"

"No, of *course* not, Sheriff. Say, what's the latest on all of this anyway? First Lathe and now Kathy? What the hell is going on here?"

"Jimmy, I'm not here to be interviewed!" Sheriff Kerry said.

"I'm not looking for an interview right now, but in case you haven't realized, people are getting *pretty* upset!" Jimmy snapped back. "This has happened *twice* now and we don't have any answers. How do you *expect* people to react when put into this kind of a situation with no information or answers about what's going on?"

"Now you listen here," Sheriff Kerry said as he took a step forward until he was so close that Jim could smell the sheriff's warm breath, "I've got the goddamn Grand Rapids Major Case Squad working on this! They're going through tons of evidence that they've collected and that's going to take some time. It's not like writing a little article, we're all doing actual *work*!"

Unfazed, Jimmy shot back pointedly, loud enough only for the sheriff to hear him, "That's *two* people killed in less than a week, Sheriff. Both of them had chunks of skin cut out of them so *obviously* we've got a serial killer running around which, I don't know about you, but it scares the shit out of me! Everybody in town is scared! Is that what you really want, Sheriff?"

"Look, Jimmy, there's really nothing to tell yet" Sheriff Kerry said, trying to control his temper and the volume of their conversation as the number of onlookers, including the deputies, began to grow, some of them giving disgusted looks at the sheriff and Jim for causing a scene at Lathe's funeral. "When there *is* something to tell, I'll let you know. Now why don't you go have a seat and have some respect for everyone around?"

Knowing that he wasn't getting anywhere with the sheriff, Jim walked hastily into the church.

The sky had begun turning dark as a group of black clouds crept toward Walkerville. As Sheriff Kerry closed the front doors of the church for Lathe's funeral sermon, muffled sounds of thunder were heard in the distance. Bill Walthes sat in the front row, just in front of Lathe's casket, and was surrounded by his two sisters and his wife's family, including Lathe's Aunt Teresa who had comforted a much younger Lathe so many years ago at his mother's rainy funeral. Bill sat quietly, watching the line of Walkerville locals file past Lathe's casket and looking upon Lathe's face one last time before approaching the family to shake hands or hug while they offered their condolences.

When the line had ended, an old, lanky priest entered the church just as the organ began playing "Nearer My God to Thee." Father Goshi was about seventy years old and his head leaned slightly forward and toward his right shoulder. He had a well-defined arch in his back that gave him an uneven gait as he walked to his podium. The old priest spoke with a gravelly voice that sounded almost as if he had phlegm resting in the back of his throat, although he persistently tried to clear it of the obstruction.

"My dear friends, how sad it is to see you all here today in this house of God," he began. "But we must remember that we are here to give a warm and loving farewell to Lathian Vincent Walthes."

He spoke of the meaning of friendship, family and love and pointed out how he had baptized Lathe when he was just a baby as he had done for most of the people in attendance of the service today. He also spoke of the funeral service that he had performed for Lathe's mother so many years ago.

As Father Goshi spoke, the congregation was still and quiet except for the occasional cough or the whimpering from one of Lathe's four aunts. Father Goshi consoled both family and friends of Lathe, telling them that, "No matter how happy we think we are here on earth, the one hundred best days we've ever had cannot compare to a split second of the happiness that Lathe has found in Heaven."

His words were kind and warm, his ideals consoling, but no one really felt any better about Lathe, and now Kathy, having been so brutally murdered, or the notion that since their killer had not been caught, that person could be sitting there in the pews along with everyone else; maybe even sitting right beside them. During the service, glances were secretly made from most of the members of the congregation. They were all looking at each other; doubting each other, studying each other's faces for just a trace of an expression that they thought only the killer would have.

As the old priest concluded his service, he instructed everyone to walk around to the back of the church to begin the procession to Lathe's final resting place. Two of the deputies opened the front doors of the church and everyone exited single file, mostly in silence, and walked around back where Father Goshi was waiting, having gone through his own exit behind the church. Lathe's closed casket was rolled out of the rear exit by four of Lathe's cousins and two of his oldest friends, Jobin, and Travis.

Most of the boys were looking down at the ground as tear drops dripped from their eyes, which were soon followed by light rain drops from the coming storm. Father Goshi, using his black umbrella as a cane, limped slowly as he led the way into the graveyard where a freshly dug hole awaited its fill. Sheriff Kerry and his deputies brought up the rear and took their place at the back of the crowd. Father Goshi read aloud from his old, tattered Bible as he held his black umbrella overhead. His quiet words of deliverance were mostly drowned out by the splatter of rain and occasional thunder.

As Sheriff Kerry closed his eyes and began concentrating on the cold rain bouncing off of his hat and face, he overheard someone saying, "Two people killed and he *still* hasn't done anything about it."

Sheriff Kerry opened his eyes and looked to his right to see who had said it, then heard a quiet voice coming from somewhere to his left, "What's *he* doing here? Shouldn't he be out finding the guy that did this?"

He heard another voice coming from somewhere I nfront of him, "Wonder if he'll be at Kathy's funeral in a couple days?" Sheriff Kerry closed his eyes again, swallowed his pride and bowed his head. He understood the frustrations of the Walkerville residents and knew that saying anything would only make things worse.

After Lathe's casket was lowered into the ground, the crowd gradually dispersed until only Bill Walthes and his family remained. Although Bill hadn't shed a tear, his head hung low and the pain of losing his son showed on his face and in his bloodshot eyes. Sheriff Kerry put his hand on Bill's back and said, "I'm so sorry, Bill."

"Eh, thanks Sheriff," Bill responded uncomfortably.

"Bill, could I have a word with you in private?" Sheriff Kerry asked as he motioned for Bill to join him under a nearby tree. Bill followed, wiping his greasy wet hair out of his face.

"What do you need, Sheriff?"

"Bill, as I'm sure you've heard there's been another murder. A girl named Kathy Peters."

"Yeah," Bill said, "I heard about that. Hard to believe."

"Yeah, well we're trying to put some pieces together but I need to ask you for a little help."

Bill looked at Sheriff Kerry with uncertainty. "I'm sorry to have to ask you this, Bill, but do you know if Lathe had a tattoo on his chest?"

"I don't know," Bill responded, somewhat annoyed. "What the hell difference would it make now anyway?"

"Well, like I said, we're just trying to figure out what happened to your son and to Kathy Peters."

"I don't know a goddamned thing about any tattoo!" Bill hissed. "Now if we're all through, I'll get back to what's left of my family!"

"Sure, Bill," Sheriff Kerry said apologetically. "Thanks for your time."

On his rainy drive back to the sheriff's department, Sheriff Kerry went through the events of the week in his head.

"What more do they expect me to do?" he thought to himself.

Just then, he remembered Lathe's girlfriend, Jessie Marconi. They had been pretty serious a few years ago and she now lived out of town.

"She was never questioned!" Sheriff Kerry said aloud.

"Linda," he said into his radio, "can you give me the address for Jessie Marconi, that girl that used to date Lathe?"

Within minutes Sheriff Kerry was driving in the opposite direction heading toward the town of Webber, Michigan, which was located about a half hour outside of Walkerville. As he drove, the storm grew stronger. The sky had become a greenish-black and lightning crashed violently over and over again. Sheriff Kerry even saw it hit the ground once, about a half mile away in a field. The heavy gusting winds combined with the torrential downpour made the drive all but impossible and Sheriff Kerry struggled to both see and keep his vehicle going straight on the road.

As he pulled into Webber, the storm had all but passed. Only a light drizzle remained as the sun peered between the dark rolling clouds. Sheriff Kerry parked in Jessie's driveway and headed up the walkway leading to her front porch. He rang the doorbell and knocked three times on the small diamond-shaped glass panel in the door before it opened slightly to a tall, skinny woman standing in the narrow opening. She had straight, dark brown hair that stopped just above her shoulders and wore a pair of black-rimmed glasses. She wasn't what most would consider attractive, although she was often told that she had a contagious smile.

"Sheriff Kerry!" she said. "What are you doing here?"

"Jessie, could I trouble you for just a little bit of your time?" he replied.

"Of course!" she said as she opened her door wide. "Please, sit down." They sat across from each other in the living room and just before Sheriff Kerry had a chance to speak, Jessie said, "I assume this is about Lathe, huh?"

"So you did hear, then?" Sheriff Kerry responded, not sounding too surprised.

"Yeah, I still have a few friends down there in Walkerville. I heard the morning they found him. Did they find the guy that did it?"

112

"No," Sheriff Kerry said disappointedly, "we're still working on it."

"Would you like something to drink, sheriff?" Jessie said as she started to stand up.

"I'd love some coffee if you've got some."

Jessie smiled and said, "Be right back."

Sheriff Kerry looked around the living room while Jessie went into the kitchen to make some coffee. On the far side of the room was a computer on a desk that was almost completely covered by various thick programming books, yellow pads of hand written notes and computer magazines.

"Almost done, sheriff!" Jessie called out from the kitchen.

"Oh, no problem Jessie. Take your time." He continued surveying his surroundings and noticed the disarray of the rest of the room. There were newspapers and a few used paper plates scattered about. It was obvious that Jessie hadn't expected any company.

"Here you go." she said as she walked back into the living room and handed Sheriff Kerry a cup of coffee.

"Thanks," he said. "Sorry about the unexpected visit, but I am glad you were at home."

Jessie smiled politely. "Well, I'm a computer programmer for a company out of Chicago. I work from home so I'm here most of the time."

Sheriff Kerry responded with a simple, "Ahh." The two sat together while Sheriff Kerry entertained Jessie's inquiry as to what had been going on in Walkerville in the years since she moved away and she told the sheriff all about the changes in her life since the move. As they were both nearing the bottom of their coffee cups, Sheriff Kerry said, quite seriously, "I do need to ask you about something, though."

"Sure, what's that?"

"Well, can you tell me if Lathe had any tattoos?"

"Yeah, he had one on the right side of his chest," said Jessie. "It was a skull with a top hat and little black bow tie. He got it years ago. He made me promise to never tell his dad that he had gotten it. I told him that it shouldn't matter since he wasn't living at home anymore and he was a grown man, but Lathe didn't care. He did *not* want his father to know about it."

Sheriff Kerry sat somewhat surprised, realizing that in this brief instant the speculation of a serial killer in Walkerville had just become truth.

"Sheriff, what's wrong?" Jessie asked as she watched the sheriff's face turn to a mixture of surprise and horror. Sheriff Kerry started imagining again the pain that Lathe and Kathy went through as a mad man ripped them open while they were still alive only to kill them after he removed their tattoos. And the worst part of it was that there were still no leads and it could be happening again at that very moment.

"Jessie… I'm so sorry, I've got to go," he said hastily as he stood up and shook her hand. "Thanks so much for your time and for the coffee."

"Sheriff, are you OK?" Jessie hollered as she watched him walk hurriedly toward his squad car.

"Yeah Jessie, thanks again!" he yelled back as he got into his car and pulled out of her driveway to head back to Walkerville.

*****

Upon reaching town and pulling into the office parking lot, Sheriff Kerry caught Captain Parker just as he was walking out of the building to get some lunch. Sheriff Kerry ran over to him and said, "Captain, we were right!" Captain Parker looked at the sheriff with great concern and peered around to see if anyone was within earshot. "I talked to Lathe's father but he didn't know anything about Lathe's tattoo, so then I went and talked to Lathe's ex-girlfriend and she verified it. He *did* have a tattoo right there on his chest where that piece of skin was missing."

"Oh hell," Captain Parker whispered as he put his hand to his mouth.

"Yeah, it's just like we thought. I've been thinking about it and I'm going to have to notify the whole town, that guy's still out there!"

"No, we can't do that," Captain Parker responded quickly. "Not yet anyway."

"No offense sir, but what the hell are you talking about?" Sheriff Kerry asked. "Two people were *killed* and it's just a matter of time until there's a third! We've *got* to let them know what's going on! They're starting to get really restless!"

"Sheriff, I understand your point, I really do, but the fact is we *don't* have enough evidence yet. If we go telling everybody that there's a serial killer on the prowl, they're going to start asking a million questions… questions we don't have the answers to yet. And guess who they're going to be asking? You! And without any answers to give back, it will just make you look incompetent and I know you don't want that. We need to wait until we get some useful information from the evidence and some leads. Even *one* lead, before we say anything to anybody. Otherwise it will surely start a panic. Imagine how *you* would feel if someone told you that there was a serial killer in town but they didn't know where the crime was committed, didn't have any finger prints or evidence, or DNA to go on and there were *no* suspects."

Sheriff Kerry put his hands on his hips and looked at the ground as if admitting defeat. "Yeah, I guess I can see your point," he said solemnly.

"Good, I'm glad you understand," Captain Parker said with a slight smile. "Join me for lunch?"

"Sure." Sheriff Kerry responded eagerly as he looked up. "I'm starving!"

*****

'SECOND HOMICIDE IN WALKERVILLE' The words seemed to jump right off of the *Walkerville Ledgers*' front page. Sheriff Kerry and Captain Parker sat together in the Eat Rite diner waiting for their lunches to arrive.

"Story by Jim Richardson," Sheriff Kerry read aloud as Captain Parker watched outside through the large front window.

"Listen to this part," Sheriff Kerry said. "Deep in the forest, the body of Kathy Peters was found early yesterday morning. This is the second murder in Walkerville in less than a week. When questioned about a suspect, authorities were unable to give a description or any useful information." Clinching his teeth together, Sheriff Kerry snarled, "That little punk!"

"Aww, don't let it get to ya," Captain Parker said coolly. "Reporters are the same all over. They always spin the story to make it more compelling to the reader. It's just the nature of the beast."

Sheriff Kerry took a sip of his coffee. "Yeah, but he's making us look bad."

"Well, Sheriff," Captain Parker said, "would it be quite as compelling if he had said 'officials are working hard, day and night, to try and figure out who done it?'"

Sheriff Kerry laughed, almost spitting out some of his coffee. "Ya know, I think there actually might be a sense of humor hiding out in there somewhere!" Sheriff Kerry said laughing as he hit Captain Parker on the arm with the newspaper.

Captain Parker smiled and said with a little chuckle, "I've taken the brunt of many a reporter in the past and it just doesn't help anything to let them get to you. We've got a job to do and worrying about what they write, which you can't change *or* control, is just pointless."

"Yeah, I suppose you're right" Sheriff Kerry said, his laughter dying down. "I guess the only really important thing, the *one* question we need to be asking ourselves right now is," and he paused and looked at Captain Parker seriously "where the hell's our lunch? *Waitress!*" he yelled as he put his hand up in the air. Sheriff Kerry watched and smiled as he finally pulled a laugh from the captain.

116

After lunch, Sheriff Kerry went on patrol and Captain Parker went into Ruby's, the local supermarket, to buy some toiletries and groceries. Because of the second murder, he needed to stay in Walkerville for a bit longer than he had originally planned.

As he walked down the cookie aisle, he heard two men shouting from two aisles over.

"Well, then where *were* you, Tom? You know you didn't like Lathe *or* Kathy!"

"I was at home *both* nights, you asshole!" Tom yelled.

"Oh, that's convenient! You live alone! Who can say you weren't there?"

"Robert, look, if I said I was at home, I was at home! And why would you think I needed to explain myself to *you* anyway? Where the hell were *you* those two nights?" Captain Parker heard Tom yell as he walked to the end of the aisle where he stood behind a growing crowd of onlookers. Tom continued, "You son-of-a-bitch! Why are you trying to make it look like *I* could have done it? Trying to take the focus off of yourself?"

With that the two men shoved each other just once before fists began to fly. Tom caught Robert with a solid right cross, knocking him back into a shelf of canned goods. Robert seemed to bounce off of the shelves and grabbed Tom by the collar of his coat as the two fell to the floor and continued beating on one another. Everyone in the store stood at either end of the aisle, just watching as two grown men, who had known each other their entire lives, pummeled each other on the floor. Blood streamed out of a cut on Tom's forehead and Robert's eye was steadily swelling shut. Captain Parker stood still, watching the mêlée with a slight grin until the two men had decided that they had had enough. Robert and Tom stood up, three feet apart from one another.

"If I find out you had anything to do with it, you're gonna wish I'd have killed you right here and now!" raged Robert, standing stiffly and pointing his finger at Tom before turning and pushing his way through the crowd at the other end of the aisle. Captain Parker just shook his head and smiled at some of the confused onlookers in the crowd.

After paying for his groceries, Captain Parker stepped outside just in time to see a van driving by with the "NBC" trademark peacock on its side. The van pulled off to the side of the road where it joined two other local network vans and two other reporters who were standing at various angles in front of a 'Welcome to Walkerville' sign, their camera men just in front of them, framing their shots.

The story of two people killed in a small town might seem like small news to some, but it is those kinds of stories that get people really interested in the news and that's what the local stations were banking on. The sleepy little village of Walkerville was quickly becoming the center of a huge storyline.

Frustrated, Captain Parker sat his groceries on the passenger seat of his squad car and headed for his motel. Along the way he opened his cell phone, pulled out the antenna, and dialed Syndi's phone number.

"Hello Syndi," he said when she picked up the phone.

"Well hello, Luke. What are you up to today?"

"Just out doing some shopping and picking up a few things. I'm going to be staying in Walkerville a little longer and I was wondering if you had plans for tonight?"

"Aww, I have to work tonight," Syndi said disappointedly. "I have to be there at 6:00."

"Well, do you want to get something to eat before you go in?" he asked.

He could hear her smiling as she said, "Sure, it would be nice to see you before I go in."

"Okay, I'll pick you up at 4:00. How's that?"

"That sounds great! I'll see you then."

118

"OK, bye," he said before closing his phone. A warm feeling coming over him. "She really *is* something special." He thought to himself as he continued on toward his motel room.

At 4:00 on the button, Luke rang Syndi's doorbell and was greeted with a kiss on his cheek. "Thanks for asking me to dinner before I have to be at work," she said, smiling and holding a small bag that contained her work uniform.

"Well, I wouldn't want you to have to be hungry all night," he responded.

They journeyed to the outskirts of town, just down the street from the Kwik-Mart, where Syndi had suggested a great pizza restaurant called Four Corners.

"It's New York style," she said, thinking back to the many slices that she enjoyed while living in New York City. "They cut the slices so big, you have to fold them to eat it!" she said excitedly in anticipation.

During their dinner, their conversation had somehow turned to travel. Syndi mentioned that in a few days, she would be going to Florida for a week to surprise her parents who had moved there about ten years ago.

"Oh really, that will be nice," Luke said. "How long has it been since you've seen them?"

"Oh, it's been over a year. I really don't get to see them as much as I'd like. I miss my family and I have some friends there, too, so I want to stay for a while this time to really catch up with everybody. Plus, it's *warm* there!" she said laughing. "You'll be lucky if I come back!"

"Well, I hope you do! It's gonna get pretty expensive if I have to fly to Florida all the time to see you!" With that, Syndi smiled warmly before taking another bite of her pizza. While they were on the subject of travel, Luke said, "I'll be going back to Grand Rapids in a couple days."

"Oh really?" Syndi asked, sounding disappointed.

"Yeah, and I was thinking, you showed me Walkerville, so it would only be right for me to show you around Grand Rapids! Maybe you could come for a visit."

Syndi smiled widely. "That would be great!" she said as she questioned the sincerity of Luke's invitation.

As they continued eating, the atmosphere, somehow, had changed. They both felt a little more nervous than they did before and their conversations became just a bit more light-hearted and silly. There was more touching than usual and, although they didn't realize it, they were sitting just a bit closer than they had been before.

When they finished their pizza, Luke left some money on the table, stood up and offered his hand to Syndi to help her up. Once she had stood up, however, she neglected to let go of his hand. Surprised, Luke looked into Syndi's beautiful green eyes and they both just smiled at each other before walking, hand in hand, out of the restaurant.

"Would you mind just dropping me off at work?" Syndi asked. "I mean; we're going to pass Seth's on the way to my house. I can just have Jackie take me home. We get off at the same time and she lives really close to me."

"Your wish is my command, my lady," Luke said as he drove toward the bar.

As they pulled into the parking lot, Syndi picked up her uniform bag from between her feet and held it in her lap. "Luke, I want you to know that I'm really enjoying spending time with you," she said as Luke pulled into a parking spot in front of the building and put the car into park.

"To be honest with you, I actually wish we could spend even more time together," Luke said as they unbuckled their seat belts. "You are a wonderful woman and I feel something I can't even describe when I'm with you."

Syndi suddenly felt nervous, a peculiar feeling for her, considering she was so beautiful and so used to men paying her special attention. But this was different. This was bigger than anything she had ever known before. She became aware of her irregular breathing as Luke leaned toward her and cupped her face in his hands. He felt the warmth of Syndi's face as she closed her eyes and leaned toward him. Syndi felt that if her heart were to beat any harder, it would beat right through her chest. She felt his sweet, warm breath on her face for just an instant before his lips touched hers. Syndi dropped her bag back on the floor between her feet and wrapped her arms around Luke as they lost themselves in each other.

Chapter 7

A large rest stop, located on a lonely stretch of highway, sits just at the border of Walkerville. It's comprised of two separate buildings – the women's bathroom and concessions in the building on the left and the men's bathroom and visitor's office in the building on the right. About thirty yards past the two buildings is the front wall of the forest's trees. Besides the restrooms, it has all the basics: maps, soda, snack machines, a changing room for parents to take their babies and, throughout the day, there's someone in the office, always willing and able to help weary travelers find their way to or through Walkerville.

It was about 11:30 p.m. when Joey Moretto, a large, hairy man, pulled his eighteen-wheeler into the rest stop with its brakes whistling and grinding as he brought the large beast to a halt. Joey had been on the road for more than six hours and was long overdue for a break. As he stepped down from the cab and headed for the bathroom, he removed his baseball cap, which had a patch on the front that read 'CAT,' just long enough to stretch his arms while he yawned and ran his fingers through his long, thick hair. At this time of night there wasn't usually a lot of traffic through this particular stretch of road and, as circumstances would have it, Joey was alone at the rest stop… or so he thought.

Eyes were upon him, watching his every step towards the men's room. They had been watching even as he pulled into the rest stop parking lot. They watched as he got out of his truck and walked up the pathway and they watched as he pushed the men's room door open and went inside.

While Joey relieved himself at the urinal, there was movement outside in the trees behind the rest stop. The final straps were being tied, transforming the large, hidden man watching from the forest into the surgeon who had taken the tattoos and the lives of both Lathe Walthes and Kathy Peters. Tonight he had been watching from the darkness between the trees in anticipation of someone going into one of the restrooms alone, and now was his chance to act.

He watched carefully as he left the safety of the veil of shadows that the trees had provided him. As he approached the rest stop from behind, he checked to see if an approaching car on the highway ahead would exit into the parking lot. As the car passed, the surgeon approached the men's room door, tire thumper clinched in his right hand, hanging down to his side. Inside, Joey was just zipping up his pants when the door flew open and the surgeon rushed in. Joey's head instinctively snapped quickly to the left to see the surgeon running toward him almost silently.

For just an instant, Joey squinted his eyes, almost as if to say, "What the hell?" Without warning, the surgeon lifted the tire thumper from his side and swung it at Joey's neck, knocking him sideways into the metal dividing wall between the two urinals. Joey bounced off before falling backwards, hitting his back and head on the bathroom floor. Through blurry eyes, Joey saw the surgeon standing above him looking down as he circled.

The sharp blow to his neck had stunned Joey. He was conscious but unable to comprehend what was going on around him and it was now impossible for him to speak or control his limbs. All he could do was lay on the floor, helpless, feeling the sharp sting from his neck radiating up into his head and down throughout his entire body.

The surgeon held the tire thumper tight as he nudged Joey's head with his foot. He could tell by Joey's blank gaze that he would not be any trouble. Time was of the essence as it was uncertain when the next person would pull into the rest stop. The surgeon laid his tire thumper on the ground behind him before quickly unzipping Joey's coat, revealing his red flannel, buttoned-up shirt. As he pulled the shirt apart with one quick jerk, tiny opaque buttons flew through the air and ricocheted off of the walls and urinals, bouncing lightly on the bathroom floor all around Joey.

"Nothing?" the surgeon wondered to himself.

He propped Joey up against his legs as he pulled his coat off of him in a frenzy, then pulled his shirt off and threw it on the ground before rolling Joey over onto his stomach. As Joey's stomach and face hit the small blue and white tiles of the bathroom floor, the cold jolt immediately began to revive him from his temporary state of shock. As he lay on the frigid floor, slowly regaining his senses, he could see the surgeon reaching down and grabbing him by the hair. The surgeon lifted Joey's hair and turned his head from side to side to examine his neck. As his eyes became more focused, Joey could make out the wooden stick with the lead tip lying on the floor just behind the surgeon and just out of Joey's reach.

The surgeon stood up and let out a very frustrated groan as he balled his fists and looked up at the ceiling. Just then, Joey shot forward and, reaching between the surgeon's feet, grabbed the tire thumper. He pushed hard on the floor and started to stand back up, but the surgeon quickly grabbed Joey by the shoulders in an effort to throw him back down to the ground. Joey grabbed the surgeon's apron for stability and, swinging the tire thumper wildly, delivered a painful blow to the surgeon's left thigh, resulting in a very loud and angered howl from behind his tight white mask. Joey reared his arm back to deliver another painful strike, this time to the surgeon's left kneecap, but was instead met with a hard, fast, right knee directly to the center of his face. The crunch of Joey's nose breaking was unmistakable and he slumped forward and fell onto the ground. The blood from his nose ran onto the small blue and white floor tiles and flowed in the crevasses between them, coursing steadily toward the drain in the floor.

The surgeon grabbed his tire thumper from Joey's hand and hit him solidly on the back of his head, taking any ounce of fight out of him

124

immediately. The surgeon then opened the bathroom door just a crack and peered out to see if any other vehicles had entered the rest stop parking lot. Seeing none, he turned back toward Joey, picked up the coat and shirt and used them to wipe up the blood from the floor, then grabbed Joey by the wrists and turned him over onto his back so no blood trail would follow as he was dragged out of the bathroom and toward a small red brick electrical shed located just behind the building.

When they reached the shed, the surgeon dropped Joey's wrists to the ground, giving himself the necessary freedom of movement needed to smash the padlock off of the door with the tire thumper. Once the lock had busted, the surgeon reached out with his gloved hands and removed what was left of the lock, opened the door and dragged Joey inside to lie on the frozen cement floor.

The room was no bigger than a jail cell. It had tall electrical boxes lining the walls and housed various plastic bottles of cleaning supplies, plastic trash bags and two ladders. The humming of the boxes drowned out the pain-induced moans coming from a barely conscious Joey Moretto. The surgeon turned on the overhead light, shut the door behind him and threw the blood-soaked coat and shirt onto the floor beside Joey as he stood above him, straddling his waist.

The surgeon sat his tire thumper next to the door, where he knew it was far out of Joey's reach. Although, he knew that Joey was unable to move, he didn't want to take the chance. Joey moved limply as the surgeon proceeded to remove the rest of Joey's clothing and threw them on top of the shirt and coat on the floor. The surgeon surveyed Joey's entire body, looking for just one tattoo, although there were none to be found.

Once again, the surgeon straddled Joey's chest. Hatred filled his eyes as he fought through the pain in his thigh and squatted to sit on Joey's stomach. Joey's breath was forcefully pushed out of his lungs with the weight of the surgeon.

Unable to breathe or move, he watched in horror as the surgeon squeezed his tire thumper tightly, lifted his arm to full extension and brought the lead tip of the stick down like a hammer onto Joey's forehead. Joey's arms and legs shot up into the air. Beneath the droning hum of the electrical boxes, the surgeon heard the crack of Joey's skull being crushed upon impact as the skin on Joey's forehead split open and blood ran out and down both sides of his face. The surgeon continued hammering away at Joeys face as he became increasingly infuriated, thinking about how violated he felt seeing Joey handling his weapon, his security, his passion.

The multiple thrusts from the tire thumper split open Joey's nose, exposing the open cavity leading into his skull. The sharp metal edge of the lead tip punctured Joey's right eye with one strike, turning it to mush as it lay inside of its broken orbital socket. The surgeon continued his mêlée until blood spilled out of Joey's head and neck and it became nothing more than a wet, mangled heap – warm pieces of meat, brain, bone, hair and teeth barely affixed to the unscathed, unlucky body of Joey Moretto.

The giant surgeon had an overwhelming feeling of satisfaction as he stood up. Looking down at what he had accomplished and seeing what could barely be identified as a head, he flipped the light off and backed out of the humming electrical shed as he said aloud, "You don't count!" The yellow light from the distant parking lot diminished over Joey's body as the surgeon closed the door and returned to his observation spot within the darkness of the trees behind the rest area buildings.

*****

"Oh man, don't get me started!" Jobin said as he broke the triangular arrangement of pool balls at Seth's Place.

"I'm just saying," replied Travis, "how do you *know* it's a drifter?"

"Because it's the only idea that makes any sense, dumbass! You have a guy that wants to kill people, he comes through town for a few days, doesn't really stand out or talk to anybody, he just kind of keeps to himself while he cases the place, then he leaves! If anybody did notice him when he was here, they'd probably figure he was just in to camp and forget him in a couple weeks. Then he comes back, like six months later and starts his killing. He knows places that are secluded, places to hide, so it's easy for him! It makes perfect sense!"

Travis took the reins at the pool table and dropped the four ball on an easy bank shot.

"I don't know, man," he said as some of the other patrons started listening in. "I think it's somebody from right here in Walkerville!"

Jobin rolled his eyes and sighed. Travis continued, "They *knew* Lathe and Kathy. Knew where and when they'd be at a specific place and took advantage of that knowledge. A drifter might be able to learn the lay of the land, but not people's schedules."

"Well, how do you know he scheduled to kill Lathe and Kathy?" Jobin retorted quickly. "Did the guy say '7:00: have dinner, 9:00: shit, shower and shave, 10:00: go to a movie, 12:15: kill Lathe?'"

Some of the other patrons in the bar laughed quietly, not sure if they really should, seeing that Lathe was just laid to rest.

"Well," Travis said, "maybe it's somebody we all know. Did you ever think of that?" Jobin looked at Travis with quiet disdain as Travis continued, "What about Scott Badalato? He's been nothing but trouble since the second grade!"

"*Hey!*" bellowed an older man from the other side of the bar as he stood up. "I don't think you need to be publicly accusing Scott Badalato of murdering two people!"

"I'm *not!*" Travis yelled back. "I'm just saying that it's possible that it's someone from here in Walkerville, that's all!"

"Well what about your cousin, Ned?" the older man screamed, now pointing across the bar at Travis, "He's a no-good asshole and he always has been!"

"Hey! Piss off, you old piece of shit!" bellowed Travis as he threw his pool cue on the table and started toward the man on the other side of the bar. Jobin stepped in front of Travis and held him back while three other men stepped in front of the older man to stop him from engaging on Travis.

"You all just settle down!" Seth yelled over the top of the crowd from behind the bar. "Now everybody just go back to what you were doing or we're closing early tonight!"

Travis pushed Jobin off of him and walked back to the pool table where he picked up his pool cue and continued the game as he said quietly, "I'm just sayin."

*****

We make choices every day: crossing the street, giving away a phone number, talking to someone we've never met before or passing on an invitation to go to dinner with some friends when we're invited. As insignificant as they may seem at the time, these choices actually change the course of our entire lives and subsequently, the lives of those around us, be they our family, friends or near-by strangers. Furthermore, the resulting actions of those whom we have affected, in turn affect those around them and so on and so on and so on. It truly is the butterfly effect.

*****

Dave and Emily had decided to go out to a club in Elbridge, not far from Walkerville, where they stayed out too late, drank too much and, when they got home, made love until just before sunrise.

"Hello, Rose?" Emily said when she heard the phone pick up and a short "Mmm..." on the other end. "Rose, this is Emily," she said in a raspy voice. "I'm so sorry to call you this early in the morning, but I was wondering if you could cover my shift at the diner for me today. I'm really sick."

"Hmm?" Rose responded, trying to wake up after having just gotten home from her night shift five hours ago.

"Rose? Are you there?" Emily asked.

"Yeah, Emily," Rose mumbled.

"Rose, would you mind covering my shift today? I'm sick."

Rose thought for a moment about her son, her mortgage and her dying car. "Yeah," she said in a depressed tone, realizing that she would be working a double shift and starting in one hour. "I'll take it."

"Oh thank you so much, Rose. I owe ya one!" Emily said before hanging up the phone, rolling over and laying comfortably in Dave's arms.

Rose Wane was a pretty, twenty-eight-year-old single mother. She had long, beautiful dark hair that went to her waist and she commonly got compliments on it from her many customers.

Rose dragged herself out of bed, showered quickly, and kissed her nine-year-old son goodbye as they both headed out the door. She told him to go to his grandparents' house right after school and that she'd pick him up after her shift was over that evening. She knew that if it weren't for her parents always helping her out with her son, and sometimes with a loan when she was short on cash, she just wouldn't be able to make it. Rose got into her yellow Volkswagen Beetle and headed back out of town to spend her day and her night on her feet. She kept herself awake by drinking cup after cup of strong, black coffee throughout her double shift until the very last customer of the night had left and she had cleaned up all of her stations.

When she walked out of the diner, she was completely exhausted and she wished that she could just close her eyes and find herself in bed at home. The drive to her parents' house to pick up her son was so long and tonight it seemed even a hundred miles farther away. Almost halfway there, Rose told herself that she could make it if she just concentrated and kept her mind off of how much coffee she drank and how badly she had to go to the bathroom. She had driven this same route for the last four years and knew that just two miles ahead was a rest stop. This didn't make it any easier for her to concentrate and the closer she got to the rest stop, the less she felt like she could hold it until finally, it was inevitable. Rose was forced to get off at the rest stop next to the highway.

As she pulled in, she noticed that only one vehicle, an eighteen-wheeler semi-truck, was parked in the heavily lit rest stop parking lot.

"He's probably asleep in his cab," she thought to herself as she parked as close as she could to the buildings and walked nervously but quickly to the women's restroom. As she pushed the door open, she heard the high-pitched whistling of water running through the pipes. Rose looked at one of the two sinks and saw a small, steady stream of water coming from the faucet. Almost instinctively, she twisted the handle but to no avail, the water continued streaming out. She turned back toward the door to lock it but found it could only be locked with a key. Walking past two stalls, Rose pulled the doors open slowly, making sure she was alone before entering the last stall against the wall and locking the door before lifting her skirt, pulling down her panties and sitting on the cold commode seat.

For what seemed like five minutes, the sounds of the water from the sink whistling, Rose urinating and her sigh of relief filled the restroom, echoing off of the bare walls and back to her ears just before the toilet flushing sounded over the rest. Still nervous about being at the rest stop alone, Rose peeked under her stall to see a thick water pipe coming out of the little blue and white tiles that made up the floor and the bottom of the shiny walls.

As she looked to her right, she could see the bottom of the two other commodes and a few brown paper towels that hadn't made it into the trash bin below the paper towel dispensers on the wall. Rose pushed her stall door open and again pulled on the two other stall doors on her way to the sink, making sure she was truly still alone. As her stall door slowly swung shut behind her, the light from over the sink illuminated the surgeon who was perched atop the bend in the water pipe that ran out of the tiled floor and into the wall a foot above. He was balanced with one hand on each wall and leaning back into the corner. He silently stepped down from the pipe and crept toward Rose. She watched herself approaching in the mirror as she walked to the sink to wash her hands.

She looked down at her hands as she washed them and then as she began rinsing them off, looked up into the mirror. She saw a worn-out young woman, a woman who was growing old before her time, a woman working hard to make ends meet so she could stop relying on her parents for her mere survival. She was trying to make a good life for her son and herself. As she finished rinsing her hands, she saw something in her peripheral vision move and she turned suddenly to stare straight into the face of a mad man. There he stood in his blue medical scrubs covered by a white apron that was splattered with Joey Moretto's blood. He wore blue rubber gloves, a blue surgical cap, and finally, a white and bloody surgical mask, fastened securely around his head so only his dark eyes could be seen.

Rose opened her mouth wide, but her scream was quickly stifled by the surgeon's enormous hand covering it as he grabbed the back of her head with his other hand and squeezed tightly. Rose's eyes opened widely and she flailed her arms frantically, hitting the large man on the chest and arms a few times before she was lifted off of the ground and thrown, head first, into the mirror over the sink.

Shards of shiny glass flew through the air, breaking in the sink and on the little blue and white tiles on the floor below. Rose hit the floor and grabbed her head tightly with one hand in an effort to stop the pain and stop the blood that was trickling down her face and neck as she frantically looked around for

131

an escape. Just then, the surgeon grabbed Rose by her long, dark hair and lifted her off of the floor only to slam her forehead into the edge of the porcelain sink.

Rose fell to the floor again but this time she lay supine and motionless, silent and unconscious, as the fresh blood streamed down her face from her forehead and into her long, dark hair. The surgeon looked down at the nametag on her shirt which simply read 'Rose.' He grabbed a handful of her shirt in each hand and tore it open. There, on her right breast, just beneath where her nametag had rested, was a small tattoo of a red rose, slightly covered by the top of her pink lace bra.

Without hesitation, the burly surgeon snatched Rose from off of the floor and threw her over his shoulder. Blood dripped steadily from her forehead onto the back of his blue scrubs as he pulled the bathroom door open just enough to see the parking lot. One semi parked toward the back of the parking lot, one yellow Volkswagen Beetle parked right in front and not a single vehicle in sight on the highway.

"Good," he thought, "no one to get in my way."

With adrenaline racing, the surgeon ran to Rose's car and she bounced on his shoulder with every step. He opened the passenger door of the car and threw her in before slamming it shut and ran around, as fast as he could, to the other side to get in. The surgeon quickly searched Rose's pockets for her keys, finally finding them in her left coat pocket. In a flash, he started up the engine, backed out of the parking spot and sped off toward the exit of the rest stop and out onto the highway. He had only driven a short distance when he pulled off of the highway onto a rural side road and then onto a dirt road that wound far back into the forest where the headlights of Rose's car brought light upon the surgeon's trusty old Blazer sitting in wait.

*****

"There, last one," the surgeon thought as he tightened the knot in the thin nylon rope that wrapped around Rose's right ankle and threaded through the metal ring that was bolted to the table.

Rose lay naked on the shiny metal table. Her wrists, ankles and waist bound tightly. Upon finishing his knot, the surgeon turned sharply to his left to begin his ritual of turning on his stereo and the water from the faucet that ran down the hose onto the floor, before removing and folding the blue towel from atop the array of surgical instruments on the stand.

The loud music seemed to act as an alarm clock for Rose who started to slowly move her eyes back and forth beneath her eyelids before opening them ever so slightly, letting the bright light from above invade her peaceful darkness. With her vision impaired by the painfully bright light, Rose felt the rubber-gloved hand of the surgeon caressing her body, starting from the bottom of her bare foot and running up her right leg to her inner thigh, past her vagina, over her stomach, up and over her right breast and finally stopping at her tattoo.

Rose screamed, "What's going on?" Which was answered only by violins playing beautifully through the speakers. She felt something warm and wet on her rose tattoo that trailed downward to her nipple. Because of the bright surgical light above her, she still could not open her eyes completely but she recognized the sensation as a tongue licking her skin. Tears ran out of Rose's eyes as she thrust them open to get a look around her at last. As her eyes burned and adjusted to the light in the room, she saw the giant surgeon that she had seen in the ladies' room of the rest stop earlier that night and her body immediately tensed up. "What are you doing? *What are you doing?*" she yelled.

The surgeon was still wearing his blood-soaked medical garb and seemed to not even notice that she had made a sound. He instead peered over his blood-splattered surgical mask while he retied the straps behind his head, looking at her almost with pity in his eyes as a surgeon would look upon a patient who had a cancerous tumor that needed to be removed.

He turned and picked up a clean, shiny scalpel from off of the stand and turned back to Rose. The classical piece on the stereo came to an end and was followed by silence. In that moment, Rose's quick, irregular and heavy breathing could be heard over the whistle of the water running through the pipes. A plethora of beautiful violins joined by the light plucking of a cello took the place of the silence as Bach's piece "Air on the G String" began to play, filling the room with the sounds and memories of a more civilized society from a time long gone.

The surgeon closed his eyes as if to enter this other period and Rose heard a desperately frantic clawing noise but could not tell from where it was coming. The surgeon opened his eyes and brought the scalpel toward the top of Rose's right breast, just above her rose tattoo. *"Oh my God!"* she screamed as the cold blade touched her skin. *"Why are you doing this?"*

With a confused look in his eyes, the surgeon froze.

"Well my dear, since you asked," he said in a dark, growling, matter-of-fact tone, withdrawing the scalpel from Rose's skin and turning down the stereo so the music played softly in the background, "I'll tell you."

He looked up at the old, brown shag carpet on the ceiling and asked softly, "Have you ever heard the expression that the body is a temple? First Corinthians, chapter six, verses eighteen through twenty."

And he quoted: "Flee immorality. Every other sin that a man commits is outside the body, but the immoral man sins against his own body. Or do you not know that your body is a temple of the Holy Spirit, who is in you, whom you have received from God and that you are not your own? For you have been bought at a price. Therefore, honor God in your body."

Rose watched the surgeon as he thrust his face toward hers, his mask-covered nose an inch from hers.

"You weren't born with that rose on your tit, were you?" he bellowed. "Did God give you that as a part of your body?" Rose flinched as he continued. "No? Then you have *defiled* a temple of God!" He stood back up and composed himself, straightening his apron and adjusting his mask.

"My mother always told me that tattoos are only for trashy people, like cigarettes and liquor. Women walk around looking pretty, they do their makeup just right, spray on beautiful perfume, and then go out and smoke cigarettes! Why would they want to ruin what they just spent so much time and effort to create? Why would they want to pervert something so beautiful that God himself has created? The exquisiteness of a woman's perfume mixed with the stench of cigarettes... that smell can only be described as a beautiful sin! It's just not right! It's an oxymoron! It just doesn't go together! Your body is wonderful."

He used the back of his fingers to stroke Rose from her neck to her thigh. Rose swallowed hard and continued crying.

"No matter how beautiful the tattoo is, it's still a sin to tarnish your body. My mother always taught me to be polite, to be a gentleman, to not consort with the likes of you." As he said this, he sounded quite snobbish as the clawing and scratching from somewhere in the room continued.

"My mother used to call people like you 'P.W.T.' – Poor White Trash. There's black people and there's niggers. There's white people and there's people like *you!* The white version of a nigger, the lowest class of my race, unsophisticated, uneducated and not at all elegant like myself or like my music!"

He closed his eyes, breathing in the pure beauty of Bach as he now felt in his heart that he was a part of the music, that it was, in fact, somehow written *for* him, written *about* him. It encouraged him and gave credence, if only in his own mind, that what he was doing was not only the right thing, but the *best* thing he could ever possibly do for humanity itself.

135

He could hear Rose unsuccessfully struggling to free herself from her binds.

"Did you know that in Borneo, there was a group of natives called the Iban tribe?" He looked down at Rose who was pulling desperately against the small nylon ropes around her wrists as she cried. She heard the nearby scratches suddenly stop.

"Pay attention now, dear. After all, you *did* ask!" He sounded as if he was smiling beneath his mask. "The Iban tribe was a tribe of head-hunters. They would get the most taboo of tattoos on their fingers when they cut off the head of their first enemy. Interesting, huh?" He raised his eyebrows and nodded his head.

"Furthermore, did you know that our word 'tattoo' comes from their word, T-A-T-U? That's the sound made when their tattooing instrument was tapped to make its mark into the skin, 'ta-tu, ta-tu, ta-tu,'" the surgeon said as he wrapped his left hand around the scalpel, its blade protruding from the bottom of his fist as he pretended to have a hammer in his right hand tapping on the handle of the scalpel to demonstrate the technique.

Rose squeezed her fists and eyes shut, as if to imagine herself away from this twisted man before he continued, now yelling.

"Tattoos were sacred, now they're just *trash*! Your culture has perverted the whole concept!" He slammed his fist down on the autopsy table just inches from Rose's head. Rose screamed as she arched her head back and squeezed her eyes shut yet again.

"Scream!" the surgeon encouraged before yelling even more thunderously. "Scream louder! Let me *know* that you're scared! Show me some *real* emotion! That's what your screams really *are*... unadulterated emotion!" Rose continued screaming, now completely terrified and fearing for her life.

The surgeon turned up the music with the back of his hand, where there was no blood, to match the volume of Rose's screams.

"Your screams are a part of my music!" he bellowed above it all. "They're like the music itself, pure emotion! They *complete* my music! People are so fake, but you can't fake emotion like this, huh?" The music grew quieter and the surgeon lightly placed his hand over Rose's mouth, stifling her screams.

"People say 'I'm sorry' when they've done you wrong. They're really not sorry, they just want forgiveness so they'll feel better about themselves. There's a *big* difference between regret and remorse!" The music changed and began playing a peaceful, light tune.

"Beethoven's 'Piano Sonata in C-Sharp Minor No. 14.'" the surgeon said warmly. "You probably just know it as 'Moonlight Sonata,'" he said smugly, figuring that everyone must have at least a basic knowledge of classical music. "Ludwig van Beethoven's opus 27, number 2. What a beautiful piece indeed."

He took his hand off of Rose's mouth as she had now stopped crying as harshly.

"Its name is 'Quasi una fantasia', Italian for 'Almost a fantasy,'" he laughed. "Ironic, huh? This moment in time, *this* is almost a fantasy, don't you agree?" Rose's lips pursed shut as she breathed hurriedly through her nose and her brow wrinkled in an effort to keep from screaming more.

The surgeon continued, "Beethoven wrote this in 1801 when he was thirty-one. He dedicated it to his pupil, the seventeen-year-old Countess Giulietta Guicciardi, with whom he was in love. Listen. You can hear him telling her how much he *worships* her. Can't you *feel* it in the music?"

The surgeon raised the scalpel and began swaying it to the music, slowly in the air.

His mood instantly changed and he roared as tears began welling up in his dark, empty eyes, "*This* is emotion! *This* is pain! This kind of emotion only *comes* from pain! Lying on the bathroom floor with food poisoning, loving someone you can never have, a woman giving birth, watching someone you love die... that's *real* emotion! That's *true* pain!"

137

The surgeon wiped the tears from his eyes with his sleeve and continued in a lighter tone, "After Beethoven died, his friends found a picture of the countess and three letters to her that were all in a hidden compartment of his desk. They weren't sure if the letters had never been mailed or if they had, in fact, been mailed and returned to him. They were addressed to his 'Unsterbliche Geliebte,' his 'Immortal Beloved.' Immortal Beloved, how beautiful is *that*? That alone *screams* of love. He began his first letter 'My angel, my all, my very self.' Can that depth of love *really* exist?"

Rose's eyes were darting around the room, trying to somehow take it all in, looking for even a hint of a means of escape.

"Have you ever listened to Beethoven's '5th Symphony,' I mean really listened to it?" The surgeon sat the scalpel down on the table, almost unconsciously just inches away from Rose's hand as he turned and walked toward the stereo and pushed a button to advance the CD to a different track.

"No, that's not it," she heard him say as he advanced through the next piece, playing only a second or two of the music. Knowing that this was her only chance for survival, Rose stretched her fingers out in an attempt to reach the scalpel. Her fingers fell just centimeters from the handle on her first try. In the silence, she could hear the surgeon advancing the CD from piece to piece.

Pulling against the nylon rope, Rose stretched her fingers all at once as far as they could reach. She felt the tendons in the top of her hand expanding as the tip of her middle finger came to rest on the warm, metal handle of the scalpel. As she began to pull it toward her a loud French horn blared through the speakers, startling Rose and causing her to jerk and push down on the handle of the scalpel, spinning it quickly on the smooth metal table. As the music played loudly, the desperate scratching that Rose had heard earlier started again as the surgeon picked up the CD case from the top of the stereo and began reading the back cover, looking for Beethoven's 5th Symphony.

Rose watched and reached for the spinning scalpel as it began to slow its rotation, moving closer and closer to her hand on each revolution. She stretched her fingers as far as they would go as the scalpel spun down, slower and slower, until its handle rested directly under the very tip of Rose's ring finger. As the surgeon began to turn around, Rose quickly flicked her fingers toward her, sliding the scalpel securely under her hand and wrist.

"I've got the wrong CD, sorry about that!" the surgeon yelled over the blaring music before turning it down a bit and walking across the room, sloshing through the water in his rubber boots to the freestanding orange metal cabinet where he began searching through a few CDs for the correct one.

Rose curled her fingers in toward her palm and pulled the scalpel out from its hiding place. Clumsily, she picked it up and bent her hand back toward her wrist as far as it would stretch and began sawing at the thin nylon ropes that were restraining her to the table. She quickly moved her fingers back and forth, slicing at the ropes until only a few threads were left and, with a sharp jerk, Rose's right hand was free. She looked over at the surgeon who was still rummaging through his stack of CDs before she reached over to her left hand and began slicing at the ropes that were holding that hand in place.

"Hey, what are you doing!?" the surgeon raged as he dropped his CD collection on the floor and ran, red-faced, toward Rose. The anger in his eyes horrified Rose and she turned back toward the surgeon, squeezing the scalpel tight and pointing it in his direction. She hadn't finished cutting through the ropes on her left hand and was pulling with all of her strength against them, trying to break free.

The surgeon stood with his face only six inches away from the tip of the scalpel, both of them knowing that if she brought the scalpel back to the ropes on her left wrist, he would advance.

"*You get away from me!*" she screamed while pulling against the ropes with her left arm and flailing the scalpel at the surgeons face with her right.

"Now, just take it easy honey," he said sweetly as he looked at Rose's naked body from head to toe, "I was just playin' with you. I wasn't really gonna' hurt you."

His voice sounded warm and soothing over the violent scratching noise. The surgeon unexpectedly shot forward, slapped the back of Rose's clinched fist with his left hand and grabbed her wrist in his right.

Through clinched teeth, the surgeon yelled, "How *dare* you touch my instrument?"

The frantic scratching noise continued as his heavy, meaty left fist landed squarely on Roses right eye. The impact from the force caused Rose's hands to shoot open and the scalpel fell to the floor landing silently in the puddle beneath. Rose went limp as the surgeon returned to the cabinet to retrieve more rope. He tied Rose's hands back down to the table before picking up the scalpel from under the puddle on the floor and dropping it into the dish of sanitizing liquid. He returned to the stereo with a new CD and began a new piece. The scratching noise again became silent.

"Beethoven's Fifth Symphony. Now *this* was music!" He said with gusto as he closed his eyes seeming to not even remember what had just happened between him and Rose.

He felt the first four notes that played loudly through the speakers and said, "Beethoven is regarded as one of the greatest composers in the history of all music."

Rose opened her eyes and, for a moment, had forgotten where and in what situation she was.

"In his early twenties he got tinnitus, which made it hard for him to hear or appreciate music. Now *that's* ironic!" The surgeon laughed slightly before continuing.

"He went deaf in his mid-twenties but still continued composing. He composed *this* masterpiece while he was completely deaf!"

The surgeon looked around the room for a moment, listening to the great work of art as tears began welling up in his eyes and fell silently down his cheeks, moistening his mask.

"He wrote this and never even got to *hear* it! Can you imagine the *pain* that he was going through, composing what was up in his head and *knowing* that he would never be able to actually hear it himself! Listen to his sadness, listen to his anguish, listen to his pain that almost led him to madness and his own suicide!"

The surgeon began to cry openly. "Can't you *feel* the pain in his work? This isn't just music – his soul is crying out, *openly*, for everyone throughout the ages to hear! That kind of emotion only *comes* from pain. It's so beautiful when I get the opportunity to mix such raw emotions. I have the gift, no...," he said hesitating, "I have the *power* to bring out that kind of emotion in everyone. You are so lucky," he whispered loud enough that only he heard it.

He continued with a slight gleam of jealousy in his eyes. "No one lives for the moment any more. Ever heard of a flow experience? That's what happens when you're doing something but not really concentrating on what you're doing or where you are. Have you ever driven somewhere and then suddenly realized that you don't know what happened for the past five minutes? That's a flow experience. Everyone lives in a kind of blur, a life of foggy thoughts and actions." He stopped and picked up a clean scalpel from the tray and looked down at Rose.

She looked up at him as her right eye was slowly swelling shut. She heard his next few words, which were as sharp as the blade of the scalpel in his hand. He spoke the words slowly: "I guarantee you that these next few moments will prove to be the clearest moments of your entire life!"

Rose began to shake and yell at the top of her lungs, "*No, please let me go!*"

The surgeon continued, seeming to not understand why Rose wouldn't want to be there. "We come into this world naked, vulnerable, screaming, and at the mercy of the doctor. You have the unique opportunity to leave the very same way!" He brought the scalpel downward toward Rose's tattoo.

Rose screamed at the surgeon, "*Fuck you!*" before spitting at him, her saliva landing just below his neck on his apron. He stopped dead in his tracks, confused as to what had just happened.

Like an explosion, the surgeon pointed his scalpel at Rose's face and roared, "*Ladies don't use that type of language!*"

Rose, more scared than ever, screamed out just as the final two notes of Beethoven's Fifth Symphony brought the piece to its close, "*OH SHIT!!*"

In the silence of the room, the surgeon's right eye twitched. "*You ruined it!*" He roared. He dropped the scalpel onto the instrument stand and picked up the dull and rusty pocket knife. Rose screamed as the voices of the choir in Mozart's thunderous 'O Fortuna' was born from the silence.

Although she knew her escape was impossible, her arms and legs instinctively pulled against the thin nylon ropes.

"Shit, huh?" the surgeon said furiously. "That's S-H," and he swiftly and shallowly sliced the letters into Rose's bare stomach. She screamed hysterically and pulled against the ropes as he continued spelling out the word. The blood streamed down her skin from each letter, hastily sliced into her, and gathered on the metal table below her.

As Rose screamed in pain, the surgeon dropped the bloody pocket knife onto the instrument stand next to all of the glistening, shiny instruments and picked up another scalpel. He turned to Rose who was writhing in pain from the slashes to her stomach. With one finger, the surgeon rubbed Rose's small red rose tattoo above her right breast, then wrapped his fingers tightly around the handle of the scalpel and quickly thrust it down into her chest. Rose yelped out in pain, her eyes and mouth open wide as the surgeon sawed at the meat below her skin, jutting up and down, as if cutting into a piece of raw steak.

The blood welled up and exited the fresh wound, running down her shoulder and chest and onto the cold, steel table and oozing toward the groove that encircled it. Rose screamed with each breath she took and the surgeon delighted in the sound. As the surgeon continued drawing the scalpel and separating Rose's skin, she shook her head violently back and forth as her hands and feet pulled hard against the unbreakable ropes. Her high-pitched screams persisted as did the surgeon until he had finished cutting a square around the rose tattoo. He picked up the hose and rinsed the excess blood from Rose's breasts and dropped the hose to the floor again.

"*You son-of-a-bitch*!" Rose screamed over the music.

The surgeon put two fingers on the side of her neck and exclaimed "Oh my, my, my, my, my. Your heart is beating a mile a minute!" And with that, he removed his fingers and quickly sliced deeply into her jugular vein with the bloody scalpel. A stream of blood shot out of her neck like a geyser, arching in the air and landing in the water puddle below. Rose's eyes shot open as she felt the sharp cut on her neck and the odd feeling of her warm blood quickly escaping through the new hole. She turned her head slightly to see the arch of blood become smaller and smaller as the music and the light in the room seemed to get further and further away until finally there was nothing but silent darkness.

The surgeon stood back and looked in horror as Rose took her last breath. He quickly moved to the other side of the table and began punching Rose's chest with the side of his fist yelling, "*No! Don't leave me! Come back!*"

He stopped and put his ear down near Rose's mouth as if to listen for a breath. Hearing none, he rested his palm between her breasts and began pumping on her chest with both hands. The surgeon pumped again and again, giggling like a school boy as each compression on Rose's chest shot blood out of her neck like a water gun.

"Oh well," he said, "all work and no play makes Jack a dull boy." He walked to the other side of the table and carefully began removing Rose's tattoo using his forceps, razor blade and rotary saw.

As he cut into Rose's chest, he realized how much easier it was to remove the tattoo once the life had exited the body and there was complete stillness, but it just didn't feel right to him. There was no excitement, no energy or love in the actions and no screams to intertwine with the classical music. He almost felt as if removing Rose's tattoo from her breast was now more of a chore than a labor of love.

The surgeon reached over to his stereo above the sink and, with the back of his hand, turned the volume up to add a bit more excitement to the room before extracting the beautiful little Rose tattoo from Rose's chest. He worked leisurely over her still, naked body, pulling the corner of skin up with the pristine silver pliers and flaying the tattooed skin away from the body with deliberate and precise slices.

Once the tattoo was removed, the surgeon picked his pocket knife off the instrument stand and hastily hacked at the wound and inner wall of skin left on Rose's chest. When he was done, it looked as if a wild beast had taken a bite out of her.

The scratching and clawing that had taunted Rose earlier began again and the surgeon yelled, "Fine! Fine!" and headed toward the door behind the slit in the white curtain. He pushed the door open and said "Come on in already!" as a small, hairless dog entered the room, his tail wagging furiously as he looked up at the surgeon excitedly. "Baby want a treat?" he said as he pinched the inner wall of skin from where Rose's tattoo had been removed and tore a small piece of meat out of the wound.

He held an inch-long piece of bloody flesh waist-high and said in a child-like voice "Come on baby, sit pretty! Sit pretty, boy!" The hairless dog sat up on his hind legs and sniffed the meat. A drop of warm blood dripped from the meat and onto the dog's nose, which he quickly licked off before snatching the meat from the surgeon's hand.

"That's a good boy!" the surgeon encouraged, "Good boy!" Once the dog had swallowed the meat, the surgeon escorted him out, told him to go lie down, and then shut the door again to keep his dog from coming back in.

"I'm sorry I have to do this." He said aloud to Rose as he picked up a bottle of bleach from the floor, "But I've got to make sure this is our little secret!"

Later that night, Rose's yellow Volkswagen sputtered down a wide dirt road deep in the forest, stopping suddenly just beneath a thick tree limb that stretched out twelve feet above the road from a giant maple tree. The surgeon got out of the car, still in his surgical garb and mask, and opened the front hood where he removed a brown blanket that held Rose's body. He gripped one end of the blanket and let Rose unroll from within; her body fell lifeless onto the thick pile of dried leaves that covered the dirt road. The surgeon shut the hood and threw the blanket out over the roof of the car before picking up Rose's body and laying her atop the blanket. The surgeon then stepped up onto the hood of the car and up onto the roof, careful to stand with his feet far apart to disperse his weight evenly over both doors. He squatted down and picked up Rose's naked body and lifted her up over his shoulder. Her long dark hair, now white from the bleach, reached down the surgeon's back toward the car. The surgeon grabbed Rose's hair and threw the end over the thick tree limb just above his head and tied it securely in a knot. He lifted Rose's body from his shoulder and gently let her go.

She dangled, naked, silently from the limb. Her hands and feet reached for the ground as her face was held upward, looking straight down the long, dark, empty road. Her right eye was blackened and swollen shut and the blood from the wound on her neck, breast and the word "Shit" that was cut into her stomach, trickled down her pale, wrinkled and bleached body and onto the blanket below as the surgeon jumped off of the roof and onto the road. He took the blanket from the roof and wiped the hood of the car to remove any seen or unseen footprints before folding the blanket neatly and placing it back in the trunk in front of the car and slamming the hood closed. Rose's blood dripped onto the hood of her little yellow Volkswagen as the surgeon got back in the car, shut his door and drove down the road just a short distance. He then abruptly turned the car around to face Rose. The headlights shone through the dust in the air, bringing Rose's body into view. She seemed to look right at the surgeon for a moment before a gust of wind blew through the trees, uprooting some of the thin brown leaves on the ground and swinging Rose ever so slightly. The surgeon revved up the engine and sped down the road, passing just inches under Roses' bare toes before spinning around quickly and racing back under her. The surgeon turned the car around yet again and sped down the frozen dirt road, passing just beneath Rose's pale and bloody body. Two drops of blood hit the windshield as he raced below her on his last pass.

"No footprints, no evidence, I'm smarter than they are," he thought to himself as he began spinning wildly in the dirt and leaves under Rose's body. Satisfied that he had sufficiently covered his tracks, the surgeon took one last look at Rose hanging in the tree by her white hair before speeding off down the dirt road and back toward his Blazer that he had parked in a different part of the forest, not far from the rest stop, leaving Rose to hang in the darkness, staring out into the void. It was official: there was a serial killer afoot in Walkerville.

Chapter 8

"Sheriff's office," Linda answered her phone as Sheriff Kerry, his deputies and Captain Parker sat behind closed doors in their daily 7:00 a.m. meeting. They were discussing the murders of Lathe Walthes and Kathy Peters as well as the latest information from the Grand Rapids Homicide Department. The fact that tomorrow would make it a week since Lathe had been killed was brought up as well as the fact that it seemed there were still no leads and because of the bleach on the bodies, not much evidence was found to help them track down who was behind it all. Just then, the sheriff's door abruptly swung wide open.

"Sheriff!" Linda said breathlessly, her face pale, "You'd better take this call!"

She covered her mouth with her shaking hands as Sheriff Kerry turned toward the captain with a surprised and worried look on his face before picking up the phone receiver on his desk and pressing the white blinking button.

"This is Sheriff Kerry," he said, fearing the worst that could come from the other end.

"Oh God, no," he said, dropping his head into his hand. "Where abouts?" he continued as he shook his head.

"OK, we're on our way." Sheriff Kerry hung up the phone and looked at Linda and then at the other men in the room.

With a mixture of sadness, helplessness and rage, Sheriff Kerry announced, "He got another one."

Everyone in the room felt the blow at the same time and they all began speaking at once.

"Now hold on a second," Sheriff Kerry yelled, quieting everyone in the room.

"It's Rose Wane," he said. The room fell silent.

"She's hanging in a tree, by her *hair* down a dirt road just off of East Hawley. Let's go."

Without hesitation, all five men in the room picked up their hats and coats, hastily left the building in silence, and headed toward their cars. Captain Parker called his team in Grand Rapids as Sheriff Kerry led the way out of the parking lot and out onto the road with lights and sirens announcing their departure.

Down at the end of a long dirt road, two loggers sat in their empty logging truck, watching the lifeless body of Rose Wane suspended from the thick limb that crossed over the road, swaying and spinning gently with the strong, steady late-October winds that whipped through the trees. Her pale skin, white hair, and the thin streams of blood running out of her wounds and down her body made her look like a gruesome spirit hovering ominously in the air.

The loggers, although both large, strong men, dared not leave the safety of their truck in fear that whoever did this could be very close. Possibly even watching them. They could hear the faint echoes of the sirens making their way through the forest and toward the logging truck. As the sheriff, captain, and the three deputies pulled up behind, the loggers got out of their truck and ran back toward the approaching squad cars. The driver of the logging truck started yelling, horrified, over the sirens.

"Sheriff, it's the damndest thing I've ever seen in my *life*! She's got the word 'shit' cut into her stomach and she's got a piece of skin missing from her chest, just like Lathe and Kathy!"

The passenger of the truck added, "She's also got a swollen right eye!"

Sheriff Kerry and the other officers turned off their lights and sirens and shut their doors behind them as they exited their squad cars and looked past the logging truck at Rose's body. Her half-open eyes looked straight ahead and her mouth hung open, almost as if she were in the midst of an unending silent scream.

"You did the right thing by calling," Sheriff Kerry told them as he pulled his eyes away from Rose's pale, naked body. "How long have you two been out here?"

"Just about a half hour, sheriff. We called the minute we saw her!" The passenger of the logging truck said nervously as the driver nodded his head in agreement.

Sheriff Kerry and his three deputies spread out behind Captain Parker as he began questioning the loggers. "Did you walk up to her or touch her?"

"No way, sir! We stopped right there and stayed in the truck!" The driver told Captain Parker as he turned and pointed to his empty truck that had been destined to be filled with freshly fallen trees by day's end but was now parked silently, thirty yards from Rose's body. "We just sat in the truck until just now when you got here."

"OK, great," Captain Parker said. "I want you two to go with the deputies back to the station to answer some more questions when my guys get here from Grand Rapids. I'll need the truck to stay where it is for the time being."

The two loggers shook their heads and proceeded to follow Deputies Charlie and Tim toward their squad cars where the deputies helped them to get into separate cars, explaining that it was procedure. The two men nervously got into the backs of the cars and the deputies headed back up the long dirt road toward town.

"The Major Case Squad will be here in a couple hours," Captain Parker said as he, the sheriff, and Deputy Julian stayed on site.

Sheriff Kerry turned to Julian and spoke boldly, "Julian, I want you to stay here with the captain. I'm going back to the station to question those two loggers, and then I'm going around town to question some of the folks there."

"What are you talking about?" Captain Parker asked confusedly. "Why would you think you need to question anyone? My men will take care of that when they get here."

"No offense, Captain, but your men haven't really gotten any useful information yet. No useful evidence, *nothing* to relieve the anxiety that everyone in town is feeling!"

"Sheriff," Captain Parker responded coolly, "these things take *time*, they don't just solve themselves."

"I understand that, Captain, and you're exactly right, they *don't* just solve themselves," said Sheriff Kerry, a bit sharply. "It's time I get out there and get my hands dirty. This is *my* town and by God, I've been pushed aside long enough."

Captain Parker responded in an authoritative tone. "Sheriff, I don't want you getting in the way of this investigation. You've got the Grand Rapids Major Case Squad working on this and I don't want you to get in the middle of it and run the chance of messing something up! We know what we're doing. We do this stuff day in and day out. We're professionals. You need to understand that, sheriff, and let us handle it."

Sheriff Kerry raised his voice even louder: "Captain, I've been hearing the folks around town saying that I'm not doing my job! I'm looking like a bumbling idiot to those people and it's high time I stop! I'm going out there and I'm going to try to come up with some *useful* information and, if I'm lucky, maybe even *catch* this guy!"

"Sheriff," Captain Parker yelled as he pointed his finger towards the sheriff who was walking away, back toward his squad car, "I've asked you nicely, now I'm telling you, stay out of the damn way. We've got it taken care of, we don't need your help!"

Sheriff Kerry slammed his palm down on top of his car. "Goddamn it!" he yelled as he turned around to look back at the captain. "Sheriff is an *elected* position and I haven't been doing my job! I have to do something!"

Sheriff Kerry felt alone, angry, depressed, and unsure of what he could do to help track down this killer. Seeing Rose cut up, streams of blood trickling down her naked body as she hung by her hair in a nearby tree was more than he could bear.

He yelled out, "I'll turn in my badge before I sit back for one more day and let someone else get murdered!"

Sheriff Kerry got into his car, revved up the engine and sped away leaving the captain and Deputy Julian behind. They watched as he sped down the dirt road and out of sight. As the two men stood in silence, Julian turned and looked wide-eyed at the captain, who turned and looked furiously back at Julian.

"I'll just go wait in the car," Julian said as he slowly backed away.

*****

Later in the morning, after Sheriff Kerry had finished questioning the loggers and getting the same story from each of them, he set out into his town with list in hand of every witness and person of interest in both Lathe and Kathy's murder cases. He tried to come up with some connections between Lathe, Kathy and Rose, but being from such a small town, they all knew each other in one way or another. He was determined to find *something* that had been missed. 'Somewhere,' he thought, 'someone had held something back, some tiny little detail that could be the thread to unravel the entire case.'

Sheriff Kerry began by visiting patrons and staff of Seth's Place who were there the night Lathe was killed. It was particularly uncomfortable questioning Syndi Bastion, as word had spread that she was spending a lot of time with the captain, although neither the sheriff nor Syndi brought it up. From there, he went to the Ace Logging and Lumber Company, the site where Lathe Walthes's body had been found in the parking lot, leaning up against a tire of one of the logging trucks. He spoke with Frank, the owner of the logging company, and a few of the men that worked there at the building.

Throughout the day, Sheriff Kerry went from place to place, questioning, prodding and trying to learn something new, something that had been thought unimportant or omitted unintentionally or even intentionally when the Walkerville villagers were questioned the first time by the Grand Rapids officers. Despite Captain Parker's opinion, Sheriff Kerry thought that he might have a better chance of gaining information since everyone knew and trusted him.

Surprisingly, most of the townspeople didn't seem to mind being questioned again as now they were all completely terrified and wanted to do whatever they could to help catch the killer and put an end to all of this. However, there were some who were irritated at being questioned again.

"How many times do I have to tell the same thing?" Said one of the townspeople to Sheriff Kerry.

"Seriously, Sheriff, this is the fourth time I've been questioned," another very unhappy and boisterous man yelled.

"Do you think anything's changed since the first time? Our faith in Walkerville's finest has been shot to hell, Sheriff! Why don't you leave me alone and get out there and actually *try* to find that bastard?"

Dealing with the negativity of the townspeople throughout the day, Sheriff Kerry's mood went from bad to worse. He was trying to do what he could to help make the people in his town safe but they just couldn't understand that. All he got in response to his efforts was criticism and un-cooperation.

'Goddamn!' he thought to himself as he drove through town, gritting his teeth. 'Can't they see I'm on their side? Why the hell am I even trying?

They're all just a bunch of ungrateful rednecks! They're vulgar, uneducated and stupid! These assholes would stick out like a sore thumb among all the sophisticates up on the island!'

His thoughts began to drift. 'Now *that* was a great job! Highly educated, financially stable, polite and friendly folks up there. Why the hell did I ever have to leave?'

*****

As the cold wind whistled through the leafless trees, the sun, high overhead, shined down on the Grand Rapids Major Case Squad as they took their time to meticulously collect evidence from the area around the tree limb that, until an hour ago, had Rose Wane's long, bleached white hair tied around it, supporting her dead, stiff, naked, and mutilated body. Captain Parker supervised the crew and was heard telling one man to be sure to get plenty of pictures and asking a few others what they had found so far. Deputy Julian stayed in his car for the most part, exiting every half hour or so to ask the captain if there was anything he could do to help, yet each time being told that everything was under control but thanks for asking.

"Dispatch to car three!" came Linda's familiar but now upset voice.

"Car three here, go ahead," Deputy Julian responded, sounding a bit worried.

"Julian!" Linda began, almost yelling, "Are you with Captain Parker?"

"He's working with some of the Grand Rapids guys here, why, what's up?" he asked.

"Someone just called in another dead body! A man was found in an electric shed at a rest stop just at the edge of town! An over-the-road trucker! The sheriff wants you to bring the captain here to the station so they can go to the rest stop together!"

"Are the Grand Rapids guys still there at the station?" Deputy Julian asked.

"No," Linda replied nervously, "They finished questioning the two loggers and then left. I don't know where they were going, though."

"OK," Deputy Julian responded quickly as he felt his face and ears warming with the impact of the sudden and terrible news. "I'll grab the captain and be back there in about fifteen minutes!" Julian got out of his car and ran to Captain Parker, briefly explaining the recent discovery. Captain Parker yelled to his men that he would be calling for them when he had some more information and he and Julian ran back to the deputy's car together and sped off down the long dirt road back toward the sheriff's office. "Did Linda say anything about the condition of the body?" Captain Parker asked Julian over the car's siren. "No, she just told me that someone just called in another dead body and said it was a male truck driver and that he was found in an electric shed at a rest stop."

"*Goddam it!*" Captain Parker yelled as he slammed his fist on the car's dashboard. "Two in one day?"

As they arrived at the sheriff's office, Sheriff Kerry sat waiting impatiently in his squad car. "Come on, Captain!" he yelled out of his open window as Captain Parker hurriedly exited Deputy Julian's car and entered the sheriff's. With a flip of a switch on the dashboard, Sheriff Kerry's siren and lights came alive before his tires spun quickly, throwing dust and gravel into the air behind them as they pulled out of the parking lot and onto the road. Although the siren blared, the silence in the car was not only uncomfortable, but also intense.

"They say his head is gone," Sheriff Kerry said uncomfortably just to break their silence. "What do you mean 'gone?'" Captain Parker asked sarcastically, which only further irritated the sheriff who pursed his lips together and shook his head slightly before answering back, "The manager at the rest stop said the truck driver's head was smashed so bad that if there wasn't a body there, he wouldn't have even been able to tell that the mess on the floor was a human head!" "Son of a bitch," Captain Parker responded empathetically. "Did he say if anyone saw anything?"

"I asked him that. He said when he got to work this morning, the mirror in the ladies' room was broken and pieces were all over the floor. He had one of his employees clean it up. Then later in the afternoon, he was out stretching his legs and noticed the lock was broken off of the electric shed behind the rest stop, so he went over to check it out. He said that after he opened the door and saw the body, he slammed it shut and ran into the rest stop where he told one of his employees to go out and stand by the shed and not to open the door or let anyone in there while he called us. He said he was the only one to see the body so far." Out of the corner of his eye, Sheriff Kerry could see the captain clinching his fists and his teeth tightly as he continued, "I told him to tell any travelers that they would have to stay put until we got there and had him tell his employees to park a vehicle across the entrance and the exit so no one else could come in and no vehicles could sneak out."

"Good thinking, Sheriff," Captain Parker said quietly.

As they approached the rest stop, a truck that was blocking the entrance rolled quickly backward and out of the way. They were met by Chris Hearding; the manager of the rest stop facility. He was a slightly built, middle-aged man with thinning, light brown hair with a restless body language that implied his nervousness. "Right back here!" he yelled and waived as Sheriff Kerry and Captain Parker exited the vehicle. Chris walked briskly, followed closely by the captain and the sheriff, around the side of the rest stop and toward the red brick electric shed.

"The mirror in the ladies' room was broken last night, too," Chris said in a shaky voice. "I had one of my employees sweep it up, but then I found the guy in the electric shed and figured you guys would want to investigate both of the restrooms, so I just locked them." Although Chris had slammed the door to the electric shed shut, it had not latched completely, or the curiosity of the employee standing guard got the best of him and he had opened the door for a quick peek inside. Either way, a half-inch crack ran around the slightly opened door and they could hear the humming of the electrical boxes coming from within.

Still twenty feet from the shed, Captain Parker said "Why don't you go wait for us back in your office?" Relieved, Chris nodded his head and turned to quickly walk back to the rest stop. "Step exactly where I step," Captain Parker said to Sheriff Kerry before the two men made their way to the corner of the red brick shed. "Are you ready for this?" Captain Parker asked the sheriff, looking him straight in the eyes. Sheriff Kerry took a deep breath before answering. "Yeah, go ahead and open it." So as not to touch the door with his fingers, Captain Parker took a pen out of his coat pocket and stuck it between the door frame and the door and began pulling it open. There in the darkness laid a figure so gruesome that the average human mind could not perceive it as being real. One would immediately think it was a set-up, a dummy body lying atop a mutilated chicken or maybe some road-kill. The mind is funny that way, it can comprehend anything we perceive to be real but only a very limited amount of anything beyond that. Our mind tends to try and rationalize what we cannot understand and we unconsciously try to make sense of everything.

The men immediately covered their mouths and noses as the warm, terrible stench wafted out of the small room and into their lungs. "Oh shit!" Sheriff Kerry muttered beneath his hand as Captain Parker, staying outside of the shed, used his pen to flip a switch just inside on the wall. It didn't seem possible for this scene to become any more macabre, however, with the bright light from above, the small pieces of bone, the wet, mashed hair and pieces of pureed brain lying in the pool of blood that covered the cement floor, could now be seen in more detail. The puddle of blood dripped out of the doorway and onto the frozen ground and as their eyes reluctantly surveyed the scene, they noticed a bloody shirt and jacket lying beside the body and pieces of bloody skin and teeth which were flung from the surgeon's tire thumper onto the surrounding floor and walls as he mercilessly smashed Joey's head into an unrecognizable gory pulp.

The men stepped back a few feet and uncovered their mouths and noses to deeply inhale the fresh, cold air. Sheriff Kerry coughed as he said "This had to be the same guy that killed the others here in Walkerville, don't you think, Captain?"

"I don't know, Sheriff – unless this guy had a tattoo on his head or under his pants, maybe," Captain Parker said after looking around. "The others were found naked and had pieces of skin missing. This guy is still wearing his pants! I'll call my men and have them come and sweep the scene and when they get to the body, we'll see if there are any pieces of skin missing from under his pants. They'll check him for some identification, too. We'll have to contact his family and let them know what happened. We'll have to ask them if he had a tattoo on his head anywhere. God is *that* going to be an uncomfortable call!" Sheriff Kerry nodded in silent agreement as Captain Parker led the sheriff away from the shed as he called one of his men from the case squad and instructed him to come to the rest stop when they were finished working the scene where Rose was found.

As he was finishing his conversation, Sheriff Kerry walked up to the captain and stood in front of him, patiently waiting and listening to his conversation. When he was through, Captain Parker hung up his phone and, with obvious aggravation, asked the sheriff what was the matter. "Nothing! I just wanted to be sure I know what's going on. I need to be kept in the loop, Captain!"

"Sheriff, I gotta' be honest, you're really starting to get under my skin," Captain Parker "It's starting to sound like you think you could do this better all by yourself!" His voice, beginning to rise, continued: "Like you alone could do a far superior job than the goddamn Grand Rapids Major Case Squad! This is what we do, Sheriff!"

"Well, it may be what you do, but that doesn't mean there's not other ways of getting to the bottom of all this!" Sheriff Kerry yelled back. "I know I'm just some small-town, slack-jawed yokel, but I'm tired of this bullshit! Don't you even *think* that you can come into *my* town and kick *me* around! That just doesn't work for me, son!" Captain Parker stepped toward Sheriff Kerry and, with his face flushed red, thrust his finger into Sheriff Kerry's chest. "I'm in charge here, Sheriff! Do you understand me? You'll know what I tell you and you'll do what I tell you!"

Both men stared at each other, their faces contorted, looking like two dogs snarling before tearing into each other. Captain Parker continued: "If you have a problem with that, you'll need to take it up with the Michigan State Department. In the meantime, get off my fuckin' back!" Captain Parker took two steps back before turning and walking back toward the rest stop building to begin questioning everyone inside. Sheriff Kerry spit on the ground and walked briskly back to his squad car.

About an hour later, Captain Parker finished his questioning and stepped out of the building and back into the freezing air outside. Reaching into his pocket, he pulled out his cell phone and dialed Syndi's number.

"Hello there, Captain Parker," she answered playfully. "Hi honey, how's your day going?"

"Pretty good, actually! I'm getting a lot of things done that I've been putting off. How about you?" By this time, Captain Parker had removed from his mind all of the disturbing images he had seen that day as well as the negative attitude he had received from the sheriff. "Not too bad," he said. "I'll be going home tomorrow for a few days to work on these Walkerville cases. Would you like to get together tonight? You *did* say you're off on Thursday nights, right? Maybe we could have some dinner!"

"*Sure*! I'd love to!" Syndi responded with delight. "Wonderful!" Captain Parker responded, also sounding excited. "How about I pick you up at 7:00?"

"That sounds good!" Syndi responded eagerly. "I'll be ready to go." Captain Parker laughed, thinking back to their first date when she made him wait for her to get ready. "OK, so should I really get there at 7:30 then?" he jokingly asked. Syndi laughed the cutest laugh the captain had ever heard.

He walked back into the warmth of the rest stop building as he was hanging up with Syndi. Two cars pulled into the rest stop parking lot and seven men from the Grand Rapids team exited the vehicles and hurriedly headed into the main rest stop building where they were met by Captain Parker. Moments later, they all exited the building again, headed by the captain, who motioned toward the electric shed. Sheriff Kerry watched from inside his car as Captain Parker pointed to the line of trees in the distance, instructing a few of his men to cover that area as well. The men spread out and began their second investigation of the day, knowing that their search and examination of evidence would take them well into the night.

Captain Parker looked out into the parking lot and saw the sheriff sitting in his car. Moments later, Captain Parker came back out of the building carrying two Styrofoam cups and a white paper bag. He walked down the walkway and to the passenger side of Sheriff Kerry's car, opened the door, and sat down in silence. Captain Parker, now in a better mood, took a deep breath before speaking. "Sheriff, I really don't mean to step on your toes. That's not my intention. Coffee?" The sheriff, who had a look of uncertainty on his face, took one of the cups. Captain Parker opened the paper bag revealing a few bagels and some small packages of cream cheese, jellies, plastic knives, and paper napkins and motioned for the sheriff to help himself. After taking a sip of his coffee, the captain continued: "Sheriff, I can tell you're a very smart man and I need to talk to you, quite candidly, about some of the information concerning these cases. Now this is *classified* information, it cannot leave this car. Do you understand?" Sheriff Kerry sat expressionless, coffee in one hand and a bagel in the other, nodding in agreement. "Do you remember me telling you that I was transferred to Michigan after working on a case in a college town up in Missouri?" Sheriff Kerry swallowed a bite of his bagel before answering, "Yeah, I remember you saying that."

"Well," Captain Parker continued, it was a case very similar to this one. There was a young kid up at the college named Billy Damballa, aka, the "Soul Reaper." He was a really big kid and a sick son-of-a-bitch that preyed on the other college kids – the college kids who had tattoos!" Sheriff Kerry became wide-eyed as he took in the shocking news. "Billy's M.O. was to cut the tattoos off of his victims while they were still alive and, from what we could gather, while they were fully awake." Sheriff Kerry closed his eyes tight, muttered and shook his head.

"Yeah, and it gets worse," Captain Parker continued. "Do you remember me telling you that most serial killers intentionally leave something for the cops to find?" Sheriff Kerry shook his head. Captain Parker continued, "Do you remember me telling you that one guy used to leave the eyeballs of his victims?" Sheriff Kerry spoke out with surprise, "That was *him*?" "That was him." Captain Parker confirmed. "Every time he killed one of the kids, he'd taunt us by leaving their bloody eyeballs.

"Billy actually sent a letter to the local paper in Cape Girardeau. It was pretty disturbing actually. He talked about how tattoos were sacred and how ancient tribes felt like their tattoos were a physical representation of their lives and souls and then he went on to describe how he would cut the tattoos off of those kids, sauté them in his skillet and then eat them, thinking he was consuming their souls. He said he was becoming stronger and stronger with each one that he ate and he thought that if he ate enough tattoos, he would become immortal!" Sheriff Kerry covered his mouth while his stomach

161

wrenched as he imagined the boy actually eating the flesh of other college students.

"He said that the eyes were a window to the soul and since he had consumed their souls, his victims no longer needed their eyes. That's how he got the 'Soul Reaper' name. We never found the tattoos so we had to assume that he actually did eat them."

"I hope you fried that sick bastard!" Sheriff Kerry spouted.

"Never got the chance!" Captain Parker responded angrily. "We found him hanging by a noose in a wooded area not far from the campus. He knew we were getting close so he just took the easy way out. We found a scrapbook of his work in his apartment. It was filled with newspaper clippings and photographs of those kids. He'd always take before and after pictures of his work. Oh, he was very proud of himself! He was very careful, very meticulous. He was more surgical than savage though – much different than the guy we're after now. We found a bunch of surgical instruments in Billy's apartment, too. We think he was trying to make it look like a surgeon was doing the cutting so we wouldn't think it was just some college kid. He was actually pretty smart because, for a while, that's just what everyone thought! Of the bodies we found, the cuts in the skin were perfect. But he started getting a little sloppy and we took advantage of that. Unfortunately, he killed seven other college kids before we figured him out." Sheriff Kerry sat silently for a moment before erupting furiously, "And you waited until this guy killed *four* people in my town before telling me that?"

Through his years of training, Captain Parker had learned that by talking in a calm voice to an irate person, the emotion is sometimes transferred, bringing the other person's emotions to a more peaceful level. And so he responded calmly to the sheriff. "Sheriff, it's too coincidental for this same thing to happen a thousand miles from Cape Girardeau, Missouri, where I headed the last case and only two hours from where I live now. Someone is messing with me and I don't want to give that person the recognition or publicity that he's shooting for. I want to just find him as quickly as possible and put an end to all of this."

Sheriff Kerry was red in the face but seemed a bit calmer when responding to the captain. "I'm responsible for the safety of every man, woman, and child in this town, Captain! Do you realize that? I need to know everything there is to know about what's going on! You can't keep this kind of thing from me anymore. You can't keep *anything* from me anymore!" Captain Parker quietly agreed: "You're right, but I hope you can see my point. Also, if anyone in town finds out about this and learns that it's a copycat killer, they'll really be out for blood, thinking that it's my fault that this killer is here in their town!" Sheriff Kerry nodded in agreement as Captain Parker continued discussing all of the information that his men had found thus far.

As nighttime fell, the case squad wrapped up their investigation, packed up their gear and left the rest stop parking lot, heading back to Grand Rapids. Early the next morning in their labs, they would start studying all of the evidence they had collected throughout the day from both crime scenes. Captain Parker and Sheriff Kerry rode back into town together in the sheriff's car. Captain Parker thanked the sheriff for the ride back and reminded him once more to keep all of the details of the case "under his hat."

*****

By 7:30, Luke and Syndi were sitting comfortably in a dimly lit back corner of Jr's Hideout, a local steak house, where they enjoyed a chilled glass of wine and conversation while they waited on their meals to be served. Luke couldn't understand it, but somehow, just being with Syndi made it possible for him to lock up the ghastly visions of horror to which he had been exposed that week, lock them into a deeply hidden chamber of his mind. Just looking into Syndi's beautiful green eyes both excited him and gave him a warm, peaceful feeling throughout his entire being that he couldn't remember ever feeling before and didn't think he ever wanted to do without. Luke knew that she was a one-in-a-million catch and, as Syndi smiled, Luke wondered if he was the only one who was starting to have these strong feelings.

"Is she just enjoying the excitement of being on a date with the captain of the Grand Rapids Police Department, or is it something more?" he thought to himself. Syndi interrupted one of Luke's disparaging thoughts by saying, "Who would you most like to meet, living or dead?"

"That's a tough one," Luke replied. "I guess it would have to be Houdini."

Syndi giggled and said, "Houdini? How come?" Luke took a sip of his wine before answering.

"I always admired Houdini. He's the world's most famous magician and escape artist and he came up from nothing. In the books I've read about him, I get the sense that he was a very confident and strong-willed man, very admirable."

Syndi smiled and looked Luke deep in the eyes as she said, "He reminds me a lot of you."

Luke was flattered and smiled back as he lifted his wine glass and said with a smile, "I'll drink to that!" Syndi tapped his glass with hers and they both finished their last bit of wine before Luke picked up the bottle from the table and refilled their glasses.

Luke and Syndi continued asking each other fun and flirty questions throughout their meal from "If you could only have one wish, what would it be?" to "What would you do for a million dollars?" They sat at their booth and chatted about nothing until their bottle was empty and their dinners were consumed. "What now?" Luke asked, hoping Syndi wouldn't be quite ready to end their date.

"How about we go to Four Corners, where we had pizza last night, and get a little ice cream?" she said, eagerly.

"It's not too cold for ice cream?" Luke asked.

Syndi grinned and said, "It's never too cold for chocolaty, cherry, gooey ice cream!" Luke laughed heartily and the two left the restaurant to continue their date. After their ice cream, while Luke was driving Syndi home, she reached over and took his hand in hers. "That was a great dinner and *awesome* ice cream! Thank you for taking me out."

Luke turned to Syndi and responded, "Well thank *you* for going out with me; I hope we can do it again sometime soon." Syndi smiled and felt a warmth fall over her body as she squeezed Luke's hand and smiled.

When they arrived at Syndi's house, Luke got out and walked around to open Syndi's door for her. "My, what a gentleman!" she said as he took her hand and helped her out of the car.

"My mother didn't bring up any uncouth boys." Luke said slyly. Luke held Syndi's hand as he walked her to her front door.

"I'll see you soon then?" Syndi asked hopefully.

"You can count on it!" Luke quickly responded. He took Syndi's other hand, pulled her in close, and tenderly kissed her before he reached around her thin waist and pulled her body tight up against him. Luke felt Syndi trembling slightly and he squeezed her tighter as they kissed goodnight.

*****

Earlier that night, after the sheriff dropped the captain off at his motel room, Sheriff Kerry had driven straight back to his office and, as he pulled into the parking lot, was greeted by an anxious Jim Richardson. Jim had been waiting for hours just to get a brief quote about the most recent murders from the sheriff, Captain Parker, or even one of the deputies. Unfortunately, up to this point, no one had anything to say. As Sheriff Kerry exited his car, Jim walked toward him, a pad of yellow notebook paper and a pencil in hand. "Sheriff, what's the latest on the killer? What has the Grand Rapids team found out? Sheriff, you've got to let us all know what's going on!" His brazen voice rose at the end, sounding more scared now than annoyed.

Sheriff Kerry walked directly toward Jim, grabbed him by the back of the neck and pulled his head in close. Stunned, Jim's body tensed as Sheriff Kerry spoke through gritted teeth, "Jimmy, I'm about to make your day! Come with me." Jim, for once, was speechless and followed Sheriff Kerry up the stairs and into the building.

As morning broke, the village was aghast as they read the headline on the front page of the *Walkerville Ledger*: "Revenge of the Soul Reaper – Copycat killer claims fourth victim in Walkerville – Story by Jim Richardson."

Chapter 9

Captain Parker packed up his overnight bag, left his motel room, dropped the key off at the front office, and began the drive through town on his way to the morning meeting at the sheriff's office.

After the meeting, he would be going back to Grand Rapids to join his team and begin working exclusively on the Walkerville murder cases from his office.

As he drove through town, he noticed stares from everyone on the streets. This was nothing new, he had been getting stares ever since he stepped foot in Walkerville, but it seemed like he was noticing them even more today. As he neared the sheriff's office, he was questioning whether he was just suddenly more aware of it, or if there were actually more people staring at him today for some reason. To his sudden disbelief, he saw nine large towers, each about twenty-five feet high and each connected to the roofs of their own news van. As his eyes surveyed the surroundings, he saw teams of local and national reporters, from both radio and television outlets. They were congregated around the faded sign stating the village's name and population and several of them were interviewing some of the village's inhabitants.

"This is Maria Claver, reporting from Walkerville, Michigan, where four people have been killed in what is now being called 'The Revenge of the Soul Reaper!' The actions of a serial killer in this small village have brought terror to this community."

As Captain Parker parked his car and strode towards the sheriff's office, he heard another reporter say,

"... the fourth victim was found naked and hanging by her hair in the surrounding forest. Officials have declined to make a statement as of yet."

Captain Parker ran inside the sheriff's building, threw open the door to the sheriff's office and eyed the sheriff sitting on the front edge of his desk, talking to his deputies. Captain Parker ran toward him and threw a hard right cross that landed solidly on the sheriff's chin, knocking him backward over his desk. Enraged, Captain Parker started heading around the desk before the three deputies grabbed him, all at once, pinning him up against the nearby wall. Sheriff Kerry picked himself up off of the floor and dizzily searched for his hat, not yet comprehending what had just happened, as Captain Parker struggled to free himself from the three deputies' grasps.

"What in the holy hell was that?" Sheriff Kerry screamed as he turned and faced the captain.

"I told you that in *confidence*, Sheriff!" Captain Parker snarled, still trying to break free.

"I didn't say shit to *anybody*!" Sheriff Kerry contended. "We were all just as surprised by that article and all the reporters this morning as you were!"

Captain Parker yelled back: "So, you expect me to believe that all these reporters are here the very next morning after I told you what happened in Missouri and you didn't have a thing to do with it?"

"You know what, captain?" Sheriff Kerry screamed pointedly as he rubbed his chin, "I don't give a good goddamn *what* you believe! I didn't say shit to *anybody* about what you told me! Maybe someone looked into your history! Maybe someone did some research into what you've been up to in the past! Did you ever think of that?"

Captain Parker, now diminishing his struggle, responded short of breath, "If I find out you had anything to do with the leak of this information, or if you do *anything* to get in the way of this investigation, I'll have your badge. Do you understand me, Sheriff?"

"Show the Captain out!" Sheriff Kerry said harshly as he stared across the room at the captain. The three deputies held onto the captain and cordially walked him out of the sheriff's office and out of the building.

*****

Captain Parker was halfway back to Grand Rapids when he heard his phone ring. It was Syndi and she was calling to see if he had any plans that evening. "Well, I'm actually on my way back to Grand Rapids, remember? I'm going home for a few days."

"I know." Syndi responded, "I was just sitting here, thinking to myself; 'ya know, Syndi, it's been *years* since you've been to the big city. Maybe tonight would be a good time to go down to Grand Rapids!' What do you think?" she asked hopefully.

A somewhat nervous little laugh escaped Captain Parker's mouth before he smiled widely and responded, "Well yeah, that would be *great!*" He gave Syndi his address and briefly explained to her how to get to his condo once she got into town.

"What time do you want me there?" she asked, sounding even more excited than before.

"How about 7:00? And I don't want you to worry about having to drive all the way back to Walkerville after dinner. You're more than welcome to stay at my place and I *promise* to be a perfect gentleman and sleep out on the couch!"

Syndi let out a nervous but excited laugh. "That sounds pretty good to me! OK then, I'll see you in Grand Rapids around 7:00 tonight then!"

"I'm looking forward to it," Captain Parker said eagerly.

"Me too! Bye for now!" Syndi said as they ended their conversation.

As his day went on, Captain Parker conversed with the separate departments that made up the team that had joined him in Walkerville to collect evidence on the various recent murders. Still, nothing was found to give them

170

any leads or direction as to which way to move from here. Surprisingly, there were no fingerprints or fibers on any of the bodies and besides the glue residue from the duct tape, no foreign matter was found on the bodies, either. They had found no footprints or distinguishable tire prints in the areas where the victims were found and had no calls from anyone stating that they saw or knew anything. It seemed like whomever was responsible was very clever. Having gone straight to the Grand Rapids Police Station from Walkerville, Captain Parker took off a little early and headed home, anticipating his hard-earned time off and his evening with Syndi.

Entering his darkened home, Captain Parker took off his clothes and went straight into the bathroom for a nice, warm shower. He reflected back on the past few days, putting everything that had happened into perspective. His mind began to relax as the water sprayed over him, seeming to wash the malevolence he had been dealing with right off of him and disappearing down the drain. After his shower, he fixed his hair and splashed on some "White Crystal" cologne before getting dressed in a pair of his nicest black slacks, a crisp, dark blue Eton shirt and a blue and silver Stefano Ricci tie.

At 7:15, Captain Parker heard a light knocking at his door. Opening it just a crack, he was surprised to see Syndi standing in the hallway, holding a UPS envelope in one hand and an overnight bag in the other. As he opened the door wide, she looked even more stunning than he had ever seen her before. In his eyes, she seemed to actually glow. Her hair curled down over her black satin shirt and she wore white, skin-tight slacks and shiny black thigh-high boots.

"Special delivery!" she said in a bouncy voice as she grinned mischievously.

Luke smiled widely. "I'm so glad you made it!" he said as she stepped inside and gave him a much-anticipated kiss on his lips. "It's so good to see you!" he said quietly as she stepped back and offered him the envelope. "What's that?" he asked.

171

"Well I ran into the UPS guy in the street," said Syndi. "He was actually here to deliver this envelope to you. I told him that I would sign for it and give it to you myself since I was coming to see you. He said it was against policy so I just flirted with him a little and won." Syndi laughed as she handed the envelope to the captain. He grabbed her, held her tightly and kissed her once more before taking the envelope and laying it on a nearby coffee table.

"Aren't you going to open it?" Syndi asked.

"No," Luke said, "it's pictures from the cases, you don't need to see that kind of stuff." Syndi smiled at his chivalrous act. Luke, beaming as he realized that this goddess had driven two hours just to see him, said, "Are you hungry?"

"Starving!"

"Good!" he responded. "I'm gonna take you to my favorite restaurant here in Grand Rapids."

"No you're not!" Syndi said sharply.

"What? Why not?" Luke asked confused.

"Because you took me out in Walkerville. It's *my* turn to take *you* out!"

"Oh, you don't have ..." and Syndi cut him off mid-sentence.

"I'm taking you out and that's that!" Luke smiled in agreement.

"Here, let me get your bag," Luke said. Syndi handed him her black overnight bag and he took it into the bedroom and laid it on a chair next to the bed.

"You've got a *beautiful* place!" He heard Syndi say from the living room.

"Oh, thank you," he said as he walked back out of the bedroom. Syndi was impressed with Luke's lavish furniture, his large plasma television and surround sound system and all of his unique art.

"Are those African?" Syndi asked about two large wooden masks that hung on the wall.

"No, those are actually from a region near Malaysia," Luke answered. "They were a gift. They're supposed to give you good financial luck!" From the look of his house, Syndi thought there might be something to that.

Luke took the UPS envelope off of the coffee table and stuck it between two large books on a bookshelf that was built into one of the walls next to the front door.

"Shall we?" Luke asked as he opened the door.

"Absolutely!" Syndi answered. "Where are we going?"

They walked outside and Luke locked the door behind them, took Syndi's hand as they walked toward his car, and said; "I know a *great* Italian restaurant. Sound good?"

Syndi excitedly said, "I love Italian food! Nice choice!" Luke grinned as he escorted her into the car.

After dinner, they decided to go out for dessert, which somehow turned into drinks at a nearby bar and grill. Luke asked the waitress if they could sit in the upstairs section of the restaurant by themselves so they could talk in private. He knew that the upstairs was only used when the downstairs was full and because the restaurant was relatively empty, the top section wasn't in use.

Syndi told Luke that he needed to try some of her favorite drinks and since she was picking up the tab, he had to drink whatever she said. Being a bartender, she had a plethora of exotic drinks in mind.

As the night wore on, the drinks flowed and the tensions between Luke and Syndi both dissipated and solidified. Luke found his arm on the back of her chair and he suddenly realized that he had been running his fingers lightly through her hair while he talked to her, almost not even noticing what he was doing. Syndi did notice, though, and it was giving her chills throughout her entire body.

"I really want to thank you for taking me out tonight," he said quietly. "I'm not used to anyone taking *me* out ... is there anything I can do to thank you?"

"Oh no," she said shyly, nervously looking down at her empty glass, "you don't have to do anything."

"But I want to," he said as his fingers gripped the back of her hair and pulled her toward him. They met in a warm, lustful kiss, the kind that only comes from previous self-restraint, from two people controlling their passions until the mere thought of holding back any longer is futile. Syndi grabbed Luke just below his ears and eagerly continued their kiss. Their tongues madly rubbed against each other as faint groans escaped from between their breaths. Syndi pushed herself out of her chair and straddled Luke, almost knocking him over backwards as she lunged toward him, throwing her body onto his, their lips never separating.

As she pressed herself against him, Luke pulled her in tight and, without hesitation, brought his hands to her firm buttocks and pulled her in even closer. He kissed her on her cheek and then on her earlobe. Syndi moaned softly into Luke's ear as he began kissing her neck and then back to her wanting lips.

They could both feel the sexual energy coursing through each other's bodies as the lights overhead flashed on and off, which was their embarrassed waitress' way of telling them that they had been caught.

"I guess we better get out of here, huh?" Luke said breathlessly as he looked into Syndi's hungry, wanting green eyes.

"Whatever you say," she said before pressing forward and kissing him again. They stood up and headed for the door in anticipation of their night of passion.

*****

Before Luke's front door was even locked behind them, she had already removed his belt. The slaps of the leather through the belt loops sounded like machine-gun fire and was followed quickly by the snap of the button on Syndi's white, skin-tight pants. Their passionate kisses continued uninterrupted as they negotiated themselves through the living room and into the bedroom. As they undressed each other, they grew feverish as their warm skin came in contact. Luke pulled Syndi close while unstrapping her bra. Her large, beautiful breasts were perfect, he thought, as he grabbed her arms and pushed her up against the bedroom wall, holding her there, as he traced her throat with moist, passionate kisses.

Standing together, Syndi wearing only a white satin thong and Luke in his boxers, he guided her to the bed and lay on top of her. He continued kissing and licking Syndi's neck and ears as her legs wrapped around and pulled him in tight. His obvious physical arousal pressed hard between Syndi's legs and she let out an uncontrolled moan. Luke slowly moved down her neck, kissing and licking every inch until he was between her breasts. He tasted the sweat that had collected there as he squeezed and pinched her breasts and nipples while her fingers ran through his hair. His fingernails scratched Syndi's stomach as he moved them downward to remove her moist panties, followed quickly by his own boxers.

From deep inside, Syndi groaned as Luke knelt on the floor in front of her and rested his tongue against her vagina. Her uncontrollable passion caused her legs to squeeze Luke's head between them and as he pried them apart, he moved his tongue up and down the entire length of her womanhood, causing her to arch her back as she screamed with pleasure. For several minutes he orally pleasured her while she writhed, squirmed and screamed above him and, just when she couldn't take it for another second, Luke stood up, lifted her legs and entered her.

Syndi's eyes opened wide and her screams stopped instantly. She momentarily held her breath before releasing a long and loud moan. Syndi looked up to see Luke's muscular physique holding her legs, just above her knees, and thrusting back and forth. She felt him rhythmically and wonderfully sliding in and out of her.

"Oh God ... Oh God, don't stop," she pleaded as she looked deep into his eyes. Luke continued thrusting slowly inside of her while his face showed pleasures he had not imagined in years. Feeling he might lose control, he pulled out of her and turned her over on the bed. At the bottom of her back, just below her waistline, he saw a small tattoo of a yellow sun with bluish-white clouds behind it. Luke bent down and licked her tattoo before kissing her buttocks and back. Syndi turned over, took Luke by the hand, and lay him down on the bed.

"It's *your* turn!" she said with a sexy grin as she knelt down on the bed between his legs and began her descent.

*****

"Mornin' sleepy head." Luke opened his eyes to see Syndi's bright, beautiful face illuminated by the early morning sun that was gleaming through the open curtains in his bedroom. She leaned in and kissed him tenderly on his lips. He smiled. "Sleep well?" she asked.

"Better than ever," Luke replied as he pulled Syndi in to lie on his shoulder. He started to scratch her back as she nudged in closer while tightly hugging him.

"That was some night, huh?" she asked with a grin.

"Sure was! In fact, that was incredible!" Luke responded exuberantly.

Syndi giggled and said "So, are you going to just forget that I ever existed when I go back to Walkerville?"

"Of course not, Amber. Um, I mean, Kelly. Wait, what was your name again?" Syndi laughed and slapped Luke playfully on his stomach. He laughed and said, "Honestly, I was kind of hoping we could see a little more of each other."

Beaming, Syndi said, "Okay, I'd like that." She kissed him passionately and ran her hand under the sheets and down his body, ready to make love again.

*****

Later in the morning, Luke headed to the Grand Rapids Police Department to start his day, and Syndi headed back home to Walkerville, which had slowly become what could only be described as a circus. Everyone was already scared, mad and suspicious of each other, which only fueled the growing fire of confusion. But now, with all of the news crews in their little village, the feeling of terror had gripped them tight. There was no going back. No longer would people leave their cars or homes unlocked, whether they were inside or not. Children that once played in the streets and parks were now home, inside, safe.

June, one of the waitresses at the Four Corners restaurant, had started wearing high boots to cover the cherub tattoo on her left ankle and Mark, one of the warehouse workers at the Ace Lumber yard, had taken to buttoning the sleeves of his shirts to avoid exposing the tiger that was tattooed on his right forearm. Everyone in Walkerville who had visible tattoos began covering them up with their clothes or with strategically placed accessories because everyone had the same fear that they would be the next person to be kidnapped and brutally murdered in Walkerville.

Unlike living in a big city and wondering if a killer could be nearby, living in this tiny village and surrounded by nothing but miles and miles of dense forest, the reality of *knowing* that not only a killer, but a *serial killer* was close, gave everyone a very real reason for living in terror. The terror drove some people out of their homes and out of Walkerville forever and those who stayed no longer stopped to chat on the street but now avoided conversation and even kept their distance from one another.

All of the local businesses felt it, too. Most everyone was staying home after dark. Only a few people went to Seth's Place at night, and those who did only talked about what they would do to the killer if they ever got their hands on him. The stout, greasy, ponytailed Oswald Rodriguez, owner and operator of Ozzys' Tattoo's, was hit the hardest financially. No one came in to get tattoos anymore, and with good reason. But there he sat, day after day in his shop, wondering what he would do to pay his bills and what he would do after the lease on his shop expired. Some of his friends would come in from time to time, but only to hang out and listen to music, smoke pot and drink beer.

It was just about closing time. Ozzy and Veronica, his new girlfriend who was, not surprisingly, a tattooed biker-type herself, sat alone in his shop, watching television and wishing he had gotten just one customer before he closed up for the night. As 11:00 rolled around, with a sigh, Ozzy locked the front door and turned off the lights before he and Veronica left through the back door of the shop where their motorcycles sat next to each other and facing opposite directions. The only other vehicle in sight was an old rusty Blazer that was parked behind the café next door. Ozzy quickly locked the back door and just as he turned around, Veronica pushed him up against it and pushed her lips to his. She could feel him smiling as he kissed her back, grabbed her around the waist and pulled her closer. The two embraced for a moment before Veronica withdrew slowly and asked flirtingly, "I'll see you tomorrow then?"

"You better believe it!" he said as she walked over to her motorcycle, climbed on top and started the engine. Veronica smiled at him before covering her head with her helmet and driving off around the right side of the building. Ozzy reached into his jacket pocket, pulled out a cigarette and lit it before climbing on his motorcycle and starting up the engine. His bike was facing toward the left side of the building where, just around the corner, a large gray dumpster sat against the wall. Ozzy put his bike into gear and headed toward the side of the building to start his ten-minute ride home. Just as he turned the

178

corner of the building, the headlight of his motorcycle illuminated the figure of a large man, dressed in blue scrubs, a white apron, cap and mask, who jumped out from the far side of the dumpster and was holding a wooden bat in his blue, rubber-gloved hands.

Before he could even hit the brakes, the motorcycle had rolled directly into the path of the bat that landed with a crack in the center of Ozzy's face. The force of the strike knocked him backward and he fell hard upon the pavement. The bike wobbled for a few feet before turning and crashing into the brick wall of the tattoo shop, its engine sputtering for a moment before dying. The surgeon watched in amazement as Ozzy, quite wobbly stood up and looked cross-eyed at this very large man holding a bloody bat. The surgeon gripped the bat tightly with both hands and brought it up to his shoulder for another swing. He watched the blood begin to pour out of Ozzy's nose and run down his mouth and chest for a brief moment before Ozzy fell sideways, bouncing off of the dumpster and landing face-first back on the pavement.

The surgeon quickly walked over to Ozzy and, using the tip of the wooden bat, nudged him a few times in his side. There was no response. The surgeon knelt down and rolled Ozzy over onto his back and lifted him by his armpits. The surgeon's bat was still in his right hand as he began to drag Ozzy to the lot next door, toward his trusty Blazer.

After stuffing Ozzy inside the back of the Blazer, the surgeon ran over to retrieve the downed motorcycle, walked it around to the back of the tattoo shop and leaned it gently against the back door before returning to his Blazer and driving safely out of the neighborhood.

*****

The beautiful violins that could be heard off in the distance sounded familiar while they played but then they were gone, just as mysteriously as they had begun. Sometime later, the vision of a large white bird flying low over a lake, the sun shining off of his wings and the water beneath, came from and

179

went back into the darkness. The slow, soft timbre of the piano music seemed to soar up a grassy hillside and back down the other side over and over and over until the sudden sound of his own scream shattered the peaceful visions his mind had so generously created for him while he was unconscious.

At once, Ozzy experienced the worst pain he had ever felt in his life. It was as if all of the pain he could ever remember feeling condensed into the center of his face and spread outward through his head and into his entire body. Although it hurt even more when he screamed, he couldn't control himself and his screams continued.

He was naked and strapped down on top of the same metal table that was the last bed for too many of the unfortunate souls of Walkerville, but unlike the rest, his right forearm, not his wrist, was secured tightly to the table by a thin leather strap.

The surgeon stood next to Ozzy and watched as he screamed, not knowing what was going on and unable to see through his swollen purple eyes. The surgeon studied Ozzy's body; he tugged on a silver ring that went through Ozzy's right nipple before looking over all of the tattoos. He had an intricate, one-inch design across his forehead and his neck. His chest and right arm were completely covered with a multitude of tattoos –almost no clean skin remained unpainted and, with all of the screaming, the surgeon simply whispered but one word: "Jackpot."

The sudden burst of adrenaline that had temporarily charged Ozzy's body was starting to wane and his screams became quieter and shorter, although the pain seemed to be growing stronger and stronger. He thought he heard a voice asking him a question, but the unimaginable pain and his screams, now turning into moans, were somehow overpowering his sense of hearing or even thinking. Ozzy started feeling a poking on his body and began concentrating to try and determine where he was being poked.

180

"This one!" He suddenly heard a deep voice yelling over his moans as he abruptly became aware of the prodding on the top of his right arm. "What is *this* one? The one that goes around your arm!"

Ozzy couldn't see through his puffy, swollen eyes, an unfortunate side effect of his broken nose, but he was starting to become aware of a man's voice yelling over very loud classical piano music. His senses were starting to come back, little by little, which would only add to his confusion.

He slowly realized what he was being asked: "What was the tattoo going around his right upper arm?" Not knowing who was asking, where he was or what was going on, he cried out, praying that his answer would somehow offer him some relief from the pain. "It's a tribal design!"

"Tribal huh?" came the sarcastic response. "Well, what tribe are you a part of?"

Ozzy couldn't understand the question or even comprehend that he was being made the butt of a joke. He was suddenly concentrating, instead, on the thick mucus in the back of his throat that tasted like blood. He choked, coughing up the blood that had run down from his exploded sinus cavity and into his throat. He spat hard and a large, warm glob of fresh red blood exited his lips and landed on his neck.

"What's going on here?" he asked as he tried, in vain, to sit up, finally realizing that he was tied down tightly and unable to move an inch, which further added to his increasing confusion.

"Your chest is *covered* with tattoos!" he heard the angry man say above the classical music. "You must be in the Yakuza! Am I right? Are you in the Yakuza?"

Ozzy couldn't even begin to understand the question. As he fought to try and open his eyes, he heard the man say,

"I *said*, are you in the Yakuza? I don't think I've ever heard of a white, longhaired, dirt bag, piece-of-shit being in the Yakuza. Have they changed their entry qualifications and nobody told me?"

"What are you talking about?" Ozzy asked, fearing the response.

"The Yakuza, you know, the Japanese mafia!" Ozzy lay still on the table, moaning in pain, feeling his naked body shivering while he listened as the surgeon turned the piano music down to just a whisper, revealing the sound of water running through pipes nearby.

"Their origins date back to the seventeenth century! They were an outlaw group, but an outlaw group with *honor*," The surgeon said glibly. "To be a part of the Yakuza was to give of one's self completely. In fact, selling your soul to the devil would be the only logical comparison as there was no going back." The surgeon headed across the room to retrieve the cart of pristine surgical instruments hiding beneath a blue sterile towel.

"You may ask yourself why I thought you were in the Yakuza. Well, I'll tell you. The members of the Yakuza often adorned their bodies with tattoos, usually their *entire* bodies from their necks to their knees both front and back. *You* have tattoos covering your back too, don't you?"

Ozzy could hear the delight in the surgeon's voice as he asked the question, but he was in too much pain and too terrified to respond. He just lay shivering and listening, unable to see where he was, what was holding him down or what was happening around him.

"The Yakuza treat the body as a canvas," the surgeon continued. "I, myself, know it's disgusting to desecrate your body like that, but I can respect their customs and traditions because the Yakuza was, and still is, the *elite* of their culture. Much like my family is part of the elite group of *our* culture!"

Ozzy could hear the surgeon's voice become muffled as he tied the surgical mask around his head.

"The Yakuza are strong. They're strong as a group and as individuals. Now I don't mean just physical strength. No, they are the elite in *mental* strength as well! For instance, if a member of a Yakuza gang does something that offends his boss, even if it was unintentional, he must pay a penance! He will cut off the tip of his left pinkie finger and show no pain on his face as he hands the severed piece of the finger to his boss."

Ozzy flinched as he felt a rubber-gloved hand slide slowly from his right thigh, up his body, to his right nipple. As the small silver ring was clinched tightly and ripped out, Ozzy's mouth shot open and he screamed out in pain as blood squirted from the center of his nipple that was now torn in half.

The surgeon turned to his right and removed the blue towel from the line of surgical instruments, the dish of sanitizing liquid, the old, rusty pocketknife and a stainless steel meat cleaver. Ozzy's screams continued as the surgeon picked up a thick pair of double-hinged snipers in his right hand and grabbed Ozzy's pinkie with his left.

"Could *you* show no pain? No, because you're really just a weak-willed piece of shit! You're only *physically* strong but your mind is *weak*!"

"No, no *no*!" Ozzy screamed as he felt the surgeon tug on his pinkie, rest the blades of the cold sniper around the knuckle above his fingernail and, without hesitation, squeeze tightly, cutting through the skin, muscle, nerves and bone of his finger. The surgeon smiled beneath his mask as he felt the crunch of the bone and watched as the one-inch piece of the digit separated from the rest of the hand and dropped onto the cold, metal table. Blood shot out in a small unending stream from the nub of Ozzy's finger and down into the puddle on the floor.

As Ozzy screamed, he was aware of the maniacal laughter escaping from behind the surgeon's blue mask as he reached above the sink and turned up the volume on the stereo to blast the sound of a Johan Sebastian Bach piece.

Ozzy would have been writhing in pain were it not for the ropes and straps holding him tightly against the autopsy table.

"It's only through pain that we are truly awake!" the surgeon yelled over the music. "It's time for *your* wake-up call, Mr. Tattoo Artist! Don't fear it! Pain is just weakness leaving the body!"

The surgeon lay the snipers down in the pan of sanitizing fluid and picked up the large cleaver from the cart. He lined the blade up with Ozzy's right arm, two inches above the wrist and two inches below the leather strap that was tied around his forearm securing it to the table. The surgeon slowly lifted and dropped the blade twice, to make sure he was directly on target. After the third lift, Ozzy heard him yell loudly as he slammed the blade down fast and hard, completely cutting through Ozzy's forearm with one strike.

Ozzy screamed loud and hard with each breath. As blood began to spray out of his forearm and onto the table, his own leg and into the puddle below, the surgeon kept his eyes on the severed hand with the now-missing tip of the pinkie finger. He gently lay the bloody cleaver into the dish of sanitizing liquid before picking up the hand by the wrist and examining it closely under the bright surgical light above.

He began to giggle as he waved the hand at Ozzy, flopping it back and forth as if it were a new toy. Ozzy's body had now taken just about all of the abuse it was capable of handling. Both the stream of blood from his wrist and his screams began to diminish, as did his awareness. He had used up his entire store of energy and was now unable to even close his mouth. The surgeon looked down at Ozzy, his long greasy hair, his swollen, purple eyes, his torn nipple and missing hand, and at all of the blood that covered him and encircled him. The surgeon giggled yet again as he held the severed hand by the wrist and began smacking Ozzy's face with it, all the while saying sarcastically, "Stop hitting yourself! Stop hitting yourself!"

Blood from the severed hand splashed out and into Ozzy's mouth, and the strong, bitter taste of his own warm blood on his tongue faded away along with the pain in his body, the fear in his mind and the music in his ears.

Seeing that his playmate had slipped away, the surgeon turned the volume down on the stereo and dropped the hand into the tub of soapy water before turning his attention back to Ozzy and to the work he knew he had to do. He began by picking up the tip of Ozzy's pinkie finger and throwing it into the trash can before unbuckling the straps that held his neck and waist. Turning his attention to the strap that held Ozzy's right arm down to the table, the surgeon pulled it tight to unlatch it, freeing the arm and hanging it over the edge of the table. As the pressure was released from the forearm, the blood that had welled up above the strap now oozed out of the open limb and poured onto the puddle of running water on the floor.

Without diverting his gaze from this faucet of blood, the surgeon began untying the thin nylon ropes that bound Ozzy's feet and left hand to the table.

"Now," he said aloud, "let's begin." The surgeon picked up one of the scalpels from the instrument tray and shoved it into Ozzy's right arm, just below the shoulder and above the tribal tattoo. He began cutting deeply into the skin until he had made a complete circle around the entire upper arm. He picked the hose up from the floor and squirted the blood off of the arm so he could examine his work more closely. When he was satisfied, he inserted the scalpel into Ozzy's armpit and dragged it carefully down the inside of the arm until he reached the wrist, where the hand had been removed.

"That should do it," the surgeon thought to himself before laying the blood-coated scalpel into the dish of sanitizer.

Because there was so much skin to remove, and so little time in which to do it, the surgeon knew that he must work quickly to complete it in one night. With his brow furrowed, he reached under Ozzy's armpit and grabbed each side of the slit. Digging his fingers in deep, he began pulling the skin apart and away

185

from the muscles and tendons below. He readjusted his grip over and over as the blood made his fingers slippery. The surgeon hastily pulled and tugged at the meat below the skin, working the fingers of each hand in and towards each other. He worked feverishly down the arm toward the forearm until, at last, he had the skin of the entire arm removed from the body and in his hands.

It wasn't pretty, he thought, and there was quite a bit of extra meat and tissue attached to the underbelly of the skin that would have to be removed, but at least he was done with the first part. As he held the long piece of skin in his hands, the surgeon looked down at Ozzy's right arm, which was now a bloody compilation of torn muscles, veins, tendons, and arteries atop of sections of bone that peeked out, here and there, below it all.

He momentarily held the skin up to the light to examine it. In between the splotches of fresh blood that ran down the skin and dripped onto the puddle below, the surgeon studied the tattoos of a green star, a spider within its webbing, several flames, and the head of a tiger with its mouth open wide. He carefully dropped the skin into the right tub of the sink filled with soapy water and the severed hand, and turned back toward Ozzy, knowing that there was still much work left to be done.

"This next part is going to be quite laborious," the surgeon thought to himself. Picking up a fresh scalpel from the cart, he went straight to work, starting with a slice down the right side of Ozzy's chest, across the stomach and up the left side of the chest. The surgeon cut as deep as the scalpel would reach as he made long, straight slices in the meat before finishing the cut across, low on the throat, and meeting back where he had started on the right side of the chest.

He was a little disappointed at the lack of blood exiting the body, especially as he cut through the throat and carotid arteries. Ozzy had already given so much blood through his wrist and his arm and his heart was no longer beating, so no blood was pumping through his body, all contributing to the lack of blood escaping through his wide-open throat.

The surgeon dropped his used scalpel into the dish of sanitizing liquid and turned back toward Ozzy. He put a bloody finger to his mask as he scanned the naked body from head to toe. As an oboe from one of Schubert's sad tales from the past played through the speakers, thin streams of blood ran out from various spots of the slices on the chest and dripped slowly onto the metal table beneath the marred body of Oswald Rodriguez. The surgeon removed his finger from his mask, leaving a bloody impression of the digit, and inserted the fingers of both hands into the gash in Ozzy's throat. Once inside, he grasped the skin tightly but pulled gingerly to see how difficult it would be to simply pull the large piece of skin off of the muscles and fatty tissue beneath.

He began pulling at the skin and could feel it tightly gripping the muscle above the collarbones. As he worked his fingers in between the skin and the muscle, he was surprised at how resilient and tough the skin actually was as he carefully pulled it, separating it from its foundation. He likened it to the feeling of separating an orange from its peel. "This just might work!" he said aloud, sounding a bit surprised. The surgeon reached into the cold dish of sanitizing liquid and pulled out the meat cleaver that he had used earlier to sever Ozzy's hand from his arm. He gripped the loose skin around the upper chest and pulled it down, inserting the cleaver below to pull the chest skin away. At the same time, he carefully used the blade of the cleaver to lacerate the connective tissue bonding the skin to the chest muscles below, hacking at the underside of the skin with small, precise strikes. The melody of Schubert's "Serenade" carried on as the surgeon persevered, working cautiously to pull the skin off Ozzy's chest and away from the muscle above the twelve pairs of ribs below and finally above the abdominal muscles on his stomach. The surgeon smiled as he neared the bottom-right corner of Ozzy's stomach in anticipation of finally removing one large piece of skin covering the entire torso of this very unfortunate man atop the surgeon's autopsy table.

"Yes!" the surgeon exclaimed upon his final slice of the cleaver to the underside of the skin. He hastily dropped the cleaver back into the sanitizing dish and picked up the large piece of skin from Ozzy's chest and held it, outstretched, under the surgical lamp. "Amazing! Simply amazing!" he yelled beneath his mask. Blood dripped off of the skin and onto the muscles of Ozzy's exposed chest as the surgeon looked in awe at his latest prize. His eyes wandered from tattoo to tattoo, finally taking it all in for the first time. The surgeon saw how beautiful the artwork actually was, now that it had been removed from its host and was no longer desecrating one of God's masterpieces. He noticed the intricate details and shading that went into the designs of the various spider webs, tribal designs, a cross and a skull, amongst many others. After admiring the skin, he dropped it into the sink, joining it with the skin that once wrapped Ozzy's right arm and his right hand.

For the next fifteen minutes, the surgeon worked carefully to remove the tribal design from Ozzy's forehead, exposing his skull beneath. When he was done, he flipped the body over and began slicing at the skin covering the entire back, using the same technique that he used to remove the chest skin. No shortcuts were taken and the surgeon was extremely careful to not pierce the skin or cut it too thin in any one place.

After removing the single piece of skin from Ozzy's back and adding it to the skins already submerged in the sink, the surgeon began his ritual of rinsing the body with water from the hose before dousing it with bleach, both front and back and from head to toe. He drained the floor of the running water and finally pushed Ozzy's body off of the table and onto the tarp and brown blanket on the floor before turning off the music and dragging the body up the two steps, across the hall and into the garage.

*****

Deep within the Manistee National Forest rests Gilbert Lake, a large and calm body of water surrounded by miles and miles of nothing but towering birch, maple and pine trees. In the summer, the lake is full of locals and out-of-towners camping, swimming, boating, water skiing, and fishing. However, in the darkness of the night and in the freezing winds of October, Gilbert Lake was now anything but entertaining.

From out of the darkness the surgeon's Blazer roared down a long dirt road, spitting up dead leaves behind it and stopping precisely in a desolate area just at the edge of the Lake. He was deep into the forest where no one had been since the weather cooled off, well over a month ago. The moon reflected in the cold, black water of Gilbert Lake.

As he turned to park parallel to the water, the headlights of the Blazer reflected off of something large and yellow in the distance and partially hidden behind a few rows of trees. The surgeon left the headlights on and exited his vehicle. He was wearing his blue scrubs and new, clean gloves, hat, apron and mask.

He opened the tailgate door, where a black garbage bag containing his used and bloody garb sat limply atop the brown blanket cocoon that enveloped the maimed and marred body of Ozwald Rodriguez. Gripping the blanket with one hand, the surgeon removed Ozzy's body from the Blazer. It pounded the frozen ground before being dragged to the front of the vehicle. Illuminated by the headlights, the surgeon dragged the blanket off of the road, through a grassy patch and into the forest where he neared a large, yellow industrial wood chipper that sat just ten feet from the lake's embankment.

In the front end of the chipper was an eight-foot high feeder hopper that required wood to either be thrown up and into it, or dropped in from a conveyer belt above. In the rear of the machine was the exit chute that pointed toward the still, dark lake. The chipper sat upon two wheels in back and a steel beam in front, just below a long trailer hitch.

The surgeon dropped the end of the blanket and walked around the chipper, noticing the worn paint and all of the scratches and dents that usually accompanied an aging and well-used piece of equipment. He found the engine, pulled a small brass key from his pocket and inserted it into the keyhole, turning it clockwise until it clicked. He grasped the start handle and gave it a quick yank. The engine popped loudly as the surgeon released the handle and the rope shot quickly back into its chamber. The surgeon grasped the handle once again and pulled quickly. The engine again popped, then sputtered, then popped again. A large, thick puff of black smoke shot out of the hidden exhaust pipe below the chipper as the engine chugged to life and the smell of diesel fuel filled the cold air.

Grinning as he felt his heartbeat suddenly quicken, the surgeon explored the wood chipper again until he found the switch controlling the chipping blades. He thought to himself, "Is this brilliantly simple or simply brilliant?" With an easy flip of the switch, he could hear the teeth inside quickly rev up. He squeezed both of his fists tightly as he yelled out "Yes!"

About a hundred yards away, Mike, a young man of twenty-five, had stumbled through the forest, flashlight in hand, searching for some firewood to take back to the campsite that he and his girlfriend, Stephanie, had made. She was waiting impatiently by their dying fire and had made it clear that she was not happy being so cold. The unrecognizable sound of the wood chipper starting up in the distance amidst the silence of the forest caused Mike to turn and instinctively follow the sound to determine its source.

"What the hell is that?" he thought to himself as he lumbered over fallen limbs and through piles of sticks and foliage toward the sound of the wood chipper.

Because of the acoustics and the echoing nature of the trees in the forest, it seemed as if the sound was just a few feet ahead of him. He walked closer and closer toward the foreign sound and thoughtlessly walked farther and farther away from his camp and from Stephanie. As the sound of the wood chipper grew louder, the light from the Blazer's headlights became brighter and brighter, shining through the trees and illuminating everything around. As Mike got closer, he turned his flashlight off and was able to make out the shape of the noisy wood chipper and the silhouette of the large, brawny man who was standing over what looked like a pile of brown leaves. At last his curiosity was relieved.

The surgeon stood for a moment over Ozzy's body, which was entombed in the tarp and brown blanket. He reached down and grasped the blanket in his enormous arms and hoisted it up and over his shoulder. Holding the blanket securely on his shoulder with his right hand, he used his left hand to climb up onto the ledge of the chipper, next to the upright hoppers opening which was now even with the surgeon's forehead.

"Well," he said as he lifted the blanket off of his shoulder, "this is your stop." Only twenty yards away, Mike watched from behind a tree as the surgeon grunted and hoisted the blanket containing the bloody tarp and the body, and pushed it up and over the lip of the hopper. The light of the Blazer illuminated the blanket and Mike knew at an instant that what he was witnessing was not meant to be seen. Ozzy fell, head first, into the spinning, hungry teeth of the wood chipper and an unrecognizable haze of wet chum shot out of the exit chute, landing twenty feet away in the frigid water of Gilbert Lake.

Mike let out a brief yell that he quickly covered with his hand as he shot around to the backside of a nearby tree, hoping the man on the chipper hadn't seen him. The surgeon climbed down and looked out into the forest for a moment before heading back to the Blazer. He grabbed the trash bag out of the back and carried it over to the chipper before removing his gloves, mask, apron and hat and throwing it all into the trash bag. Mike began shaking as he peeked around the tree just in time to see the surgeon throwing the trash bag, which landed inside the hopper and was spat out the other side into the lake.

Frozen in fear, surrounded by thick, dark forest and only having a slight idea from which direction he came, Mike slowly began backing up, keeping his eyes on the surgeon who was obviously not aware of his presence. Mike was telling himself that everything was going to be all right if he could just get enough distance from this massive madman, get Stephanie, and go for help. As Mike crept backwards, the surgeon flipped a switch and the giant wood chipper quickly died down and became silent. The sounds of crickets, tree frogs, and the other melodious creatures of the night could be heard.

Mike's crackling steps, over the large brown twigs and leaves that had recently fallen, now echoed throughout the forest, signaling his approximate location. The surgeon turned just in time to see a distant figure falling backward. Mike had tripped on a long branch and was now on the ground, feeling nothing but his heartbeat racing. He sat up quickly to see the surgeon lumbering toward him. Mike screamed as he shot to his feet and began running away from the dimly lit forest toward total darkness.

He looked over his shoulder to see the surgeon illuminated by the Blazer's headlights, only about forty feet behind and barreling down on him. Mike turned on his flashlight and continued through the forest, jumping over downed trees, making his way through bushes, and running through shallow puddles of mud that had not yet frozen over. He thought his flashlight was his saving grace, but it was only a beacon for the surgeon, showing him in exactly which direction he should be running. Mike looked back again but couldn't see the surgeon in the dark forest behind him. He stopped and pressed up against a tree before turning off his flashlight.

Through deep breaths, Mike listened in complete darkness to all of the sounds around him while he looked frantically for any sign of his campfire. He heard a bird calling out and, as he looked up, he was able to see the pale moonlight on the very tops of the trees. He heard the echo of cracking wood coming from somewhere around him although he couldn't pinpoint the exact

192

location. His breath quivered as his eyes darted back and forth, trying desperately to see something – to see anything – in the darkness. Holding his breath, Mike turned his flashlight back on and pointed it down to the ground as he took three steps forward.

The light shined upon the immediate area around him, dimly illuminating the surgeon who was standing ten feet behind Mike with a large log that he held high above his head. He threw the log as hard as he could, which smashed Mike directly in the back of his head. The flashlight flew from Mike's hands as he crashed to the ground and rolled onto his back, tightly holding his bleeding head. The surgeon ran toward Mike as he attempted to get to his feet. The surgeon threw himself forward, tackling Mike to the ground and using his weight to hold him there. Mike feverishly clawed at the ground when he felt the surgeon's arm wrap securely around his neck and squeeze tightly.

*****

Mike was unconscious and didn't realize that the surgeon had quickly stripped him naked in search of at least one tattoo. He didn't realize that upon finding none, the surgeon had carried him back toward the Blazer where he had tied his feet and hands together with nylon rope and donned a new, clean set of surgical garb. All Mike realized as he began to slowly wake up in the silence of the forest was that he had an incredible pain in his head and under his chin.

As he regained consciousness, the first thing he noticed was the light coming from the Blazer and the eyes of the surgeon that were, strangely, just inches below him. From there, it didn't take long to realize that the surgeon was holding Mike's hair and his chin was resting on the edge of the hopper of the wood chipper. The chipper sat quietly; the still blades just inches below Mike's bare, bound feet.

"Ahh, you're awake!" the surgeon said spryly from beneath his mask. With most of the weight of his body resting on his chin, Mike was in too much pain and had too much pressure on his mouth to open it, even to scream. The surgeon let go of Mike's hair, releasing the rest of Mike's body weight upon the bottom of his mandible. Mike felt excruciating pain as his chin dug into the edge of the hopper. He could feel the nerves and bones on both sides of his chin absorbing all 175 pounds of his body and he tried to move slightly to alleviate some of the pain and still hold on to the edge for dear life. The surgeon smiled beneath his mask and winked at Mike before climbing down from the chipper and walking around to the other side where he gripped the pull handle tightly and gave it a sharp tug.

The motor responded immediately and black smoke and diesel fumes permeated Mike's nose and lungs. He coughed through his nose and through clinched teeth as he leaned his head forward in an attempt to relieve the pressure on his jawbone. Mike pushed his bare toes onto the inside wall of the hopper, trying to get a grip and somehow climb out. His hands and feet were tied up and Mike knew he wouldn't be able to get away even if he did manage to get out of the hopper but at this point, anywhere was better than where he was now! His toes pushed hard on the wall and he pushed his head forward, gripping the rim of the hopper closer to his throat, making it possible to open his mouth.

Mike was able to look down over the side of the hopper as he readjusted his toes just a couple of inches higher than they were before. He could see the surgeon on the side of the chipper looking up with squinted eyes as he smiled beneath his mask. With a flip of the switch, the teeth beneath Mike began to rev up and spin. It made the same horrible sound that Mike had heard from a distance just a short while ago. He screamed as he tried to wiggle his body forward, away from the blades. He could feel the wind below his feet from the whirring razors just inches below them and he tried over and over again to grasp the inside wall of the hopper with his toes and push himself upward. As he began to cry between screams, the surgeon wandered around toward Mike and climbed upon the ledge of the chipper.

Only two feet away from Mike's face, the surgeon lifted his hand and pointed at Mike. Mike looked at the surgeon with undiluted terror on his screaming, crying, young face. Without notice, the surgeon poked Mike gently in his right eye. Mike's eyes quickly squeezed shut as he continued writhing inside the noisy hopper, trying frantically to lift himself out. The surgeon again pointed at Mike and poked his right eye again, much harder than before. Mike's head instinctively snapped back. His chin caught the edge of the hopper just at the tip of his jawbone and his mouth clinched shut again, silencing his screams.

His toes were now just two inches above the spinning blades. Mike bent his knees to avoid being pulled into the chipper. The pain on his jawbone was excruciating as he pushed with his toes and pushed with his jaw, through the pain, to lift himself up and over the edge of the hopper once again.

"Very good!" the surgeon said and smiled, impressed at Mike's perseverance and agility. Mike's screams erupted again. The surgeon began laughing as he placed his left thumb on Mike's right eye and began slowly but steadily pressing in. Mike squeezed both eyes shut again and his screams of horror and pain grew closer and closer together, almost as if he were hyperventilating his screams. The surgeon continued applying constant forward pressure to Mike's eye as he watched the young man wiggling and trying with all of his might to somehow escape this fateful predicament.

With the additional pressure on his eye, Mike felt his eyeball shift in its socket just before he began losing his grip on the edge of the hopper. His head leaned back and his body weight again rested on the tip of his jaw. Mike's stifled screams escaped through his teeth, which were again clinched together.

The surgeon giggled as he gave one final hard thrust to Mike's shut eye. He felt it explode beneath the eyelid just as Mike's chin slipped off of the edge of the hopper and he dropped down, feet first, onto the ravenous, speeding blades. Mike felt the pull and the chopping of the blades on his feet as they were severed upon impact, then on his ankles and shins. Mike let out a last terrible, horrified scream as he was pulled down farther and farther as if it were death itself chewing and dragging him down into hell. The surgeon watched the spatter of Mikes' legs, groin and lower torso being shot out of the exit chute and landing far out in the lake.

Mike felt the angry blades chew away at his stomach and chest. His long scream finally ended as his chest and shoulders were ingested and regurgitated from the wood chipper. All that remained was Mike's head, which bounced around in the hopper a few times before the blades got a firm grip, pulled it inside, and spat it out the other end.

The surgeon, having had his fun, jumped down off of the chipper and flipped the kill switch, putting the giant machine back to sleep. Blood and tissue splattered the inside of the hopper and dripped in clumps from the exit chute. "No evidence!" the surgeon said aloud and he headed back to the Blazer, returning with four jugs of bleach. He spent the next half hour picking up the wet clumps of bloody tissue that had collected on the ground below the exit chute and throwing them out into the frigid lake. He then doused the hopper of the chipper with bleach and poured an entire bottle into the exit chute hole. When he had sufficiently cleaned the wood chipper, the surgeon threw all four bleach bottles, three that were empty and one only half-empty, into the hopper. He then started the beast back up. Light slivers of wet plastic shot through the air and fell silently on top of the lake. Satisfied that he had effectively cleansed his newest crime scene, he flipped the kill switch on the chipper, silencing it once more.

The surgeon looked around, wondering if the young man he had just disposed of was alone in the forest. "Surely not," he thought to himself as he looked out past the reach of the headlights, into the black abyss of the forest. "Somebody's waiting for him to come back!" he muttered quietly.

He bent over and picked up Mike's flashlight from the leaves on the ground and walked back into the forest, listening for distant yells and looking for the light of a campfire or another flashlight. The surgeon walked deeper and deeper into the forest with a slight rush of adrenaline, imagining the thrill of finding someone else that he could overpower and bring back to the wood chipper. Someone who may even have a tattoo! However, back at Mike and Stephanie's campsite, the fire had burned down to mere embers. Stephanie had retired to the tent to try to get warm and had fallen asleep waiting for Mike to return with more firewood. There would be no yelling and no fire to lead the surgeon back to her. Having no clue as to where Mike had come from, the surgeon listened once again, just for a moment, to the music of the forest before returning back to his Blazer and driving away.

Chapter 10

A shrill scream cut through the icy morning air as the sun arose on the first potential customer of the day at the Roll In Bakery and Café. Judy Presley, a somewhat pretty, middle-aged woman of about fifty was on her way to pick up a box of doughnuts for the other girls in the beauty parlor where she worked, when she noticed something precariously perched on top of the door knob of the tattoo parlor next door.

Unable to tell what it was from the café door, Judy headed curiously toward the tattoo shop, squinting as she walked. As she got closer, she noticed spots of red on the ground below the strange object and upon closer examination, a shock of terror and disgust shot through her entire body as she realized that resting atop the door knob of the tattoo parlor was a bloody, severed right hand that was missing the tip of its pinkie finger. Judy immediately lost control of her senses and her legs buckled beneath her as she screamed. She fell to the ground, staring at the hand just three feet in front of her face as she continued screaming in horror.

Judy and the other girls in the beauty parlor had just lost Kathy Peters to the serial killer in Walkerville and seeing the gruesome severed hand on the door knob was just too much for her to handle.

Hearing her screams, two waitresses and the cook came running out of the café, stopping a few feet behind Judy. Four other pedestrians ran in the same direction, crossing the street and effectively stopping the two cars that were approaching. The drivers and passengers of the cars exited their vehicles and headed over to the growing crowd as everyone gasped and screamed at the sight of this lifeless, rigid hand that was severed two inches above the wrist. The fingers and thumb gripped the doorknob and the inside of the wrist leaned up against the cold metal door panel. One of the waitresses grabbed the cook tightly and began to cry into his apron as a man in the crowd took out his cell phone and hastily dialed 911. Overcome with panic, Judy rose to her feet and ran as fast as she could, separating herself from this ghastly image that she had discovered and pushing herself through the crowd of onlookers, where any one of them could be responsible for everything that had happened in Walkerville in the past few days. She ran to her car and sped away, crying hysterically as the crowd grew steadily larger.

As Sheriff Kerry's sirens wailed in the distance, the mood of the villagers was turning from horror to confusion, nervousness and anger. Sheriff Kerry was met with an infuriated crowd as he exited his car. "Look what he's done *this* time, Sheriff!" One man yelled angrily. "Why haven't you caught this guy yet?"

"Believe me, folks, we're doing everything we can to put an end to all of this," Sheriff Kerry said. "Now I need everyone to go into the diner to be questioned."

Hearing this only further angered the crowd and some of the men started to move closer to the sheriff as they yelled. "We're going to be questioned again? Why aren't we getting any goddamned answers ourselves?" asked one man as he stared Sheriff Kerry boldly in the eyes.

"You need to do your god damn job, Sheriff!" another man yelled as he pushed Sheriff Kerry's shoulder.

"Now everybody just calm down!" Sheriff Kerry yelled over the overexcited crowd. "You know we're working with the Grand Rapids Major Case Squad on this. They're the best in the state!"

Another man stepped up to Sheriff Kerry and pushed him solidly in the center of his chest, causing the sheriff to take three steps back, as the man yelled out, "If they're so great, then why is there a hand on that door knob?" The crowd agreed and quickly transformed into an angry mob with Sheriff

199

Kerry as their focal point. He knew that he was in danger and had to regain control of the crowd before they eventually became more violent.

Reaching to his side, Sheriff Kerry pulled out his wooden nightstick. His expression quickly changed from the good-natured, small-town sheriff that everyone knew, to a trapped and enraged animal as he yelled at the man who had just pushed him and told him to lie down on the ground. "I said 'get on the ground', Karl!" Sheriff Kerry bellowed. Karl, now enraged, lunged toward the sheriff and grabbed him by the neck with his left hand as he drew back with his right hand that he had balled into a tight fist. Sheriff Kerry shot his left hand forward to stop the punch while rearing his right arm back. He smashed his nightstick down upon Karl's left outer thigh, effectively dropping him to the pavement. Karl grasped his leg as he moaned loudly.

Red-faced Sheriff Kerry turned around to engage the others in the crowd, but seeing the sheriff in this state for the very first time, everyone took a few steps back and fell silent.

In this instant, everyone in the crowd realized that Sheriff Kerry was not a man to be trifled with. They realized that he was a strong-willed man who had, until now, always kept his composure, treating everyone in Walkerville kindly and fairly. They understood this now and, for some reason, seeing this reaction from the sheriff actually put everyone a little more at ease knowing that he was on their side. Sheriff Kerry knew that he had now restored order.

In the distance, two sirens made their way toward the sheriff as he corralled everyone in the crowd into the café while he stayed out on the sidewalk with Karl, helping him to his feet and offering a shoulder to lean on as he, too, headed silently toward the café.

Three deputies arrived and hurriedly joined the sheriff to begin questioning the group sequestered inside. Everyone told the same story of hearing a scream and rushing over to see what was going on. Except for Judy Presley, no one had touched the hand or even gotten within a few feet of it.

Everyone mentioned that Judy was the one who had found the hand and it was her screams that led them over to it before she ran away and drove off. Sheriff Kerry and his deputies continued questioning until they had spoken to every last person in the café, including the wait staff and the cook.

Sheriff Kerry gathered his deputies together, just inside of the café and set out the order of business. "Julian, I want you to call down to Grand Rapids and tell them what's going on," he said. "We'll have a couple hours to do what we can before they get here and take everything over. Then I want you to patrol the streets, talk to as many people as possible and get as much information as possible throughout the day.

"Tim, I want you to stay right outside this door and make sure nobody goes into or leaves the café and nobody gets near that hand! I'm sure the Grand Rapids guys are going to want to question everyone again when they get here. Charlie, I want you to go outside and put up the tape about twenty feet in front of the tattoo shop and around the sides and back too before you go out on patrol. I don't want *anybody* getting anywhere near that hand until the Grand Rapids guys have a chance to get as much evidence from the area as possible. Got it?"

The three deputies shook their heads in agreement. "I'm going to look up Judy Presley's address and go pay her a visit," Sheriff Kerry said.

*****

"Dispatch to Sheriff Kerry," he heard Linda say through the radio as he drove. He pushed the button on his microphone to reply.

"Sheriff Kerry here. What's up, Linda?"

"Sheriff, there's a girl named Stephanie here at the station in hysterics. She says she and her boyfriend, Mike, were camping last night and he went off for firewood and never came back to their camp."

Sheriff Kerry responded "Maybe he got lost in the dark."

After a brief silence, Linda said, "Stephanie says he had a flashlight with him but the fire had died down to embers so, yeah, he might have gotten turned around and not have been able to find his way back." After another brief pause, Sheriff Kerry heard Stephanie crying loudly in the background as Linda said empathetically through the radio, "God, I *hope* he's just lost!"

Sheriff Kerry instructed Linda to keep Stephanie in the office while he radioed Deputy Julian to head back to interview her, in order to get an accurate description of her boyfriend and to take her back out to their campsite to look for Mike in the daylight. Sheriff Kerry went on, half-heartedly reassuring Linda that Mike may have even found his way back by now. "God, *please* don't let him be another one," Sheriff Kerry said to himself as he hung his microphone back on its hook and continued toward the Presley's home.

Removing his hat and sunglasses, Sheriff Kerry pressed the button next to a beautiful, cherry-wood door and heard "Westminster Chimes" ringing from within. He could hear heavy footsteps growing closer before the door opened wide and a large, middle-aged man of about fifty-five stood in its opening. He had a kind but concerned face, was dressed in khakis and a white, sleeveless t-shirt and was holding his black leather belt and a blue, button-up shirt in his hand. "Good morning, Mr. Presley, is it?"

"Ye-ye-yeah, Mick Presley," he responded. "I've k-kind of been expecting you, Sh-Sheriff. My wife came home hy-hy-hy-hysterical and told me about the hand she found on a-a-a doorknob in town. I couldn't believe it!"

"Yeah, I know!" Sheriff Kerry continued, ignoring Mick's stutter, "Is your wife at home right now? I need to ask her a few questions about it."

"Yeah, she's u-upstairs resting right now. She works at the b-b-b-beauty parlor where Kathy Peters worked and after finding out that Kathy was killed a-a-a few days ago and then finding that hand today, it was all I c-could do to calm her d-down when she got home."

"They worked together?" Sheriff Kerry asked, sounding surprised.

"Yeah," Mick responded, "they worked together for quite a while. Please, c-come on in, sheriff."

Sheriff Kerry smiled cordially and nodded as he stepped into the house and the two men walked into a large, two-story living room. "This is a beautiful house, Mr. Presley!" Sheriff Kerry said warmly, obviously impressed as he looked around.

He noticed the crystal chandelier hanging above a white grand piano and an antique glass and wooden curio cabinet filled with porcelain vases that looked quite old, as well as a few crystal bells and various ceramic figurines. Below the glass were several ornately carved wooden drawers, each with a shiny brass handle. The curio cabinet sat next to a beautiful trickling waterfall built right into the wall.

"Well thank you, Sheriff. We li-li-like it!" Mick said humbly with a slight smile.

"I've seen you two around for a while, but you're kind of new to Walkerville, aren't you? You've only been here a couple years now, right?" Sheriff Kerry asked in a friendly tone.

"Three, actually," Mike said. "W-w-we just moved into this house about six months ago. We were living in a sm-smaller house just-just outside of town for a couple years while we were looking for a nicer, bi-bi-bi-bigger one."

"Ahh," Sheriff Kerry continued. "Where did you live before you moved to Walkerville?"

"Oh, w-we were out in Co-Colorado. Beautiful out there!"

Sheriff Kerry agreed. "Yeah, I've been there a few times. I love Colorado!"

Mick turned toward the open staircase and said, "I'll go up and ge-get my wife. Be right back. M-m-make yourself comfortable!"

Sheriff Kerry smiled and wandered around the room while Mick went to get his wife. As he waited, he watched the brilliantly colored, exotic fish swimming in the immense salt water tank that was built into a dark rock wall and marveled at the striking white-stone fireplace, far on the other side of the room and the seventy-two-inch television mounted above its mantel where he noticed an old black-and-white photo of a handsome young man in an Army uniform. Sheriff Kerry headed over to a nearby bookshelf and read such titles as, *Etiquette of Man* and *Beautiful Pieces of History.*

His perusal of the Presley's library was interrupted as Mick helped Judy down the staircase. "Ah, good morning Mrs. Presley," Sheriff Kerry said somberly as he looked into her bloodshot eyes from which she hadn't even taken the time to wipe away the running mascara.

"Morning, Sheriff," she responded sheepishly.

"P-p-please, sit down, Sheriff." Mick said as he helped his wife to the large white couch beside the waterfall. Sheriff Kerry sat on the chair across from the couch and pulled out a small notepad and red pen from his shirt pocket.

"Your husband tells me that you worked with Kathy Peters," he began. Judy looked down at her hands in her lap and responded with tears in her eyes.

"Yes, we've worked together for a couple years now. She was such a sweet girl." As Judy thought about the condition in which Kathy was found, she burst into tears and Mick held her tightly. Judy spoke as she sobbed, "I just can't believe anyone could do something like that to someone like Kathy." Sheriff Kerry made a note in his notebook before gingerly asking Judy how close of a relationship she had with Kathy.

"We were pretty good friends. There's only a few of us that work together in the beauty parlor and when you see someone day after day for that long, it's hard not to be friends."

Sheriff Kerry proceeded to ask several more questions about Kathy and Judy's relationship before asking questions pertaining to the hand that Judy had found earlier that morning, including what time she saw it, what time she

204

usually got to work at the beauty parlor, if she saw anyone strange nearby, or if anyone had touched the hand.

He wrote in his pad as Judy answered all of the sheriff's questions, stating that she hadn't seen anyone that she didn't know and no one had touched the hand while she was there. Just saying those words brought up the horrible and all-too-recent vision of finding the hand and Judy again burst into tears. Mick pulled her in close and kissed her on top of her head. "It's OK, honey. It's OK. They'll find whoever did it. Don't worry, baby."

Sheriff Kerry spoke out, "Mrs. Presley, I'm sorry I have to ask this, but where were you last night?"

"I was home all night. We both were." She tried to stifle her crying. "My husband is a taxidermist and he was working on a deer down in the basement all night and I went to bed early, around 9:00."

Sheriff Kerry turned his attention to Mick. "Oh, you're a taxidermist? That's pretty interesting. I've always wanted to do taxidermy myself. Heh, actually even thought about picking it up after I retire! How long have you been doing it?"

"Well," Mick said quietly, still holding and comforting Judy, "I just d-d-do it part time for some of the folks in town."

"Really?" Sheriff Kerry asked looking around the beautiful living room. "I hope you don't mind me saying this, but this sure doesn't look like the home of a hairdresser and a part time taxidermist to me."

"Oh, m-m-m-my parents were well off," Mick stated in a matter-of-fact tone. "My-my-my father came from old money – he died when I was very young and whe- whe- when my mother passed away, I was left wi-wi-wi-with a considerable amount."

"Oh, I see," Sheriff Kerry replied, now understanding the situation. "Did you ever have a full-time job then?"

"Yeah, I was a medic in Vietnam!" Mick responded proudly.

"Yeah," Sheriff Kerry said, "I thought that was you in the picture on the mantle. How long were you in the service?"

"I actually st-started out in the reserves. M-m-my mother said it would look good on my resume. I was in medical school when I was called. I was s-s-s-studying to become a surgeon, but during Operation Ivory Coast, I was shot in-in-in the arm and have some minor nerve da-a-a-amage, so no hospital would accept me when-when I got back."

The expression on Mick's face showed his anger and the feeling of betrayal from his country that he once so proudly served. Although he didn't say it, since his arm wasn't perfect, Mick had always felt like *he* wasn't perfect – like he was less of a man and less of a *human being*. He hung his head and squeezed his wife tight as he rubbed her arm before stating, "I always loved hunting and I l-l-learned taxidermy when I was just a boy."

Their conversation was briefly interrupted when a small, wrinkly, hairless dog wandered silently into the room, its tail wagging incessantly. He meandered over and jumped up on the couch next to Judy and laid his head in her lap.

"Wow!" said the sheriff. "What kind of dog *is* that?"

"He's a Peruvian Inca," Judy said as she petted the dog on the top of his wrinkly head. "They're very rare and really expensive," she said, looking down at the dog. "His name is Kojak."

An unintentional "Ha!" escaped Sheriff Kerry's mouth as Judy pushed Kojak back off of the couch and rested her head on Mick's chest. As Sheriff Kerry continued questioning the Presley's, Kojak walked out of the room and stuck his paw into a small gap between the basement door and the doorframe and pulled the door open just enough to squeeze through before heading down the stairwell. Seeing this, Mick excused himself for a moment, headed out of the room and shut the basement door tightly, ensuring that they would not be disturbed again. Returning to the living room, he said, "OK, sorry about that."

Kojak reached the bottom of the stairwell and came upon two wooden doors across the hallway from each other. He stuck his paw into the crack of the door on the left, which slowly swayed open, revealing a darkened room. The light of the hallway revealed a cement step down and a slit running the entire length of a clean, white sheet that hung directly in the doorway. Sniffing quickly, the dog entered the room, stepping down to the cold cement floor. As the slit in the sheet pulled open, the light briefly reflected off of a metallic table ahead and to the right. To the left was an old green, five-wheeled swivel chair that had a fresh white apron strewn over its back and a pair of black rubber boots to its side. Kojak continued inside, sniffing and wagging his tail all the while as the light from the hallway dimly illuminated the room through the white sheet.

The wagging dog neared the metal table and the drain beneath, which housed a hose that rose up to the bottom of the hole at the head of the table above him. With his head down near the drain, he began licking the hose and pulling at something that was stuck between it and the drain. Kojak began biting, pulling and pawing gently at the object until he had pulled out a three-inch long piece of thick flesh and fatty tissue that had rolled toward the drain the night before but had inadvertently become lodged behind the hose on its way down. Gnawing and pulling at the meat with his paw, Kojak ripped it in two and began to devour the first half. When he had swallowed it, he took the second half in his mouth and happily exited the room, ran up the stairs and began scratching at the closed door. At once, Sheriff Kerry, Mick, and Judy all turned their heads toward the sound. "Stop it Kojak!" Mick yelled, but to no avail.

"Aww, he wants to come back up, Mick." Judy said sadly before standing up and walking over to the door to let the dog in.

Mick, now feeling panicked, tried to divert the sheriff's attention back to their conversation. As he began asking the sheriff about the recent murders, he saw out of the corner of his eye, Kojak trotting toward the sheriff as he chewed on something that was hanging partially out of his mouth. Mick felt the pounding of his heart beneath his ribs and he released a quick breath as the sheriff turned to pet Kojak just as the hairless dog pulled the last bit of flesh into his mouth and swallowed it whole.

"Well folks, I want you to know, I really appreciate your time. You've been more than kind. Mrs. Presley, don't worry, we'll find this guy soon enough." Sheriff Kerry tried to comfort Judy, but didn't actually feel comforted himself as he spoke the words.

Judy replied, sounding worried, "I'm so scared, Sheriff! I don't even want to leave the house! This is the only place where I feel at least *somewhat* safe. Like whomever is doing this can't get to me in here."

Sheriff Kerry nodded in agreement and stood up to leave but as Mick and Judy walked him to the front door, he turned around and asked, quite enthusiastically, "By the way, I was just wondering, would you mind if I took a look at the area where you work on your animals? Oh, uh, stuffing them, I mean."

Judy spoke up and said, "Yeah, honey, why don't you show him around your dungeon?" She let out a slight laugh; it was the first sign of levity the sheriff had seen come from her.

"It's disgusting down there," Judy said. "All those dead animals all over the place. It gives *me* the creeps!"

Sheriff Kerry turned to look at Mick, silently waiting for him to invite the sheriff down.

"Oh, sh-sure!" Mick said. "I'll show you around my workspace. R-r-right this way, Sheriff!"

Mick turned to Judy and said, "You-You've had a rough morning honey. Why don't you go b-b-back upstairs and rest? I'll-I'll-I'll bring you up your medicine later on after I'm d-done with the sheriff."

Judy agreed and excused herself as Mick motioned for the sheriff to lead the way down the stairs, shutting the door behind them as they headed down.

Mick looked down at his right hand, which was still holding his black leather belt, and noticed it beginning to shake as he and the sheriff neared the bottom of the stairwell. He grabbed his belt with his left hand and squeezed it tight as Sheriff Kerry continued downward. As he watched the back of Sheriff Kerry's head, Mick started breathing heavier and his heart seemed to be beating even harder than before when he saw the meat hanging out of his dog's mouth.

As Sheriff Kerry took his last step down the stairs, Mick gritted his teeth and pulled the belt taut. Sheriff Kerry suddenly turned around and asked, "Which door?"

Mick relaxed his grip on the belt and pursed his lips together, trying hard to control his nervousness before saying, "The left one." Sheriff Kerry stood back and let Mick step inside and flip on the switch behind the white sheet before joining him inside the meticulously clean room.

It even smelled clean, the sheriff thought, like a hospital. There, behind the metal table, hung a mid-sized deer. The hooks hanging from chains in the ceiling pierced the deer's chest at its front armpits.

"Well that's a nice-sized deer, Mr. Presley!" Sheriff Kerry said as he walked toward it.

"Yeah, Jamie Bumgarner brought that over for me to clean and mount just yesterday," Mick replied, sounding a bit out of breath. "I had planned on working on him today, but th-then my wife came home and, well, I guess I w-w-won't be starting on him today. I n-n-need to stay upstairs with her today. I'm gonna move this guy back into the cooler un-un-u-u-until tomorrow, I guess."

Sheriff Kerry stood next to the head of the table, just in front of the sink, where hidden below were various items including two gallon jugs of bleach and an old paint can that contained several salted tattoos wrapped up in a chamois.

"What's this, here?" Sheriff Kerry asked, looking down at the left sink tub that was filled with rock salt, which, buried just inches beneath, were the flayed skins of Ozzy Rodriguez's arm, chest, back, neck and forehead. "Tha-tha-that's rock salt. You put the animal hides in there for a while be-before you separate the meat from the back side of the skin. A-a-actually, I'll fill that sink wi-wi-wi-with water and use the salt water solution to be-be sure the salt gets worked in between the hairs and in-in-into the p-p-pores."

Mick felt his legs begin to tremble and felt warmth around his head where sweat had begun to bead up. He thought that, by now, Sheriff Kerry would surely be able to actually *hear* his heart crashing against his ribs.

"So, Mr. Presley," Sheriff Kerry asked, a bit confused, "why do you have sheets hanging around the whole room and carpet on the ceiling?" Mick held his breath for a second, trying to control his speeding heartbeat before answering. "Those kee-keep the room more sterile so-so-so the skins don't become infected with-with-with anything. The-the carpet on the ceiling is really jus-just for muffling my music so-so-so m-m-my wife doesn't hear it. I like to-to-to play classical music when-when I work. It helps relax m-m-me."

Sheriff Kerry smiled as he replied. "Yeah, that's a pretty good idea! Maybe I should do that to *my* basement so I can turn up my TV at night and not have to hear about it from *my* wife!" Sheriff Kerry laughed heartily and Mick laughed nervously. "Classical music, you say? I love classical music!"

"Oh, y-y-yeah, I love classical m-m-music too!" Mick responded with a hint of a smile before continuing. "There-there-there's so much *emotion* in classical music. The greats, like Mozart, Vivaldi, Bach, and Rachmaninoff, they s-spoke out in their music."

Sheriff Kerry watched as Mick closed his eyes and continued on.

"Each piece is like an entire relationship, like-like an entire lifetime! If you listen really closely, you can not only hear, but you can actually feel, the emotion that the composer was trying to convey. And the best part about it," Mick paused as he opened his eyes and looked directly at the sheriff, "is that that it has survived the test of time! You don't think that in 200 years, anyone's going to be listening to *rap* music, do you?"

Sheriff Kerry smiled as he thought about the question and then laughed out loud. "No," he said laughing as he turned away and walked over to the metal cabinet on the left side of the room and casually opened it up, "I really don't think anyone will!"

Inside the cabinet, Sheriff Kerry saw a few stacks of classical music CDs, some unopened boxes, '20 Mule Team Borax,' it said on their labels, various shiny medical instruments, surely used in his craft and two thick leather straps, each with belt holes and a buckle.

"What are *these* for?" he asked.

"Oh, some-some-sometimes people bring me animals ri-right after they killed them and they s-s-s-sometimes tend to jerk when-when they're on the table, so I strap-strap them down so they don't f-f-f-fall off."

"Ah," Sheriff Kerry said in acknowledgement before reaching into the cabinet and pulling out a pair of double hinged pliers and giving them a quick squeeze. "I'd hate to run into a guy that had *these* in a dark alley!" Sheriff Kerry quipped. He and Mick laughed.

"Hey," Sheriff Kerry went on, "why don't you let me help you move that deer to your cooler!"

"Oh, you-you don't have to do that, Sheriff!" Mick said nervously.

"Oh, it's no bother!" Sheriff Kerry said in a friendly voice as he and Mick headed toward the deer and lifted it from the thick hooks that hung from the ceiling, negotiated it over the table, across the room and up the step, Mick leading the way. When they reached the hallway, they turned left and rounded the corner into a larger, dimmer room that was lined with shelves of antlers, mounted animals, various skin-cutting tools including the fleshing machine with its round blade, and several very sharp scalpels of various sizes, lined up, shortest to longest, one thumb's-width apart on the work table.

"Here it is," said Mick with a smile as he grabbed the handle of the large metal door and pulled it open.

Inside of the walk-in cooler were several shelves of various meats wrapped in cellophane. From the ceiling hung three cuts of meat but by the size and shape, Sheriff Kerry was unable to tell what kind of animal they were. As they walked the deer into the cooler, Mick looked around the room in a panic as he grabbed one of a few metal hooks hanging by a chain from the ceiling. "We-we-we can hang it on th-these," he said as he and Sheriff Kerry hoisted the deer and thrust it down onto the pointed tips of two hooks, precisely using the same holes that it had been hung on previously.

"I-I-I-I sure do appreciate the help, Sheriff. You know, I-I'm gonna make some jerky from this deer. I'd b-b-be happy to bring some by the station if you'd like some."

Sheriff Kerry wiped his hands on his pants and said, "Well, I'd love some, if it's really not too much trouble!"

Mick answered politely, "N-n-n-n-not at all, Sheriff!"

Sheriff Kerry excused himself, telling Mick that he had a few more stops to make and was led back upstairs and out the front door with a smile and a wave from Mick. After coming back inside, Mick fell to the ground, pushing his back up against the closed door and covering his face with his trembling hands as he bent over and breathed deep in and out, in and out.

"That was too close," he said into his hands, sounding almost as if he were about to cry. "I'm smarter than they are!" he said aloud before he got back up to his feet, quickly threw open the door to the basement, ran down the stairs, into his skinning room and slammed the door shut behind him. "I'm smarter than they are!"

He cried out as he slapped both sides of his face hard with his hands. His cheeks instantly became a bright pink.

"I *am* smarter than they are!" he continued. "Gotta be more careful! Got lazy! *Gotta* be more careful!"

He hastily opened the cabinet beneath the sink and grabbed a gallon jug of bleach, two rubber gloves and a large sponge.

"Gotta be more careful! No fingerprints!" he yelled as he began pouring bleach onto the table, the sink counter, the floor and onto the sponge before quickly rubbing down every surface he could reach. The cabinet doors, the stereo knobs, the chair and the doorknob were all wiped down before moving onto the many other surfaces in the room.

"No DNA!" he yelled as the vapors from the bleach invaded his sinuses and lungs and burned his eyes. He coughed and turned his head to the side to try and inhale some fresh air as tears streamed down his thick, grimacing face.

"I'm smarter than they are," he said, turning back to wipe down the table. "No DNA, no fingerprints. I'm smarter than-than-than they are!" Mick paused for a moment in silence before pointing his finger at the thin air and screaming loudly, "*Yes I am*!"

Chapter 11

A long, black van, emblazoned with the words 'Crime Scene' on its side and the Michigan state shield on its doors was led into the parking lot of the Roll In Bakery and Café by an unmarked, brown Crown Victoria squad car. Although Deputy Tim was among those inside the cafe, the mood was noticeably anxious and fearful.

Everyone had been sequestered inside for hours and no one spoke of anything but the murders in the village. Each person had their own idea of what had happened to the victims and how each one of them was killed. The more they talked, the more scared everyone else became, visualizing each other's thoughts and picturing the different scenarios that each person in the café had portrayed. No longer did everyone have only their idea, their *one* vision of the murders, but now they had the shared visions of *everyone* in the café, which only further confused and frightened everyone inside. To make matters worse, everyone worried that the serial killer could be right there in the café among them, possibly even sharing the true stories of what he had done to each victim.

Three men, including Captain Parker, entered the café while four other men exited the crime scene van and headed next door to the tattoo shop. There they began to carefully mark and photograph any and all suspicious-looking items. They marked each drop of blood on the ground beneath the hand on the door knob with numbered yellow sticky notes. They also diagrammed the pools of blood around the side of the tattoo shop nearest the café, just next to the large grey dumpster.

Inside the café, the room fell silent as Captain Parker and two other men from the Grand Rapids team walked in. They were greeted by Deputy Tim, who explained to the captain that he was instructed to keep everyone in the café until the Grand Rapids team arrived.

"Good job," Captain Parker said supportively as one of the captain's men informed the villagers in the café that they would be questioned shortly. Tim was quiet about the fact that he and Sheriff Kerry and the other two deputies had already questioned everyone inside and was worried about how the captain would react when he found out.

"If you don't need me then, I'd like to go ahead and start my patrol now," Tim said nervously.

"Sure," Captain Parker replied, "We've got it from here."

Relieved, Deputy Tim quickly left through the front glass door just as he heard one man inside the café ask sheepishly, "Do we really all have to be questioned *again*?" Tim didn't dare look back to see the captain who was turning red-faced and glaring at the back of Tim's head.

For the next hour, the three Grand Rapids detectives took everybody aside, one by one, and asked a battery of questions, hoping to find someone who had some useful information that might help get them at least one step closer to the person responsible for this and all of the other murders in Walkerville.

When they were down to the last three people in the café – the two waitresses and the cook – Captain Parker asked the two detectives from his team to finish up so he could go next door to see how things were going.

Outside, two detectives, who were clad in black rubber gloves, had finally reached the hand on the door after their slow circular sweep of the parameter of the tattoo parlor. Captain Parker approached the men just after one detective had finished his close examination of the hand under a magnifying glass and the other detective, Jeff, had begun to carefully remove the hand from the door knob. He would place it into a large clear plastic re-sealable baggie and take it into the crime scene van where it would quickly be fingerprinted.

215

"Find anything useful, Jeff?" the captain asked.

"Yes sir," came the swift reply. "There's a motorcycle propped up against the back door and a pool of blood on the side of the building, right next to that dumpster." Jeff pointed toward the back of the building. "We're pulling prints off of it now." Captain Parker looked toward the back of the building. "Have you contacted the owner yet?" he asked.

"No, we haven't been able to reach anyone yet. We called the number on the door but we could hear the phone ringing inside and then it went to the answering machine."

Captain Parker opened his notepad and read through some of the notes he had just taken inside the café. "The owner's name is Oswald Rodriguez. Have one of the guys call local information. Get his home number and give him a call to come down here and open up his shop so we can continue this inside. I wonder if this was some sort of a warning for Mr. Rodriguez?"

Jeff nodded and carried the baggie with the hand toward the back of the building where he conveyed the information about the owner to the two other detectives. Then, he headed back to the crime scene van and climbed inside through the back door.

About a half hour later, Jeff exited the van and headed straight for Captain Parker, who had been wrapping up the investigation outside of the tattoo shop and was just finishing a phone call.

"We still haven't been able to reach the owner of the tattoo shop," Captain Parker said as he saw Jeff approaching.

"Yeah, you're not *going* to reach him, Captain." Jeff responded. "That was his hand on the door."

Briefly, Captain Parker raised his eyebrows and his mouth fell open. He gathered all six men from his unit and filled them in on the latest news. "Okay, we're going to need a locksmith and we're going to need to get a hold of," he paused as he looked through his note pad, "Veronica Benington. She was the owner's girlfriend."

As he continued briefing the men, Captain Parker explained that he had some other business to attend to and left orders to find and question Veronica and all of Oswald's friends as well as thoroughly search inside the tattoo shop for more evidence and clues. He would have had them question Ozzy's family as well but, according to his notes, his parents were deceased and he had no other family in Walkerville to speak of. When everyone knew what was expected of them, Captain Parker told his team that he would meet up with them later in the day back at the Grand Rapids station.

As Captain Parker drove to another part of town, he passed a news truck that surely was headed toward the tattoo shop to try to be the first on the scene to report on the latest murder in Walkerville. His concentration unshaken, Captain Parker continued to drive through town until he pulled into the driveway in front of Syndi's house. After knocking on her door, Syndi appeared with a bright smile and greeted Luke with a long, warm kiss as she pulled him inside and wrapped her arms tightly around him.

Without hesitation, they began to undress each other. Luke spoke out between their kisses, "I'm so glad you called!" Syndi opened his shirt and began rubbing her hand down his toned chest and stomach.

"I'm so glad you could come over," she said before he pulled her closer and pressed his lips to hers while he unsnapped her pants and hurriedly began pushing them down off of her hips. They worked their way into her bedroom where they spent the next two hours hungrily exploring each other's bodies.

*****

Nearing the point of exhaustion, Syndi breathlessly staggered naked from the bed as Luke smiled, watching two images of her beautiful, perfect body as she passed by a full-length mirror on the wall.

217

She headed into the kitchen where she grabbed a bottle of cold water and took a long refreshing gulp before bringing it to Luke and lying next to him as he drank the rest of its contents.

"You're amazing," she said and smiled, nuzzling into the crook of Luke's arm and rubbing his chest.

"You're not so bad yourself!" he quipped with a smile. "It's been a long time since anyone's made me feel like this," he continued.

"Well," Syndi said tenderly, "You deserve it for your efforts!"

They both laughed and Luke squeezed Syndi tight, saying, *"You* are amazing, honey! You're beautiful and sexy and funny and smart and amazing!"

Syndi giggled as she sat up. "How do you *really* feel about me?"

Luke just smiled and looked into Syndi's eyes adoringly. "I'm going to really miss you while I'm in Florida," Syndi said sadly.

"Yeah, you'll be gone a whole week," Luke responded softly. "I'll really be looking forward to seeing you when you get back!"

"Me too," Syndi whispered.

"When's your flight?" Luke asked.

"Tomorrow morning. I'm leaving out of White Cloud airport. I *am* getting kind of excited though!" she admitted.

"I'll bet!" Luke responded agreeably.

"My friends there throw the best Halloween party every year! They decorate their entire house with some horror movie theme, even their front and back yards. And everyone comes in costume and they give prizes for the best ones and it's just a lot of fun!" Syndi said excitedly.

"Sounds like it!" Luke responded before she continued.

"And the best part is that they don't even know I'm coming! I'm going to show up in my Cat Woman costume and surprise them all when I take my mask off. I can't *wait* to see the looks on all of their faces!"

Luke responded enthusiastically, "Oh that's gonna be *great*! I want to see a lot of pictures when you get back!"

Syndi agreed and lay back down in Luke's arms. She then spoke in a more serious tone; "My parents are really worried about me being here in Walkerville now."

Luke's silence signified both his understanding and his agreement. Syndi continued. "I told them about you ... well ... about us. They both feel a little better knowing that you're here with me, even if it's only every now and then."

Luke rubbed her arm and said, "You can tell them that I'm looking out for you."

Syndi squeezed Luke tight and said solemnly "You better have this guy by the time I get back!"

"I'll do my damndest," Luke said assuredly. He continued, "When *do* you get back?"

Syndi responded, "Well, I leave tomorrow morning, Halloween is Wednesday, my friend's party is Saturday and I'm coming back Sunday afternoon, probably hungover!"

They both laughed, effectively breaking their brief somber mood. "I was hoping we could get together when I get back," Syndi said hopefully.

"I think I can arrange that," Luke said, sounding quite happy to hear Syndi's words.

"I was hoping we could see a lot *more* of each other when I get back," Syndi continued. Luke didn't speak but pulled Syndi's naked body on top of his and began kissing her more passionately than ever.

Later that afternoon, after Luke had left Syndi's house and was driving back to Grand Rapids, Sheriff Kerry and his three deputies met in the sheriff's office to discuss the discovery of the severed hand found earlier that morning, the death of Lathe Walthes and everything in between.

The four men brought all of the notes, pictures, statements and evidence that they had collected and had been privy to from the Grand Rapids team.

"He's *got* to be someone from around here," Tim said. "It's someone that knew about everyone's tattoos!"

"Yeah, but Joe Moretto, the guy found in the electric closet out at the rest stop, he didn't have any tattoos." Sheriff Kerry replied. "The Grand Rapids guys said they spoke to his wife and she confirmed that he didn't have any tattoos on his head either."

The room was silent, just for a moment, before Julian spoke up. "Who in town, or out of town for that matter, would want other people's tattoos?"

Charlie chimed in: "Obviously it wasn't the only tattoo artist around for twenty miles. If he hadn't been killed, I'm sure he would have been one of our main suspects."

Sheriff Kerry looked around at his men silently before saying, "Well, we only found his hand. He *could* still be alive somewhere!"

The three deputies looked back at the sheriff in silence as they pondered his horrific suggestion, envisioning Oswald tied up in a chair somewhere, reeling from the pain of his amputated right hand.

Sheriff Kerry looked down and studied the compilation of notes as the three deputies continued speculating on the possibilities of various villagers and out-of-towners.

"What about doctors?" Julian proposed.

"Yeah," Tim interjected, "a doctor might know who had tattoos and even where they were on the bodies!"

Sheriff Kerry rummaged through the stack of information in front of him and said, "Their medical records show that only a couple of them had the same doctor. It was a good thought though!"

Frustrated at losing the only possible connection linking all of the victims together, the deputies grumbled and festered in their seats. Their analysis of the numerous people questioned went on throughout the afternoon. Multiple statements were read aloud, opinions were offered and discussed and possible scenarios were presented, but still no one in the room felt sure about any one suspect.

"You know," Sheriff Kerry mentioned, "that taxidermist – the husband of the woman who found the hand – something about that guy just struck me as odd."

"How do you mean, sheriff?" Tim asked.

"Well, he just," Sheriff Kerry paused, "I just got kind of a weird feeling in their house." He went on, "I went down in their basement to check out his taxidermy stuff and seeing all the equipment, it was just a little eerie, really. He was practicing to be a surgeon a long time ago and now he uses surgical equipment on the animals."

Julian said, "Yeah, but the tattoos weren't removed with scalpels and forceps! They were messy, like the skin was ripped off of the bodies, or hacked out by a dull axe or something."

Sheriff Kerry looked down and shook his head. "Yeah, that's true," he said, sounding unsure of himself. "But I still get an uneasy feeling about that guy. And they've only lived in Walkerville a few years."

The four men sat in silence until Julian said, "Do you think we should go back over there and bring some equipment to check the place out?"

Sheriff Kerry looked up at the three deputies and said, "I don't think that would be a bad idea at all.

*****

The setting orange autumn sun flickered through the brown, lifeless trees lining the roads of Walkerville as Sheriff Kerry and Deputy Julian drove toward the Presley's home. After entering the newly developed subdivision, the

221

light from the large chandelier hanging between two giant white columns guided them toward the beautiful home of Mick and Judy Presley.

Sheriff Kerry and Julian stepped out of the car and walked up a red brick pathway, past the fountain in the front yard and up the porch to the dark mahogany front door. Sheriff Kerry removed his hat after ringing the doorbell as his deputy stood next to him, holding a large black case that had 'Walkerville PD' stenciled in white on one side. Sheriff Kerry noticed the light from the peephole in the door briefly disappear before he heard the sound of a deadbolt and chain lock being undone. The door opened just a crack, revealing Judy Presley in a black sweatshirt, sweatpants and slippers.

"Good evening Mrs. Presley," said Sheriff Kerry.

"Good evening Sheriff," came her confused and nervous response. "Is everything OK?"

"Yes ma'am, everything's just fine. I don't know if you've met my deputy, Julian."

"Good evening ma'am." Julian said straight-faced.

"Deputy," came Judy's quick response.

"Please," she continued, "come on in out of the freezing cold."

Sheriff Kerry and Julian stepped inside the warm home and immediately unzipped their bulky green coats.

"Is your husband home?" Sheriff Kerry asked.

"No, he went hunting," Judy responded anxiously. "He won't be home until tomorrow morning. I asked him not to go. I'm so scared, Sheriff!"

Sheriff Kerry shook his head in agreement while Judy continued to talk.

"Mick told me not to worry since we have an alarm system and the house is so well lit, but I'm still scared. He told me that we couldn't stop living our lives because of what's happened here in Walkerville. I told him that I was worried that he might get killed out there but he just laughed it off and reminded me that he was going hunting so he'd have a loaded rifle in his hands the whole time."

Sheriff Kerry responded supportively, "I'm sure he'll be okay, Mrs. Presley." Seeing the pain and anguish in her face, Sheriff Kerry had to force his next words out, "Ma'am, the reason we're here is because we'd like to have another look around your basement if that's OK."

Judy showed a puzzled look on her face before asking why. Sheriff Kerry went on to reassure Judy in his kind, small-town sheriff way that they were not suspects in the murders. He lightheartedly went on to tell her that they were checking up on a few things around town, including her house, and asked her kindly to stay upstairs while they looked around.

Although surprised, Judy agreed and Sheriff Kerry and Julian headed down the stairwell as Judy returned to the living room where she had been watching television. She sat upon the couch and began to cry for what must have been the twentieth time that day.

Reaching the hallway at the bottom of the stairs, Julian set the black case on the ground, opened it up and took out two pairs of white rubber gloves. He and Sheriff Kerry pulled the gloves on tightly over their hands before Julian reached inside the case and took from it a spray bottle of Luminol, a reagent liquid. He began spraying the two doors, the doorknobs and the floor in between.

Sheriff Kerry looked inside the case which contained various empty, sterile vials as well as vials of blood testing liquids – one to determine if blood is human and one to determine if it is from an animal. There were several scalpels that could be used to scrape evidence off of hard surfaces or to cut pieces off contaminated fabrics. There was also a magnifying glass, tweezers, various hand tools, swabs, and resealable baggies. At the bottom of the case was a portable black light that, when shown on the reagent liquid, would cause any traces of blood to glow.

Sheriff Kerry reached into the case and pulled out the black light and turned it on before flipping a switch on the wall to turn off the overhead hallway light. As he waved the black light in front of the door to the garage, the entire door glowed a bright bluish white.

"What the hell?" Sheriff Kerry exclaimed. As he drew the black light down the door, the two men watched in amazement as the hallway floor and the door that led into the skinning room all glowed the same bluish-white hue. Not an inch of either door or the tiled floor was left unglowing. Confused, Julian turned the knob of the door leading into the skinning room. The pungent smell of bleach was evident. Julian reached behind the slit in the curtain and flipped the overhead lights on and began spraying the reagent liquid onto everything – the back of the door, the floor, the table, the hooks hanging from the ceiling, the sink, the stereo above it and the cabinet doors below it, the green swivel chair, and the orange, upright cabinet.

Sheriff Kerry flipped the switch on the black light wand and Julian flipped the switch behind the slit in the curtain to turn off the overhead lights in the room. Sheriff Kerry and Deputy Julian stood silently in utter amazement as everything in the room glowed a bright bluish-white. "Well I guess that explains the smell of bleach down here!" Sheriff Kerry said, exasperated. "He must have just cleaned this place."

Julian furrowed his brow and said, "Yeah, but why would he clean the doors, top to bottom, with bleach?"

Sheriff Kerry thought back to his conversation with Mick Presley and explained that Mick said he kept the room sterile so the animal hides didn't get infected and that's why there were sheets hanging around the room as well. "He said he was a surgeon for a while." Sheriff Kerry explained. "He had to be in a sanitary environment when he did his surgeries and I guess he still likes to work in that type of environment. It's a bit odd, I'll give you that, but it's nothing we can bring him in on. What gets me," he went on, "is that all of the victims have been covered in bleach. Maybe it's a coincidence, maybe not. Let's see if we can find anything tangible."

Sheriff Kerry flipped the switch next to the door behind the slit in the curtain. The bluish-white glow disappeared as the overhead lights, including the round surgical light over the autopsy table, came on. The two men began looking diligently for something, for *anything* out of the ordinary. They didn't vocalize it, but they both wondered what would be out of the ordinary in a taxidermist's workroom?

Sheriff Kerry opened the orange cabinet against the far left wall and searched its contents while Julian pulled a magnifying glass from out of the black case and got down on his hands and knees and began to look closely at the floor around the table.

Inside the cabinet, Sheriff Kerry riffled through a stack of CD cases, opening each one to check for anything that might be hidden inside. Julian was scouring the legs of the metal table and the concrete floor where they were attached, searching for any kind of foreign object such as hair, a drop of blood or even a fiber of material.

Finding nothing, he turned his search to the drain that housed the rubber hose leading out of the bottom of the table. Julian pulled the hose out from the drain and was surprised that it had been submerged a full five feet down into the drainpipe. Upon further investigation beneath the magnifying glass, the hose looked as if it were brand new. With cotton swabs, Julian wiped some of the sludge from the drain off of the outside and inside of the hose and stored them in resealable baggies, writing on each baggie with a felt tipped marker of what it contained and where the sample was taken.

Having finished looking through the orange metal cabinet, Sheriff Kerry approached the sink next to the autopsy table and bent down to open the cabinet doors below. Inside he saw a few boxes of table salt, a half bag of rock salt, an opened box of borax, and an old paint can. He reached into the black

225

case and rooted around until he pulled from it a standard screwdriver that he used to sift through each box of salt before giving them a quick sniff. Satisfied of their contents, he put the boxes back, pulled out the bag of rock salt and repeated the same procedure. When he had gone through the salt, he pulled out the box of borax. It too was sniffed and sifted through. It gave off a light, clean scent and the sheriff was sure it was actually laundry detergent.

After replacing the borax, he reached into the back of the cabinet and pulled out the paint can. Thin white lines of dried paint originated from the lid, which was tightly hammered down, and when he shook it, Sheriff Kerry could tell that it did not have any paint inside but felt, instead, like there was something else bumping the walls of the can with each shake.

"Have you got something, Sheriff?" Julian asked from the far side of the autopsy table where he had been examining the two hooks that hung from the ceiling.

"Not sure." Sheriff Kerry replied as he inserted the end of the screwdriver into the lip of the paint can and worked it around the edge to pry the lid open. Once he had removed the lid, he looked inside, only to find a large, green, bleach-filled sponge. "Naw, just an old sponge," Sheriff Kerry said. "Doesn't look like there's really anything out of the ordinary in here. We didn't find any tattoos, no clothing, no skin. Hell, we didn't even find a *trace* of skin."

Julian walked around the table toward Sheriff Kerry and said, "What now?"

Sheriff Kerry motioned with a tilt of his head for Julian to follow him. They exited the room, turned left in the hallway and headed back to the walk-in cooler. Inside, Jamie Bumgarner's deer still hung on the hooks and although Sheriff Kerry didn't notice that a few pieces of meat were missing from a nearby shelf, it all looked just as he had remembered it. Beside the deer, there were a few cuts of meat hanging on the various hooks and there were some cuts of meat sitting on the shelves wrapped in cellophane.

Sheriff Kerry and Julian began looking closely at the different meats, inspecting them for anything that might be hidden within. They checked the cavities of the meats hanging from the hooks and even used a screwdriver to remove the grate over the fan that circulated the cold air inside the cooler. There was nothing hidden and nothing to find.

"Well," said Sheriff Kerry, "Let's go upstairs and look around the rest of the house."

With Judy Presley's permission, Sheriff Kerry and his deputy looked around the house for the next half hour. They went through drawers, looked in closets and cabinets and under all of the furniture only to realize that there was nothing sinister to find in the house. Nothing at all.

After thanking Judy for being so patient and understanding, Sheriff Kerry and Julian left her, alone, in her home.

*****

In a house not far from Seth's Place, the music from a Halloween party was thumping loudly. The high school and college kids inside had put their fears and sorrows aside for just this one night as everyone came together to celebrate. There were sexy witches and vampires, a few monsters and superheroes, as well as an Indian, a ninja, a hippie, a zombie, and a werewolf.

The front door opened and a young man came in yelling with both hands held up in the air. He had blood splattered on his face and was dressed in torn and bloody overalls. In one hand he was holding an oversized plastic bloody meat cleaver, while in the other hand he held a bloody rubber arm with a hastily drawn anchor and the word 'MOM' written on a banner below it. A sticker on his overalls read, 'HI, My name is Billy Damballa Jr.'

Everyone looked at him in disgust and he heard a few "Boo's" before one boy was heard over the music yelling, "You're an asshole!"

227

Dropping his hands down to his sides in defeat, he yelled back, "Come on! Where's your sense of humor?"

The party raged on for just over an hour, with everyone drinking the spiked punch, beer and various different Halloween-themed shots of liquor. Suddenly the lights began to flicker on and off and the music was abruptly stopped.

"My friends!" one obviously intoxicated reveler, dressed as a cowboy, said from the fourth step of the open stairwell leading to the upper level of the house. "My friends, I have a special surprise for you this fine All Hallows Eve."

One equally inebriated party-goer piped up, "It's Saturday! All Hallows Eve isn't until Wednesday!"

The cowboy took a long drink from his cup before yelling back. "You … can just shut the hell up, sir!" Everyone in the house roared with laughter at once as he continued. "Where was I? Oh yeah. My friends, thank you ever so much for coming to my party! I have a very special surprise for you this fine four days before All Hallows Eve!" Everyone laughed once more.

"If you will follow me out back," he said, "you will surely be rewarded!" The cowboy carefully made his way down the four steps and headed through the crowd to the back door where he led everyone out into the darkness and across his large backyard which was lit by the full moon, and toward the dark, surrounding woods.

Amongst the yelling and cheering for the host, one high school girl, dressed as a cheerleader, spoke out. "I don't like this! I'm scared!" she told her boyfriend who was dressed as a football player.

"It's okay. There's a bunch of us. What's the worst that could happen?" He sounded brave, but he was nervous himself.

As the long line of shivering kids disappeared into the darkness of the woods, the cheering was quickly subsiding as everyone began to feel the loss of warmth and safety that they had inside the house. With the feeling of vulnerability creeping into each person with every step they took deeper into the forest, true fear took the place of the excitement of the party. Their only solace was the fact that there was strength in numbers.

Although no one could see him, there was someone else in those woods. He was watching, hidden, as everyone from the party made their way into the darkened confines of the forest. He sat, anxiously, but patiently, listening to their whispers and waiting for the right moment – for everyone to be at the right spot for him to act. He could feel his heart beating stronger and faster as the group of kids made their way farther and farther into the woods until they finally reached a large, dark clearing. The cowboy suddenly stopped walking as he looked out into the darkness.

"Did anyone hear that?" he whispered as he looked around. The line of inebriated, costumed teenagers quickly turned into a tight grouping as the cowboy slowly crept ahead of the silent crowd. From the stillness of the forest, everyone heard a crack like the sound of a fallen branch being stepped upon, out in the distance.

"I *know* I heard something that time," he said a bit louder in a very nervous tone.

Everyone froze in place, straining their eyes to see into the darkness and suddenly aware of their complete vulnerability.

All at once, a huge blast of fire erupted from a mountain of carefully grouped lumber. The crowd screamed out in surprise and excitement and from the release of their tensions as the college boy who had been waiting in the dark and had ignited the blaze from behind the wood, ran around the fire and hugged the cowboy who had led the group.

"The Bonfire Boys strike again!" he yelled as he drunkenly hugged his friend. Everyone screamed and cheered before circling around the bonfire to warm up and to escape the forbidding darkness behind them.

For the next hour, the atmosphere changed back to a party mood, mostly due to the host who had returned to his house and brought back a portable stereo that was turned up loud, playing their music throughout the forest. But it was because of the loud music and the bright fire that no one had seen or heard the one extra person in the forest around them who had not been invited to the party but was about to crash it nonetheless.

A large man was making his way over the fallen leaves, branches and sticks and was walking directly toward the clearing where the bonfire was raging high into the air.

"I gotta go pee!" the boy who was dressed as the tattoo serial killer proclaimed before standing up and heading away from the fire and back out into the darkness of the woods until he was out of sight.

About forty feet from the clearing, the man in the forest stopped as he looked to his left and saw the boy peeing behind a tree. The man in the woods turned sharply and quickly headed straight toward the boy.

Back at the fire, almost everyone was completely drunk. Half of the crowd was screaming along to the rock song playing through the stereo while the others were sharing stories, making out or *trying* to get someone to make out with them. Moments passed before the man in the woods loomed from the darkness. He held the young man, who had gone in the woods to urinate, tightly by the arm. The yellow light of the bonfire reflected off of the silver metallic star on the chest of his uniform as Deputy Tim escorted the young man out of the woods and back into the clearing.

"OK!" he yelled, "Turn the music off!"

At once the only sounds were that of the crackling fire and the whispers of everyone at the party.

"Alright kids, time to break it up. Are you guys *crazy* being out here in the woods after what's been going on here in Walkerville?"

There was no response from anyone in the crowd. Tim continued, "Time to go back into the house and anyone under twenty-one, time to go home."

Everyone moaned their disappointment to which Tim asked rhetorically, "Or do I need to ask everyone for their IDs?"

At this point, they all thought it best to cut their losses. Tim followed everyone back through the woods, across the long back yard and watched as some went back into the house while others headed straight to their cars.

*****

On another street in Walkerville, a house sat quiet and unassuming in a dimly lit area at the opposite end of the street from a single lamppost. The sides of the house were lined with a plethora of tall, full Evergreen Perennial bushes strewn with cheerful, bright red berries. Next to the garage, behind the first bush, Mick Presley had been sitting silently in the dark for almost an hour, squeezing his tire thumper tightly as he shivered in the cold, pressing himself up against the house in a desperate effort of staying behind the bushes to avoid the freezing, gusting wind. His wore his blue scrubs and cap, blue rubber gloves and a clean white apron and surgical mask. Under his apron, around his waist, he wore a large brown hip bag.

As he sat freezing in the bitter cold, Mick could actually feel his anger welling up within him. By the time he saw headlights nearing and heard the sound of an engine getting closer, his anger was almost irrepressible. Mick pulled his legs in tight so as not to be seen when the garage door began to open and a truck turned into the driveway and pulled slowly into the garage.

Mick quickly crawled on his hands and knees, with tire thumper in hand, from out of the bushes and into the garage behind the truck. He was careful to stay as low as possible to avoid being seen in the truck's rearview mirror.

Mick reached under his apron and into his hip bag where he pulled out a pair of clear plastic work goggles. He strapped the elastic band around the back of his head and adjusted the goggles securely over his eyes just as the garage door lowered, shutting tightly just a foot behind him.

Chapter 12

The 10 a.m. service was fuller than Father Goshi could ever remember. Fuller even than the Easter and Christmas services or the recent funerals. It seems that in times of crisis, people often turn to religion for comfort and for a feeling of safety.

During his sermon, Father Goshis' tilted face smiled as he quipped about the packed church and the current situation in their village. "Apparently there *are* no atheists in a foxhole," he said with a grin, which was a rare spark of levity from the old priest. This caused his congregation to laugh and lightened everyone's mood, which, actually, was his intention.

Upon leaving the sanctity and security of the church, the congregation's mood promptly became far less jovial as the reality that there was evil hidden somewhere among them snuck back into their minds, returning them to the feeling of sheer panic. The fact that Halloween was only three days away only worsened their fears. Everyone in town thought that if someone else was going to be murdered, it would be on Halloween and although they all resented him for bringing this lunatic to Walkerville, everyone felt much safer when Captain Parker was in town. Word had spread that he had gone back to Grand Rapids yesterday. Knowing that they still had Sheriff Kerry and his three deputies in town didn't really help the genuine feeling of vulnerability that overwhelmed everyone in the village.

For the next few gray, snowy days, all was quiet. Captain Parker and his men worked steadily in Grand Rapids. They focused primarily on the killer in Walkerville when they weren't working on their many other local cases.

When Sheriff Kerry and his deputies weren't making their presence known even more thoroughly than usual throughout town, they were taking turns driving and walking through the forest, near the area where Mike and Stephanie had been camping, looking for Mike or any clues that might help them find him. On Tuesday, Charlie discovered the giant wood chipper that sealed Mike's fate a mere four days earlier.

He brushed a bit of wet snow off of the chipper but even upon thorough investigation of it and the immediate surrounding area, found no traces of anything unusual. Charlie looked out into Lake Michigan, noticing the developing sheet of ice that had grown ten feet outward from the bank and wondered if maybe Mike would someday be found at the bottom. He imagined Mike walking through the forest and tripping on a log. "Maybe his flashlight broke when it hit the ground," he thought. "Maybe he was walking around aimlessly in the dark and walked onto the ice and fell through." Charlie continued deeper into the forest while yelling for Mike, feeling that his efforts were probably futile.

Everyone in Walkerville breathed a slight sigh of relief as Captain Parker pulled into town Halloween morning. It wasn't long until almost everyone in the village had gotten word that he was there. Although most of the people of Walkerville stayed inside the safety of their works, schools and homes, their paranoid minds relaxed ever so slightly knowing that he was there to protect them.

Captain Parker visited Sheriff Kerry to get caught up on the latest goings-on in Walkerville. Their meeting was brief and tense as both men were extremely uncomfortable in the presence of each other.

After their meeting, Captain Parker spent the bulk of his day driving around town, stopping at several restaurants just to make sure everyone knew he was there. As he drove, Captain Parker noticed that, strangely, none of the houses were adorned with any Halloween decorations. There were no carved pumpkins or scarecrows, no bails of hay, not even paper witches or black cats taped to the windows of the homes. It was apparent that the Walkerville serial killer had successfully established a very tight grip on the fears of the entire village.

Captain Parker continued driving the streets of Walkerville, passing by Syndi's house at one point and desperately wishing that she was back from Florida. As the sunlight faded away, the streets became empty. Not one trick-or-treater ventured from door to door. This was either by choice or under the duress of their parents. The village was quiet and still.

Everyone stayed in their homes; every door and window was locked, every curtain was closed, and all of the lights outside of the houses were turned on to hopefully deter the serial killer in Walkerville from getting too close. In fact, the terror of becoming his next gruesome victim was so intense, that more than one family had barricaded themselves inside of their homes by pushing couches and dressers up against their doors and windows for the night in hopes of keeping the madman away while they slept.

Outside in the darkness, only four vehicles were on the streets that night; their drivers were Captain Parker, Sheriff Kerry and three deputies. All five men rotated between sleeping at the station and driving around the village.

As the eerie night crept by, the officers were diligent in their task of covering every inch of the snowy roads in Walkerville. They drove slowly as they swept their directional spotlights into every darkened crevice, surveying the town through their windshields and passing each other several times into the wee hours of the morning.

As the sun rose, everyone rushed out to work and to school to find out if there was any news – to see if anyone was murdered in Walkerville on Halloween night. Conversations about several people evolved into rumors of their demise, which were eventually put to rest once they were found to still be alive. With all that had happened in and around Walkerville in the past thirteen days, people were actually surprised that they had all gotten through the holiday unscathed.

Since he was in town, Captain Parker invited himself into the sheriff's morning meeting to keep abreast of the latest news in town. He kept surprisingly quiet while Sheriff Kerry headed the meeting, hoping that the sheriff would realize that he was there, on his own, to help find the killer. This silent gesture helped regain a bit of the sheriff's trust and removed some of the negativity that had plagued the two men.

Sheriff Kerry commended everyone for staying diligent the night prior and said that they all needed to be on the lookout today for a couple other victims; for Mike, the camper who had gone missing, and for Oswald Rodriguez, who was still presumed missing because no body had yet turned up.

Although no one had reported anything, there could very easily be a dead body in the snowy forest just waiting to be found. At the end of the meeting, Sheriff Kerry politely asked if the captain had anything else to offer. The captain only added that the entire Grand Rapids department was proud of the way the team in Walkerville helped out when needed and how much of an asset they were by following up with certain suspects and trailing several others when asked to do so. As the sheriff and his deputies tried to hide their proud grins, Captain Parker said how invaluable their doing what was asked of them actually was.

For the rest of the day, the five men drank several cups of coffee to help them stay awake and aware as they drove around Walkerville, looking on and off of the roads for a discarded body and hoping all the while that they wouldn't find one. They searched in abandoned houses and sheds, as well as out in the forest, under bridges and in frozen creeks. By the end of the day, to their great relief, no bodies were found and there were no new reports of anyone missing. It seemed that they had gotten through Halloween with no casualties.

Captain Parker called to the sheriff on the radio to inform him that he was heading back to his motel room and would join the team again tomorrow afternoon.

"Ten Four, Captain," came the response from his radio. "Thanks much for your help today!"

Captain Parker headed back to his motel room where he showered, shaved and lay in his bed to watch some television until finally, exhausted from working a full day after driving around the village the night before, he drifted off to sleep.

*****

Six a.m. came and went and Captain Parker, away from the eyes of the Grand Rapids team, enjoyed four extra hours of sleep. After waking up, he lazily turned on the television to see a live report from right there in Walkerville. An eager and very pretty blonde reporter was doing a follow-up report on the recent slayings. Even though there had been no new killings for about a week and there was nothing new to report, it was still one of the hottest topics in the nation. And why wouldn't it be? A serial murder case in such a secluded area, surrounded by nothing but forest for miles and miles, four people slain and two still missing, all within just under two weeks – it was the makings of a great slasher movie!

Captain Parker let out a slightly amused "heh" before getting out of bed and brushing his teeth. Then, he dressed in his uniform and ran out to the Eat Rite diner where he picked up some food and brought it back to his motel room. He had just finished eating when he heard a knock at the door. He looked out of the window of his room and saw a brown UPS truck in the parking lot and a delivery man at his door. Captain Parker opened the door and signed for a large envelope that the delivery man handed him in trade for his signature pad.

"Thanks very much," Captain Parker said before closing his door and walking to the other side of the room where he sat down at a small table and grasped the tear strip on the back.

He paused for a moment as the story on the television caught his attention. The pretty blonde reporter had tracked Sheriff Kerry down and was

238

trying, albeit in vain, to pry some information out of him. Sheriff Kerry gave a nervous but brief and candid account of what had been happening, stating only that which was common knowledge of the cases before excusing himself.

Captain Parker chuckled and turned his attention back to the large envelope, tearing off the strip in the back. Turning the envelope upside down, a six-inch square of aluminum foil dropped out and onto the table. Captain Parker eagerly tore off the foil, revealing two pieces of cardboard that were taped together. He pulled his pocketknife out of his pants pocket and carefully pierced the tape along the tiny gap between the two pieces of cardboard.

From inside of the cardboard, a small, two-by-two inch square fell out and landed flat on the table. It resembled a piece of beef jerky but was much lighter in color. Captain Parker picked up the object and turned it over to look at the other side. He dropped it and jumped back, covering his mouth. There on the table, to his horror, was the tattoo of a yellow sun with bluish-white clouds behind it. He knew this tattoo. He had *licked* this tattoo. This was the tattoo of the most beautiful woman he had ever known. *This* was the tattoo of Syndi Bastion!

In a sudden fit of blinding rage, Captain Parker picked up the heavy wooden table and flung it across the room where it splintered and broke apart upon impact, leaving a gaping hole in the yellow wallpaper. Unable to control himself or even think, he grabbed the television set and ripped it off of the dresser where it had been secured with thick double-sided tape. He lifted the television high overhead and threw it down with all of his might, yelling *"NO!"* The plastic body and the glass from the television set shot out in every direction like shrapnel. He looked on the floor where the table had sat and saw the sun and cloud tattoo and imagined it on the soft curve of Syndi's back. *"NO!"* he screamed. *"NO, IT CAN'T BE! HE DIDN'T DO THIS!"* Captain Parker grabbed the closest thing to him, the Gideon's Bible, off of the nightstand and turned around to see his own distorted, red-faced, furious reflection in the large mirror over the dresser. *"GODDAMN IT!"* he screamed at himself as he threw the Bible at the mirror. His opposite image shattered with a loud crash and then, was no more.

In a rush, Captain Parker grabbed the tattoo and his coat and ran out of the room as the door automatically shut and locked behind him. He got into his squad car and, as the tires spun, snow shot up into the air as he tore out of the parking lot with the lights flashing and the siren screaming as he sped away. Moments later, Captain Parker came to a screeching halt in the driveway of Syndi Bastion's house. He got out of his car and ran to the front door. Without even slowing down, he kicked the door wide open and ran into the house yelling Syndi's name at the top of his lungs.

The putrid stench of rotting meat overtook him and wafted past him through the open doorway. With his mind racing, Luke ran through the different rooms of the house. Although he had several years on the force and numerous years of training in dangerous and extreme situations, he was unable to think clearly and his vision became tunneled. Luke ran towards Syndi's bedroom, seeing only the open doorway, and felt his mind finally snap as his eyes fell upon Syndi's naked and bloody body that was tied to a wooden chair. Her throat had been sliced from ear to ear and trails of dark dried blood ran out of her neck and down her chest. The white bedroom carpet was damp with a large puddle of bleach and blood under and around her.

Luke squeezed his eyes shut to somehow remove himself from this reality and when he opened them, he saw Syndi's beautiful blondish-brown hair that was now bleached pure white. As he cried out loudly, Luke fell to his knees in front of her, landing in the moist puddle as he looked up at Syndi's angelic face which hung down.

Light blue veins showed through her pale, translucent skin and her mouth, hanging agape, exposed her dried and chapped lips and tongue. Luke gazed into Syndi's once deep-green eyes that were now grey and opaque.

Horrifically, her lifeless eyes gazed back out at him from another place and from another time. Luke clinched his fists and set them upon Syndi's cold and rigid knees before bringing his forehead to rest on them. He began to tremble while trying to control the anguish and the fury that was steadily overtaking his senses. He breathed deeply, unaware of the cool dankness of the blood and bleach soaking through his pants to his skin.

At once, Luke jumped up and screamed loudly as he looked down at Syndi's bloody, maimed and defiled naked body. With rage in his eyes, he backed across the room; he wanted to take his eyes off of his beautiful Syndi but was unable to do so until he was all the way out of the room and back in the living room where he had sat, just a couple weeks earlier, waiting for her to get ready for their first date. With this memory, he felt undiluted fury. Luke ran out of the house, got back into his car and sped away, swerving briefly in the snow.

"Sheriff's office." Linda answered the ringing telephone, abruptly cutting off her conversation with Deputy Julian.

"Captain Parker, please. This is Detective Richard McKenna from the forensics division of the Grand Rapids Police Department," came the deep voice from the other end.

"I'm sorry, detective, Captain Parker isn't here right now. Can I help you with anything?" Linda asked sweetly.

"We found a whisker," the man said.

"A whisker?" Linda asked innocently.

"It's a whisker from a dog. We found it in the hair of one of the recent victims from Walkerville. She was victim number four – a Ms. Rose Wayne."

Linda gasped and said, "The girl that was found hanging by her hair in the forest!"

"That's right, but this whisker is pretty unique," Richard continued. "We ran some tests and confirmed that it's from a Peruvian Inca hairless dog.

We need to get this information to the captain but he's not answering the phone in his room or his cell phone. Do you have any idea where he might be?"

Linda stammered briefly before saying, "No, I'm sorry, I have no idea where he might be right now. We can try him on the radio!"

Obviously frustrated, Richard said, "Do that and please have him call us the moment anyone finds him."

"I sure will!" Linda answered.

She hung up the phone and ran into Sheriff Kerry's office. "Sheriff," she said anxiously, "I just got off the phone with a man from the forensics department down in Grand Rapids. He said they found a dog whisker in Rose's hair!"

Sheriff Kerry's eyes widened. "Really? Do they know what kind of dog it's from?"

"Yeah, he said it was from some sort of Incan hairless dog. The guys in Grand Rapids are trying to get hold of Captain Parker but he's not answering his cell phone or his motel phone. I told them that we would call him on the radio!"

Without hesitation, Sheriff Kerry shot up from his desk, grabbed his coat and ran out of his office toward the front door. He yelled for Julian to follow him in his car and for Linda to call the other two deputies and have them meet him in the parking lot. "Right *now* goddamn it!"

Within four minutes, all three deputies were in the parking lot and congregated around Sheriff Kerry. He hastily filled them in on the situation, explaining that the Grand Rapids forensics department called and said that they had found a single whisker of an exotic breed of hairless dog and that the Presley's have this breed of dog.

With this news, the despair of the deputies seemed to instantly disappear and was replaced with vigor and determination.

"Let's go get that son of a bitch!" Tim shouted, which was followed by the other two deputies simultaneously yelling, "Yeah!"

"Okay boys," Sheriff Kerry said loudly, "Follow me and keep your sirens off – we don't want him to hear us coming."

They climbed into their cars and the sheriff said, "I called the captain on the radio but he didn't answer. Let's stop by his room and see if he's there!"

Sheriff Kerry sped out of the parking lot, followed by the three other squad cars and raced toward the All Seasons Motel where Captain Parker had been staying. Arriving moments later, Sheriff Kerry ran from his car to Captain Parker's motel room and banged loudly on the door.

"Captain Parker!" he yelled. "Captain Parker!"

From behind him, Sheriff Kerry heard deputy Charlie yell, "I don't see his car! I don't think he's here, Sheriff!"

"Okay, Charlie, try the captain on his cell phone," Sheriff Kerry shouted back. "If he doesn't answer, leave him a message telling him that Mick Presley is our suspect and we're on our way to his house now!"

"You got it, Sheriff!" Charlie yelled as Sheriff Kerry ran red-faced through the crunchy snow back to his car and flipped on the blue and red lights. All three deputies flipped on their overhead lights as well, and followed the sheriff out of the motel parking lot, speeding toward the other side of town to the home of Mick and Judy Presley.

Chapter 13

Captain Parker, almost blind with rage, threw the car into park and ran through a snowy front yard. Reaching the front door, he turned the knob. The door was unlocked and Captain Parker quickly rushed into the house and slammed the door behind him. There, sitting on his large white couch, was a very surprised Mick Presley.

With wide eyes, Mick jumped up from the couch and watched in fright as Captain Parker ran into the living room toward him, grabbed Mick by the throat with both hands and squeezed tightly. "*You son of a bitch*!" Captain Parker yelled loudly. His face contorted with anger and pieces of spittle escaped his lips. "*You killed her!*" He screamed, his face only two inches from Mick's.

Captain Parker cocked his right arm back and delivered a solid and very painful blow to Mick's face. Mick fell backward, bounced off of the white grand piano and fell into a heap on the floor. Mick looked around the room both sorry and glad that his wife was at work at the beauty parlor downtown.

As Captain Parker neared, Mick crawled under the piano and cowered with his arms in front of his face, like a scared child trying to hide from an abusive parent. "Y-y-y-you d-d-don't u-under-understand!" he said awkwardly from beneath the piano. "We-we *had* to!" Captain Parker grabbed Mick by the head with one hand and used the curled fingers of his other hand to dig into the soft tissue under Mick's jaw. Against his will, Mick rose from beneath the piano as he yelled in pain.

Captain Parker released Mick's head and watched as Mick folded his hands together and curled his shoulders forward and down as he inched backwards, actually making him appear much smaller. As he twitched slightly, Mick looked down at his feet while he spoke quietly in his deep, growling voice, "I-I-I'm sorry. I j-j-ju-just w-w-wanted …" Captain Parker cut him off abruptly. "Goddamn it! God*DAMN* it!" He took a step toward Mick and grabbed him by his shirt with both hands. Mick winced and tried to turn away before continuing.

"I-I-I've been wa-watching everyone in W-W-Walkerville for three years now. I learned whe-whe-where everybody lived and where they w-w-went during the day and night. I-I-I even knew where a-a-a lot of people ha-had their tattoos."

Captain Parker grabbed Mick by his shirt and pulled him in close as he spoke through gritted teeth. "I told you to leave her alone! You said you understood!"

Mick, looking straight into the Captain's wide eyes replied, "I know, I know. And-and I w-w-w-wasn't going to, bu-bu-but we had already p-p-planned on getting her tattoo before they called y-y-you in and I c-c-c-couldn't fight it for-forever! I couldn't s-s-stop myself! It was already p-p-p-planned! We-we-we figured it w-w-was for the best a-a-anyway."

Captain Parker squeezed Mick's shirt tightly in his hands before throwing him backward onto the white couch. "For the best? For the fuckin' *best*? You stupid son of a bitch!! You're only here because of *me*!" Captain Parker yelled down at Mick. "You would be rotting in a cell right now if I hadn't saved you!"

Mick looked down at his folded hands in his lap and replied, "I know, I know."

"Years ago, I found you running away from that young boy's body in Colorado when I was there teaching that two-week training course!" said Captain Parker. "Do you remember? I had the barrel of my gun to the back of your head and I explained your choices to you!"

"I-I remember." Mick said quietly.

Captain Parker continued to yell loudly. "I told you that I could blow your brains out or you could work with me. I transferred to the Grand Rapids Police Department and you moved into this little piece-of-shit town in the middle of nowhere. No one would ever put it together when you started killing people in Walkerville and I came up from Grand Rapids to help out. There's no *way* anyone would ever figure out that you and I had this symbiotic relationship – that I was actually here to help you out! You've got the brawns and I've got the brains! Remember? How much better could things have turned out for you? You can get off in your own sick, disturbed way by murdering whoever you want and not getting caught and I get more tattoos for my overseas buyers! It was perfect! It was a win-win situation! You got what you wanted and I got what I wanted! I even told the sheriff about the Soul Reaper which *really* paid off. When that story got out, you wouldn't *believe* how much more valuable tattoos from Walkerville became! I even have a few buyers on *back order*! They're just *waiting* for the next story to come out of Walkerville. Everybody wants one! Believe it or not, the bidding has gotten so high that Ozzy's skins are reaching the million-dollar mark!"

With his adrenalin spent, Captain Parker started to become a bit more clear headed. His breathing slowed down and he was becoming more capable of controlling his emotions and thoughts. Mick looked up from his couch in silence with tears in his eyes as Captain Parker continued scolding him.

"I had all of our bases covered. I interviewed every last person in town to see if anyone had seen anything or if anyone had any ideas of who was doing all the killings and no one had a clue! A lot of them actually suspected different people around town but your name never even came up *once*! I even had some of the deputies tailing different people in town just to divert their attention and to keep them out of our way. Do you remember me teaching you all the things you needed to know so you would never get caught or even look like a suspect?"

Mick nodded his head silently. Captain Parker continued his tirade. "I taught you to use bleach to destroy any DNA and to cover up the appearance of blood. I made you cover your body up so no dead skin floated off of you and onto the bodies. I made you shave your head so there was no way any hairs could be transferred to the bodies."

Captain Parker took a deep breath before continuing. "We had a system! You leave the body, or a part of the body, somewhere that it will be found and I would call you from a payphone five days later, when you were done tanning the skin, to tell you where I would be so you knew where to send the tattoos. *That* was the plan!"

Mick looked up at Captain Parker and said timidly, "We were careful. We always used a fake name when we mailed them to you!"

"Goddamn it! How many times do I have to tell you, there's only *one* of you? You're the one that stalks and kills and cuts the tattoos out of your victims down in the basement and *you're* the one that lives here in this house with your wife! It's just you, Mick!"

Mick hung his head low, he didn't dare argue with the Captain. "And I know you were careful! I'm the one that told you to use a fake name! Remember? I also told you to wear rubber gloves and destroy your clothes and your shoes each time so no one could find any trace evidence on them and prints couldn't be traced back to you.

"I'm the one that told you to wear a different kind of shoe each time so the treads would all be different just in case they did find a shoe print. After the sheriff came by the other day, I even told you to move the tattoos to the shed at your old house so if anyone came back, they wouldn't find anything! And who was smart enough to take one of the wood chipper keys from the wall in the office of the lumber yard where you left Lathe's body?"

Mick just sat on his couch, wiping tears from his eyes as he responded quietly, "You were."

Captain Parker ran his fingers through his hair and walked around the room, trying to regain his composure and control his emotions, even though he was starting to lose that battle and felt another wave of anger building up within him as he thought about Syndi, the feelings he had for her and the feelings she had for *him*.

Mick stood up from the couch and spoke in an assertive voice. "We're still a good team!"

Captain Parker, overcome with rage, screamed, *"We're not a team anymore you stupid asshole*! This is *over* goddamn it!"

Confronted with the sudden news that he must put an end to his killings, put an end to his only release, Mick yelled back at the captain. "I'm not done yet! There's still five more people I have to clean!"

"You're done!" Captain Parker yelled back, red in the face.

"You can't stop me!" Mick replied angrily.

Captain Parker had heard enough. His anger had built so intensely that he was barely in control of his fists that began flying quickly and steadily at Mick's head and face. Captain Parker grabbed Mick and threw him into the white rock wall next to the grand piano. Mick bounced off of the jagged stones and rebounded toward Captain Parker who threw a hard right cross to Mick's sternum, effectively dropping him to all fours and causing him to gasp for breath. Captain Parker drew his right foot back behind him and delivered a solid kick to Mick's well-exposed rib. Mick fell over onto his back and grasped his side with both hands as he labored to inhale.

Captain Parker peered down at Mick and yelled, "This didn't work out with Billy Damballa either!"

As Captain Parker continued his assault on Mick, Sheriff Kerry and his three deputies were racing from the other side of town toward Mick's house with flashing red and blue lights signaling any traffic ahead to move to the side of the road.

With clinched fists and a red face, Captain Parker roared at Mick, who was rising to his feet with great effort. "How did you do it?" Captain Parker screamed. "I want you to tell me exactly what you did to her!"

Mick backed away from Captain Parker as he cried out, "You d-d-don't really want t-t-t-to know! I c-c-c-can't tell you! I can't tell you!"

Captain Parker approached Mick and slapped him across his tear-soaked face, resulting in a loud pop. Mick winced as he felt his cheek immediately heat up.

"*What the hell did you do to her?*" Captain Parker screamed. Mick continued backing away from the captain, looking down and shaking his head all the while as his bottom lip protruded and quivered nervously. Captain Parker grabbed Mick by the throat and pushed him hard into the antique glass and wood curio cabinet. The glass door shattered as Mick fell backward into it. Small pieces of glass shredded Mick's shirt and back and the vases, bells and figurines inside fell and crashed onto the floor beneath.

Mick's face instantly transformed from scared child to enraged psychopath as he reached down and opened one of the wooden drawers, pulled out a pistol and swung his arm hard, hitting Captain Parker in the ear with the butt of the gun.

Captain Parker fell sideways and landed on the ground amongst the shattered remains of the curio cabinet. He was looking down the barrel of Mick's gun that was pointed directly at his forehead.

Mick's face quickly changed, revealing the ravenous killer that dwelled inside and he yelled out in his deep, growly voice, "Do you know who you're fucking with, captain?" Captain Parker raised both hands in front of his face as Mick neared him. "I'll tell you *exactly* what I did to her!" Mick bellowed breathlessly before kicking Captain Parker in his ribs.

"I *had* to kill her!" he began. "I had planned on killing her at Seth's a couple weeks ago, the night that I killed Lathe … before you even *met* her! It

249

was our destiny; hers and mine! I'd been planning on cleaning her for a long, long time! She was *so* beautiful but I wanted to make her *perfect!* She always parked at the back of the parking lot when she was working at Seth's. I knew nobody would hear or see us that night, way out there, but that was all blown to hell when that big buffoon walked her to her truck. He ruined my plan!" Mick screamed. "I wasn't about to let him ruin my entire evening! I waited on the side of the building and watched him walk back in. I was going to wait there in hopes that he would come out by himself at closing time. You could imagine my surprise when he came out through the *back* door no more than a minute after he went in the front! I just snuck up behind him and bashed him on the head! I was even more surprised when I opened his shirt and found that little gem on his chest! But I digress," Mick said calmly.

"I saw Syndi's little tramp stamp about a year and a half ago. I went into Seth's to bring him a mounted turkey that he'd shot and I saw that sun and clouds tattoo when she stretched for a bottle on the top shelf behind the bar. It was right above the crack of her ass, which, by the way, she didn't mind anyone seeing."

Captain Parker gritted his teeth as he scooted back across the jagged pieces of the previous curio cabinet contents as Mick went on to describe how he had savagely slaughtered Syndi Bastion.

"I decided to try something *different* this time," he snarled. "I knew I was smart enough to do it right there, in her own house, and get away with it!"

Mick explained how he had secretly followed Syndi home the night that he dropped off the mounted turkey at Seth's to find out where she lived and how he had gone back to her house last Friday night, dressed in his surgical garb and carrying a hip bag under his apron. He explained to the captain how he had snuck into her garage after she pulled in and how he quietly crept into her house after she went inside.

Mick had hidden in a closet, just outside of the bathroom in Syndi's basement after she had gotten into the shower. He stood in the closet, quiet and still while Syndi took her shower. With one eye, Mick watched through a tiny crack between the door and the frame as Syndi opened the glass shower door, dried off with a large white towel and wrapped it around her body before heading out of the bathroom, past the closet and toward the stairs. She was only halfway up when she heard the thud of someone slamming into the wall at the bottom of the steps behind her.

Startled, Syndi looked over her shoulder to see an enormous man, dressed as a surgeon and wearing clear plastic work goggles. After bouncing off of the wall at the bottom of the stairs, he began heading up the stairs toward her. Her eyes and mouth widened as her shriek echoed in the stairwell. She ran, as fast as she could, toward the top of the staircase. Mick reached out and grabbed one of her ankles but lost his grip, as they were still slick from her shower. Syndi reached the top of the stairwell with Mick just six steps behind her. Screaming frantically with Mick right behind her, reaching for her towel. Syndi ran across the living room and into her bedroom where she turned and slammed the door as hard as she could. Just before the door latched shut, it was met by a firm kick from Mick's foot. The door shot back open, its edge hitting Syndi in the face. She fell backward and the back of her head hit the clean, white bedroom carpet at the foot of her bed. Her scream of terror was stifled as Mick ran into the room and fell on her, straddled her hips and delivered a solid punch to her jaw. Syndi was unconscious even before her head bounced on the soft white carpet.

Mick stood up and looked down at Syndi. She looked pretty, peaceful and calm. Gingerly, Mick picked Syndi up off of the carpet and laid her on her bed before grasping the thick white towel and tearing it open. He couldn't help but gaze upon her stunningly beautiful face and body. When he had his fill,

Mick rolled Syndi over on her stomach to observe the tattoo of the yellow sun with bluish-white clouds behind it on her lower back.

"I've waited so long," he said aloud. He brushed his blue, rubber-gloved fingers over the tattoo as he let out a short chuckle. "I can't believe you'd ruin this perfect body," he said as he shook his head in disbelief. "Don't you worry, honey," he said happily, "I'll clean that off for you!"

Mick walked out of the room, grabbed a chair from the kitchen and brought it into the bedroom where he sat it in front of the full length mirror on the wall. He then picked Syndi up in his arms and carried her limp body across the room and sat her in the chair. He reached under his apron and pulled from his hip bag, a small spool of thin, white nylon rope and tied Syndi's hands to the tops of the two back legs of the chair and her ankles to the two front legs. When he was done, Mick grabbed Syndi by her hair, lifted her head up and looked at her in the full-length mirror.

"See sweetheart, I'm about to fix your terrible mistake." His eyes squinted behind his clear goggles as he said, "No, there's no need to thank me – I'm *happy* to do it!"

Reaching back into his hip bag, Mick pulled out a round, white plastic toothbrush case and removed the top half, revealing three shiny stainless steel scalpels. He took one from the case before closing it back up and setting the case on the bed behind him.

"Now," he began as he placed the tip of the scalpel an inch above Syndi's tattoo that was framed between two black bars, the seat and the back rest of the chair, "This might sting a little!" He plunged the scalpel into Syndi's back and drew it across the top of her tattoo.

As fresh blood coursed out of the slice and covered her tattoo, Syndi's eyes shot open and her scream of pain was deafening. With wide eyes, she gazed into the mirror in front of her to see her own naked body tied down to a chair and, peering from behind her, the evil, dark eyes of the surgeon behind his plastic work goggles.

With no classical music and no soundproof room, Mick was fearful that Syndi's screams might be heard from someone outside. He quickly removed the scalpel from her back and reached around Syndi's face. Mick thrust the bloody scalpel into Syndi's neck and pulled it across her throat, slicing her deeply from one jugular vein to the other. With her wrists and ankles tied securely, Syndi was unable to do anything but feel the extreme pain in her throat and watch the horrific sight as blood squirted out from the side of her neck and then poured out of her throat, down her chest and onto the clean white carpet beneath the chair. Her terrified screams turned into gargles as she choked on her own blood. Syndi looked straight ahead and watched in horror, anguish and sadness as her life was so gruesomely taken from her.

With tears in her eyes, her thoughts went from her parents to her friends and as the light in the room slowly faded away, she saw the face of Luke Parker. The face of the man that she had fallen deeply in love with. Her head slowly dropped down and her body convulsed and twitched several times, until finally, Syndi Bastian was no more.

Mick continued cutting an inch around Syndi's pretty little tattoo and when he was done, he placed the blood-covered scalpel back into the toothbrush case and reached into his hip bag to pull out a pair of pliers and a razor blade.

Down on his knees, he worked carefully to pull the corner of the skin away from her body and sliced it free with the razor blade. With the tattoo in his bloody, blue, rubber-gloved hands, Mick smiled widely beneath his mask. He tucked the tattoo into his hip bag and removed from it his old pocketknife. He began slashing at the meticulously cut inner-walls of skin where Syndi's tattoo had been, sawing and hacking at the skin and muscle until all traces of the surgical instrument's cuts were erased.

"Lucky for me," he said, with a laugh to Captain Parker, who was standing two feet from the end of Mick's gun, "she had bleach in her laundry room so I didn't have to sneak down the street to my Blazer and bring some back!"

Enraged, Captain Parker swiped at Mick's gun, knocking his arm to the side and delivered a right cross that landed on Mick's left ear before rushing in and grabbing Mick around his chest. Mick reared the gun back and slammed it on the top of Captain Parker's head. The captain fell to the ground and grabbed his head as he moaned in pain and felt the warm, wet sensation of blood trickling out of a fresh gash.

He tried to stand back up but found that his legs were wobbly and his body felt like it weighed a ton, causing him to fall back on the floor. Mick set his gun on the piano and rushed back toward the captain. Captain Parker felt his body lifting off of the ground as Mick hoisted him up and pressed him high overhead while walking toward the open basement stairwell. With an enormous heave, Mick threw Captain Parker down the stairs and watched his body bounce off of the railing and the walls as he fell, like a rag doll, down the entire flight. As he landed at the bottom, he lay still; the sounds of their mêlée were replaced by silence.

Mick stood motionless as he looked down the stairs and began devising a plan to dispose of the captain's body.

"I could take him out to that wood chipper," he thought. "I still have the key." As his mind worked through the situation, Mick noticed the wall beside the stairwell doorway start to strangely flash blue and red. As he touched the wall in front of him, he heard the slam of several car doors and the yells of Sheriff Kerry and his deputies.

Mick spun around quickly, ran across the room and grabbed his pistol from the top of the white grand piano. When he turned around, he hid his gun behind his back as he saw the front door of his home fly open just before

Sheriff Kerry and his three deputies ran inside, guns drawn and pointing at Mick.

"*FREEZE!*" Sheriff Kerry yelled as loudly as he could.

"Get down on the ground, *now!*" Deputy Charlie screamed.

Terrified, Mick raised his empty hand and pointed toward the stairwell as he looked pleadingly at Sheriff Kerry and said, "H-h-h-he… he… m-m-ma-made…"

A single blast rang out and Mick's head jerked backward and pieces of blood-soaked brain escaped the back of his skull, spraying the top of the white grand piano. Mick's pistol dropped to the ground between his feet as he fell backward into the piano and down to the soft carpet.

Sheriff Kerry and his deputies turned their guns toward Captain Parker who was holding onto the wall with one hand and his own gun at arm's length with the other. While gray smoke escaped the barrel and fresh blood trickled down Captain Parker's already bloody face and neck, Sheriff Kerry and his deputies lowered their guns. The sheriff ran over to the captain who fell heavily onto the sheriff's shoulder.

"*Captain!*" Sheriff Kerry yelled. "Are you alright?"

Captain Parker, unable to speak through his rapid breathing just shook his head as he wiped blood off of his eyes with the back of his hand.

"I guess you got the voicemail, huh?" Sheriff Kerry said with a slight grin, figuring that was the reason for the captain getting to the Presley home before they did.

Captain Parker kept his stare on Mick's body, which twitched a few times before finally settling down and going limp. Mick lay lifeless, staring up at the white ceiling while a thick, dark red puddle of blood grew steadily around his head.

Epilogue

I remember everything that happened back in Walkerville. The victims still appear to me all the time and, you know what? When I see them, it kind of makes me chuckle! Hell, I even remember all of Billy Damballa's victims back in Cape Girardeau, Missouri in the late eighties! He was a stupid, crazy kid, but damn, he made me a rich man!

Back in Grand Rapids they called me a hero and I was even promoted to Deputy Chief. Not long after that, I told them that I needed to get away. I told them that I needed to get *far* away and I moved to Hawaii. Everyone said that they understood, seeing as the woman I was romantically involved with was murdered during *my* investigation. Most of them just patted me on the back and told me that they didn't know if they would be able to handle what I've been through.

The side business I had in Walkerville has really helped me out financially and made the move possible. I only use my tattoo cash sparingly and keep the rest tucked away so nobody comes around asking any questions. I joined the force here in Hawaii and am really quite happy. I can't believe it's actually been three years since I was in Michigan.

Yeah, being a cop in Walkerville was simple once... until I got there anyway. I still remember *everything* that happened back then. I'm sure I always will. But that's the past and I'm living a new life now. I've got a beautiful girlfriend, a great new job and I live in paradise. I've even picked up the side business again! I'm working with a young man named Bane. He's the crazy, psycho type that just needed a little direction in his life. He was living on the streets and was quite surprised the night he stabbed a young woman to death in an alley and was interrupted just before he could have his way with her body. I rested the barrel of my piece on the side of his head and made him my special offer to come and work for me. He agreed, as long as I let him finish up with the woman's body in the alley first.

Can you believe the balls on that guy? As I sat patiently and watched him rape her lifeless body, I thought to myself; you know, they say that there's a fine line between the criminal mind and the mind of a cop. I tend to believe they're one in the same.

The End